Shine
out of
Bedlam

a novel
Jeffrey Hillard

Cover design by Jennifer Vogel

ISBN – 978-0-9970365-0-3

Printed in the United States of America Library of Congress Cataloging-in-Publication Data

Hillard, Jeffrey

Shine out of Bedlam (A Shine in Bedlam Novel) – 1st Edition

.

For Chelsea Joanne Hillard

& For Kendall, Charlton, and Nelson

LEVIATHAN

WHATEVER CAME OUT OF THAT train last night left lazy strings of smoke and broken tree limbs at the edge of the woods. Something like trash was still burning.

Shine Ross and Moondog Weasel stared at the remnants of a campfire.

The train tracks were about fifty yards uphill from a rusted fence next to a path that snaked into a stand of trees.

They could see the smoke-wisps from where they stood outside the fence.

Someone, last night, had barreled out of that train and never thought twice about making a fire or getting too warm, after setting a match to a poor excuse for a pile of tree limbs.

This was hobo territory and Shine knew it.

This was where the wandering men with no money and no real home could hop off a train and find luxury under trees. Places under which they could escape a storm.

One morning a few weeks ago, walking near these woods, Shine and his friend Moondog saw a man wearing a

1

greasy scarf and ratty coat in the heat of summer. Dirty coat down to his knees. He'd likely hopped out of a boxcar and moved so swiftly into the woods that Shine swore he vanished. Like dust.

But, today, the boys missed this new hobo who appeared to have scattered the tree limbs with his feet. The hobo must have known the arrival time of another train before the morning sun pressed down.

The grass was crusty brown, and it wasn't mid-summer.

This new hobo had hopped a train and never looked back.

Yep, hobo territory. Peering at the camp, Shine could see empty soup cans. Rubber boots by the cans had holes in the toes.

A patch of the bottom of the tall fence had been pried upward by someone with decent strength. The fence bordered this section of the woods. Apparently, someone had squirmed his way through the upturned fence-bottom.

Shine squirmed through the hole only as wide as a small body. He was no stranger to these woods. His parents' house sat on the other end of Garland Park, or the Woods, as it was known in Bedlam.

Moondog followed him through the hole. He held his ham sandwich with mustard in the air so it wouldn't scrape the ground, taking bites of it once he reached the other side. He walked a few steps behind Shine. He bit into the last half of the sandwich. Moondog's father had cooked a ham for lunch. Before the boys left for the woods, his father motioned to his son and Shine to slide the plates out of the kitchen cabinet and grab forks. They proceeded to shovel mounds of meat and pinto beans onto their plates.

In the woods, Shine could hear Moondog's mouth at work. "Can you chew that thing a little more quietly?" he said.

"Sorry."

"Pay attention. You don't know what's in here."

"I know," Moondog said.

"You know what?"

"I know I don't know what we're looking for." Moondog bit into his sandwich.

"Look for more of that hobo camp, maybe another whole camp. Stay with me," Shine said. "Let's look."

In spite of sunlight behind them on the slope leading from the train tracks to the fence and woods, Shine leveled his flashlight toward a dark spacing of trees. Oak trees filled the park. With his other arm, Shine wiped his nose on his shirt sleeve. Hayfever season. Shine's nose paid a heavy price in Garland Park, with its nasty honeysuckle and ragweed.

Moondog flipped a piece of bread into a patch of poison ivy. As Shine angled the flashlight every which way, he realized he was still several hundred yards from crossing into an open expanse of fields where two baseball diamonds and picnic areas with barbecue pits existed. The woods bordered the ball fields opposite from the bent fence and hobo camp.

The Millcreek ran near the ball fields, forming a split between the park and a garbage dump and, a little further away, a street of apartment complexes and small houses near the post office.

Shine raised his hand for Moondog to stop.

They looked at the small clearing. Shine never hesitated exploring something that fascinated him, and these hobo camps fascinated him. Moondog wanted in on the action, but usually if Shine first declared the need to explore.

Just beyond the camp were a brown blanket and a pair of dirty red gymshoes. They walked back to the hobo campfire. One log next to the tree limbs had been saturated with creek water.

"Bet that hobo put out the fire less than an hour ago," Shine said.

"Bet that puddle was made this morning. He carried creek water in those shoes and cans."

"Bet he maybe tried to catch a rat, kill it, and fry it," Shine said. "No, wait. He'd have to use a real gun or a BB gun."

"I bet he fills creek water in an old milk bottle. He carries it on trains. He's got to carry something to drink. All that train dust."

"I wouldn't drink a lick of that creek water. Those hobos. Hobos are always catching a train. Always heading north or west."

"Where you think that train's going today?"

"Michigan."

"Up near Canada?" Moondog said.

"Detroit. The track goes straight north. It runs alongside the highway, same kind of north path. The highway ends up top of Michigan. There's good stuff for hobos in Detroit. Coats and shoes. People that work at the auto factories throw away good stuff. That's where I'd head."

***

SHINE ALWAYS HAD AN ANSWER to Moondog's routine questions.

Not once, but many times Shine assured Moondog that the Pennsylavania & Ohio railroad, at the top of the embankment that descended to the base of the Garland Park fence, went past Detroit.

The track stretched far past the car-making factories in Detroit, Michigan. It was a north-south train line, with train cars hauling tons of sheet metal and, yes, coal from southern states, and the line was critical to places like the Ford Motor Company and General Motors in Detroit.

Shine's father, a long distance truck driver, would send him the same postcard from Detroit on which a red line down the middle divided two photographs: Lake Michigan on the right side and on the left, a new Pontiac Firebird parked in perfect grass with a buxom woman in a skimpy bathing suit waving from the driver's seat. His father delivered machine parts to places like Ford, GM, and Chrysler.

If Shine was lucky, his father was home only two or three days before leaving again on a three-state delivery. Home, then gone. Home and the eventual sight of his father walking to the end of Monte Avenue where he parked his rig. Home and the *click-click* of the front door lock in the middle of the night, his father slipping out to begin another road trip.

Always another trip.

His father loved collecting stamps, so that each postcard to Shine and his sister Allison was accompanied by a different stamp from a different city.

It was 1968, and when Shine read his father's last postcard just two days ago – the one from Kansas City, Missouri – he connected the smokestack on the stamp to the factory smokestacks that populated Bedlam. Whenever he looked at a card, his eyes first drifted to the stamp: what did his father put on this one? Two days ago, Shine's mind wandered to the four factories that pierced the city heart of Bedlam, whose smokestacks spewed streams of smoke night and day.

Shine thought of 1968 as the year of smoke.

He imagined 1968 as the year that the sky over Bedlam was really a roof held up by elastic pillars of smoke, pillars undamaged by even the worst thunderstorms.

Now, Shine heard a train. It would arrive in minutes. He heard three whistle blasts.

He and Moondog hadn't been chased today by the hobo who'd littered the camp. They'd tossed the broken shoes and greasy blanket in the creek. They were alone. They made the discovery. The camp had been vacated, yet at one time there had been woodsmoke, cans of beans, shoes, a blanket.

IT WAS AROUND ELEVEN WHEN the train approached and the boys heard the whistle and heard it chugging not far from Garland Park. Shine realized their plan was forming perfectly in its arrival.

With Moondog behind him, Shine crept up the embankment, crawling on his knees. He saw the train coming, and it was moving very, very slowly. In fact, it looked like it was going to stop.

"Good timing," Shine said. "Going five miles an hour, if that."

"Look at all those boxcars," Moondog said. "Probably a hundred. We got our pick."

"It's like a leviathan," Shine said. "Think of it as a leviathan. A long monster. A sea monster on land."

"A what?"

"A leviathan. Like a long-tailed sea monster. A leviathan has a long body. Comes out of the Bible somewhere. A leviathan is bigger than whales."

"Oh. That's it," Moondog said. "Well, I'm watching."

"Watching what?"

"Watching for an empty box car."

"I already see one," Shine said. "Don't forget, when you jump on, hold on tight to that car ladder with me. Don't let go."

They had become semi-expert train-hoppers in the last month since school let out for the summer.

ON HIS 15TH BIRTHDAY, THREE weeks ago, Shine cut across the creek, which separated west Bedlam from north Bedlam. Shine lived in north Bedlam, Moondog in west Bedlam. He balanced himself walking across the bridge of rocks, walked up Cooper Avenue, and zigzagged down Moondog's street to his corner house. He knocked on the door early in the morning and Moondog answered.

"Let's go," Shine said.

They walked the quarter mile to a hidden part of the train track near the water plant. They waited over an hour for a train. It appeared, and it, too, was moving very slowly. Heavy machine equipment and coal bins, Shine thought. There were always empty box cars.

The train rolled slowly enough for Shine and Moondog to jump and grab the box-car ladder. While Moondog hung on, Shine was the first to kick his right leg upward to catch the lip of the box car's opening. Simultaneously balancing and pushing with his left leg, Shine slid into the empty car which smelled like burning garbage.

Moondog followed Shine flawlessly.

They chewed on toothpicks and Sugar Babies on the ride north. They hopped off the train as it slowed near a cornfield not far from the General Motors plant in Hamilton.

SO, HERE THEY WERE AGAIN, three weeks past Shine's 15th birthday-boxcar ride.

An hour later, the train arrived in Hamilton. They hopped off at the edge of a cornfield. Within twenty minutes, after throwing rocks at the track, telephone poles, and high electrical wires, they returned to squat in that same cornfield and waited for another train heading south. The train would travel an hour before it slowed outside

Bedlam. When it slowed to about 10 miles an hour, Shine would be the first to jump and roll down the embankment.

Here, now, he sat with his back against the metal boxcar, legs propped on flattened cardboard boxes. Moondog squatted, holding his stomach. "I ate too much," he said, when Shine asked why he was moaning. They were opposite each other next to the boxcar's opening. They hung their heads out once in a while and peered at the repetitive brown fields and suburban houses.

The train jostled them as its speed varied. Mostly, it was slow. The long endless trains were slowest.

In Hamilton, Shine had counted forty-eight boxcars before they decided to hop on one heading south.

Around two in the afternoon, it seemed the trains were most plentiful and the slowest. Shine could tell when the train chugged back through the quaint village of Irondale, a couple of miles from Bedlam. He stood, spit his toothpick out the open door, and watched it disappear. He watched the large houses in Irondale, owned by factory executives, vanish from view, as if the houses were sucked into the curtain of trees.

A few minutes later, the boys leaped out of the boxcar and rolled with reckless freedom down the embankment.

***

THE BOYS WALKED PAST THE neon clock-and-thermometer in Bettman's Grocery store window which read 3:22, 86-degrees. It was when Shine said, with a yawn, *I'm heading home soon*, that they looked at one another when they heard the piercing fire truck and police car sirens.

A cop car sped past them, its siren blasting through the street, red lights twirling on top. Shine and Moondog stared at the cruiser. Shoppers came out of Bettman's. People emerged two and three at a time from the fish market, a corner drugstore, an auto body shop, and some of the houses and two-story apartment buildings lining Cedar Avenue. Everyone tended to look down the street to watch the route of the fire trucks and cop cars.

Shine wanted to run down the street and follow the parade of flashing lights, but he'd promised Moondog's father he would help carry old furniture out to the street curb, as an exchange for the ham and cornbread his father fixed this morning. Moondog's father, whose name was Henry "Pop" Weasel, said he'd slid out of bed at four a.m. because he couldn't sleep, and that he decided to do what he naturally desired: cook food.

"You boys catch wind of those sirens?" Pop said. "We're gonna have to head down and take a look, see how bad that thing is."

"I counted three fire trucks," Moondog said.

"Fellas, we got us a fire. But, first, this old raggedy desk and broken chairs and old carpet – out to the curb. Give me a hand."

Shine saw Pop Weasel's good, right eye open wide with excitement. He lost sight in his left eye at eight-years old, when one of his friends accidentally threw a large rock, hitting Pop's young eye. The blunt-force trauma from the impact tore the retina and caused internal bleeding.

Soon after the accident, Pop Weasel was told he would not regain sight in his left eye.

For that reason, too, he was called Seeing Eye by friends, even by Shine and Alphonso Peace, Moondog's older cousin who lived with him and his father. Pop encouraged it: "Call me Seeing Eye. I hear young folk saying that behind my back, and it don't bother me. I heard young folk say, 'He got that seeing eye on the right side of his head. He can't see nothin' out that left eye.' So, go ahead. Makes me sound like a prophet."

Once they hauled the desk, chairs, carpet, and coffee table outside, Shine and Moondog sat down at the kitchen table, drank ice water, and watched Pop Weasel take his trumpet out of his bright orange case.

"Let me play you a few quick licks, before we go see that fire."

He stretched his fingers and positioned the mouthpiece against his lips and blew a few notes. He arched his short fingers on the valves. He rolled those notes, unleashing a flurry that formed the *bop-bop-bop* melody of the song, "Tighten Up." It was a top-10 tune by Archie Bell and the Drells that Shine and Moondog heard on Shine's transistor radio last week, as they shot basketball. The tunes came non-stop, and among them Shine recognized two that Seeing Eye could play: "La-La Means I Love You," by the Delfonics, and Sly and the Family Stone's "Dance to the Music."

Shine's attraction to listening to Seeing Eye play trumpet coincided with his own desire to keep playing his trumpet. Shine had been in the high school band one year now. He tried not to let the frustration of practicing scales send him into panic mode, because he regarded Seeing Eye's routine as a kind of gift to him.

"Seeing Eye, you could wake up the dead with your playin'," said Alphonso Peace, who had come into the living room. "What's you blowin' now?"

Alphonso Peace was the oldest son of Pop Weasel's sister, who died a year ago. After dropping out of Bedlam High School at seventeen, right after his mother's death, Alphonso Peace was invited by Pop to live in his house with Moondog and his older brother, Ulysses, who was seventeen to Moondog's fifteen.

Pop Weasel ignored Alphonso. He played. When he stopped, he looked at his nephew, his eyes peering over his reading glasses. "I always do something with my life, young man."

"And what's you in this house for?" Alphonso said, shifting this question at Shine.

"Hanging out. About to go check out that fire."

"Y'all go on," Alphonso said, studying his hands. "Take notes and tell me about it." He wore a long silver chain, and he pinched it in the middle, sliding two fingers up and down the chain. "Bring me a report, boys. Especially you, white boy."

To Shine, Alphonso Peace looked anything but peaceful. He tended to look frustrated, even stern and nervous. He couldn't recall a time when he saw Alphonso smile. Each time he had passed Alphonso in the school hallway, Alphonso walked right by him. He remained aloof, selectively speaking to only a few students that Shine was aware of.

This was even way before Alphonso dropped out of school.

Alphonso Peace wore a sleeveless white T-shirt with the words "Black Power" inscribed in the shape of a heart on the left side. Like Shine, he cherished toothpicks and matchsticks. Alphonso was constantly gnawing on a toothpick.

"White boy," he said to Shine, "they better not catch you hanging around that fire too long."

Shine said nothing, admiring Pop Weasel's soft note-playing.

"I'm going with him," Moondog said.

"That should make anybody feel safe." Alphonso laughed. He studied a tiny splinter of wood he'd ripped from the underside of his chair. That was the first time Shine could remember Alphonso Peace's looking cheery. His face turned somber quickly. "I got nothing on you guys."

"Who's at that window, Dad?" Moondog said.

"Might be another friend of theirs wanting to come in," Alphonso said.

Pop heard the sound, too, and went to a living room window and pulled the white drapes all the way back. Shine followed Pop, feeling far more at ease near him.

They discovered the neighbor boy, Fremont Jones, crouched outside and just beneath the window.

Pop unlocked and raised the window. "You old enough to know better," he yelled, looking down at Fremont Jones. "Boy, what I told you about putting your nose up to windows and staring at folk inside their houses? Somebody gonna take you for a thief."

Although Shine took Fremont Jones as a harmless kid at nine or ten, he wondered if Pop would do the next logical thing and contact Fremont Jones' family. As he shut the window and closed the drapes, Pop said, "I'll give that boy one more chance. Some nights I see that boy out the window before I go to bed, and I'm not the only one who's seen him. Nobody said much about doing anything yet."

***

SHINE, MOONDOG, AND POP WEASEL walked toward fire smoke.

They followed people who turned on Franklin Street and then Hooper Street. The smoke hovered over small stores and houses in the opposite part of west Bedlam from Pop's house. They found that they could walk no further. Yellow police tape, wrapped around telephone poles and stretched nearly two blocks, kept onlookers at least five hundred feet from the fire.

Using their arm strength, firefighters braced thick fire hoses extending from three fire trucks, as other firefighters handled water pressure gauges and controlled the hoses' movement. Firefighters aimed plumes of water gushing from the hoses toward the top and middle of the building.

Flames swallowed the Empire Freight Company. Along with the crowd of onlookers, Shine could feel dispatches of heat. The Empire released wave after wave of hot air from its burning sides.

An old wooden warehouse standing alone on that part of Hooper, the Empire supplied Bedlam factories with assembly tables, flatbed carts. It contained shelving, racks, work benches, and paint.

Shine bit his toothpick until it snapped. He replaced it with bubble gum. Two Bedlam cops continued to tie more "Emergency – Do Not Cross" tape around parking meters and telephone poles and drag the tape a decent distance down Larkin Avenue, a main drag.

"No one's getting anywhere near that place," Shine said.

"It's all over for the Empire," Moondog said.

Shine saw a mixture of facial expressions. He heard cussing, grumbling, speculation. He heard confused voices. He heard kids beg their parents for explanations. He realized that several of the men and women who sat in yards might be watching their jobs disappear in Empire smoke. It took ninety minutes for the firefighters to overpower the blaze, cornering a last few flames. Even when the fire was diminished to weaker flames, firefighters kept pummeling the low parts of the warehouse with water.

Shine realized a majority of the onlookers were the black residents of west Bedlam, far exceeding the whites from other sections of Bedlam who'd wandered over to gawk.

The acrid heaviness of smoke snaked its way up the street and over west Bedlam.

He heard Pop say, "Let's go, fellas. We can't get any further."

Shine looked up to see Pop's good right eye bearing down on him, and he elbowed Moondog.

JOJO

"O GOOD GOD" WERE USUALLY the first words Shine uttered when he saw his mother lying on the couch in the dark with an ice pack on her forehead.

Mid-afternoon: blinds and curtains closed. Window air conditioner pounding full-blast. The hum of soap opera voices from the t.v. suspended in the dark living room.

"Holy crap" were usually his next words.

Shine walked quietly into the kitchen. He got a bowl from the cupboard and filled it with ice cubes. There was a tinge of guilt Shine wrestled with when he saw his mother down with a migraine headache. Those mind-numbing blows would put his mother down for two, sometimes three straight days.

"Holy crap," he said, again, wondering if his mother heard him last night bouncing a basketball in his bedroom well past midnight, and thus triggering her frustration, which in turn could have triggered the migraine. Did overbearing frustration knock her down like this?

Was it frustration that came with her choice to not yell at Shine for dribbling the ball in the house, believing he was only practicing?

Really, Shine thought of himself as that dutiful son when he wasn't hopping trains, or thinking of an excuse not to sweep the porch, garage, or not to rake their backyard, or not do chores when he had something important to do.

"Crap."

Shine looked at her sleeping.

Should I do this, he thought. He realized the contents of her ice bag were now reduced to water. He lifted the bag, trying not to breathe.

His mother opened one eye.

"Don't spill," she said.

Shine emptied the bag of water in the kitchen sink. He refilled it with the ice cubes. He'd decided not to have a conversation with his mother about the fire, although he was certain she heard sirens. He saw her lift her head off the pillow a few inches and glance at the t.v. A man and woman in the soap opera, "As the World Turns," flashed smiles at one another. Shine was not fooled by the phony emotion in their body language. He suspected his mother had tried to listen only to their voices; otherwise, it would intensify the pain if she tried to watch the black-and-white t.v. screen – and listen, too.

Still, Josephine Ross attempted to talk with her youngest child and only son, Benjamin "Shine" Ross. His mother Jo's plain face exuded a sweet smile even held prisoner by the pain of a migraine.

With a flick of her hand, she motioned him over.

"Your sister here?" She kept one eye closed.

"No. I imagine she'll be here soon. You need her?"

"Not now. What did you do today?"

"Just walked the creek."

"Did you hear the sirens?"

Shine changed his mind about mentioning the fire. "Moondog, Pop, and I watched a fire, mom. The Empire warehouse is burning down. We stood down the street. I don't think it can be saved."

His mother's expression did not change. "A shame. A real shame. Where your grandpa works, at Diamond National, well, it has a connection with the Empire."

"I heard they keep a bunch of paint in there, too," Shine said.

"Do you think your sister will go back out later? Tell her to not stay out late. Tell her from me. Please." She rolled that word "please" slowly off her tongue. With that open eye his mother looked at the ceiling.

"I just don't know. I think Allie said she plans on going to a movie." He had no clue what his sister was planning.

His mother made a failed attempt to sit up. "I'll be ok tomorrow. I hope. You know my cast iron skillet I make cornbread with?"

"That heavy one?" Shine said.

"That heavy one. It's like someone hit me with it. That's what I'm dealing with. That skillet could hurt a bear."

About that time, Shine heard the creaking sound of the back door opening. His mother obviously didn't hear it. She covered her forehead again with the ice pack.

In the dark house, Shine strained to see the figure of his sister, Allison, enter the kitchen through the side door. Her normal disposition was to walk briskly. And she did so, leaving a scent of powder perfume as she closed her bedroom door without acknowledging her brother.

Two minutes later, she let him in.

"Don't order me again to unlock this door," she said.

Allison was 17, with gorgeous brown eyes and wavy brunette hair that illuminated her attractiveness, which caused some guys to wonder aloud, within earshot of Shine, if she was ever dating anyone.

In fact, Allison was seeing someone.

With an allegiance one would have to keeping a secret, she was fond of Moondog's brother, Ulysses, and she told no one.

Allison was white and Ulysses was a black young man, and she understood any risk in publicizing such fondness.

In 1968, the town of Bedlam, in southeastern Ohio, inundated with factories, small stores, and a wide creek, was a town divided. '68 was already a crazy year. Confusing year.

Far from a miraculous decision some men made in the early half of the 20th century to pave over once-busy canal water and its locks with a magical new highway, Shine couldn't even decide if he wanted to spend more time playing basketball, playing trumpet or dating Cynthia Reynolds.

Far from those days when two men plotted a parcel of land by the locks and called it "Bedlam," Shine wondered if Cynthia Reynolds was the girl he 'd truly always liked, but never openly admitted. Or even admitted to himself before he went to bed at night.

One man was named Stuart Bedford and the other, Jonathan Lamkey. So they joined the first part of their names: Bed-Lam. And called the plotted land Bedlam. It was a perfect match of the real word, "bedlam," and a kind of running joke to Stuart and Jonathan, because those locks were critical in the time it took for every kind of material imaginable to be delivered to industries on the canal. It was a time loaded with anxiety, brilliance, struggle, luck, misfortune, big fortune, and, definitely, bedlam.

That canal reached the Ohio River. It was pure gold. Pure bedlam.

Three-quarters of the town were populated by whites, while one-quarter, known as west Bedlam, consisted of black-owned houses, apartments, and a smattering of businesses.

Bedlam School District became integrated in 1963, leading to new black-white friendships and new expected tension. Shine surely felt the tension in 1968.

His sister Allison and Moondog's brother, Ulysses, had met in civics class. It was during a boring discussion of federal treasury bonds that Ulysses passed a note to Allison: "Your eyes, I can't take them any longer. They melt me when I look at you." He'd signed it, "U.S." U.S. had been his nickname since first grade.

Allison read his note right there in civics, turned around, and smiled at U.S.

"I'm telling you, Shine, don't order me around this house or my own bedroom. Hear me?" Her brother stood against a bedroom wall. "Now, are you going to help mom or not?"

"I already did. That's not what I want."

"What did you do? How did you help mom?"

"Ok, the ice bag was full of water, so I changed it back to ice. She opened an eye. I hate looking at mom when her face looks like that."

"She's really down today," Allison said. "What else did you do?"

"Told her not to worry about me for dinner. I'll eat leftover meatballs."

"She'll be down another day," Allison said.

"You think she might be thinking of you and U.S.?" he said. "You think that's making her nervous? You think she knows you hold his hand?"

"Yeah, she saw. Now, drop it."

Allison gazed at her poster of singer-heart-throb Bobby Sherman. "How was I supposed to know Ulysses would walk over here at night – walk in *our* neighborhood in pitch dark. And I sure didn't know Mom would peek out like she was spying on me."

***

THE PLAN OF SHINE'S UNCLE Jerry and aunt Ruth was to haul JoJo the parrot back to their house in the backseat of their Pontiac Bonneville. They'd finished vacationing in Florida. His uncle would ease JoJo's cage into the car and drape it with a bed sheet.

This afternoon, however, they had to dump their plan. JoJo never made it to the backseat of the Bonneville.

It was a cavernous car that reminded Shine of a black hearse. The inside the Bonneville seemed as large as his bedroom.

Before he carried the cage with JoJo from the house, Shine's uncle unlocked the cage from the base unit, making it easier to carry the cage sideways and slide onto the enormous backseat. The cage, along with the wide base, would not fit together in the Bonneville's backseat. Jerry had to separate the units. Usually, Jerry came to pick up JoJo in his truck, a Chevy C-10. Its wide bed allowed him to anchor the cage with cords and two leather belts that locked into the truck's sides.

But, today, a first, he had the Bonneville.

Shine held the front door open. Aunt Ruth walked behind her husband as he carried the cage with JoJo. Jojo appeared comfortable enough with the bulky cage tilted sideways. JoJo stayed in place, shifting on his perch. Shine admired JoJo's 20-year old, bright green body and yellow head: a male, double yellow-headed Amazon parrot that his family frequently watched while his aunt and uncle traveled.

Just as he bent to put the cage in the backseat, Jerry bumped the side of it against the car door. The cage clanged loudly enough. And just as Shine jumped, wondering if the cage cracked the door window, JoJo flew out of the tilted open end of the cage.

When Jerry bumped the cage against the car, it startled the parrot enough for it to exert its flying power.

A clumsy flight, they watched in absolute shock as JoJo flew toward roofs and gutters, traversing two houses, and veering toward a neighbor's backyard oak tree, where he landed.

Shine looked at his uncle who appeared paralyzed. Speechless, Jerry had not yet yelled for JoJo.

It was a few moments before the disaster registered with aunt Ruth and she screamed, her voice carrying down the street.

Her husband ran toward JoJo.

Shine followed. It became a race.

When Shine caught up with his uncle, he told him he'd help get JoJo back. He would camp by the tree all night. He'd tell every homeowner in north Bedlam, if necessary. He saw his uncle's eyes redden. Shine saw the onset of such devastation slowly overwhelm his uncle.

Shine wondered if his uncle was thinking that JoJo may never come back.

After Jerry tried coaxing JoJo, in the promising absence of neighbors, he sat down in the neighbor's yard. "It's his freedom." That was all Jerry said, face in his hands.

Two hours later, with a cycle of neighbors anxiously coming and going and staring at JoJo in the tree, there was movement. Shine and his uncle coaxed JoJo down a few branches. They were patient with words and tone.

"Here, JoJo. Pretty boy. Good JoJo. That's it. Come on," they said.

Yet, when another new neighbor ran into the yard, JoJo stirred, hopping up a few branches. And soon he did the unthinkable: he flew off.

JOJO TREE-HOPPED DOWN THE woodline.

The denseness of the woodline took on a new shape for Shine whose neck throbbed from scanning tree tops for several hours. His arms ached from holding them out, trying to coax JoJo down. The trees were daunting now, appearing to swell in order to take in and protect JoJo. The parrot's own vivid greenness melded with the leaves. Shine's uncle Jerry, speechless again, sauntered back to his car, defeated.

Aunt Ruth napped in the Bonneville's front seat, her neck and head tilted back at an awkward angle on the seat. She clutched a fistful of Kleenex tissues.

There was only one thing Shine could do and that was go home, get his sleeping bag, and ask the Kempers for permission to sleep in their backyard, the last house along the woodline into which JoJo had flown.

In the morning, on blank paper, Shine would write and draw in bright colors. Draw and color furiously. Draw and color JoJo's head, torso, and feathers.

He would snatch a stack of paper from Allison's room and, in towering letters, write the four-letter word which already made him cringe: "LOST…Amazon parrot. JoJo."

Using bold colors, Shine would write the words, "GREEN BODY, DOUBLE-YELLOW-HEADED AMAZON PARROT."

He would take his time creating that one word, "LOST."

EMPIRE

ON TOP OF A HEAP of burnt wood and broken glass sat two birds.

Shine picked up a piece of a hotdog bun from the street and flung it toward the birds.

He'd crossed the creek, gone by Moondog's house, roused him away from watching "Dark Shadows," and convinced him to revisit the remains of the Empire Freight Company. Shine heard Seeing Eye practicing trumpet scales in his self-proclaimed music room, which also doubled as the t.v. room.

The boys had not turned the corner of Hooper before they spotted a city of Bedlam police car coming their way. Shine noticed the driver, too. Elmer Klump.

25

The boys called him "officer Breezy," as did their friends. Elmer Klump was notorious for running his cruiser's air conditioner full blast and opening the window only two inches when he pulled up next to someone and chatted.

When Shine approached the slit-like opening, he could feel the cold air ooze out. Although he was not about to let much air seep out, Breezy was considered the friendliest of Bedlam's cops.

Breezy and his wife lived across the street from Shine's family. He let Shine, Moondog, and a few other kids swim in his unique, five-feet-deep, above-ground swimming pool. They called Breezy's wife Little Bit because she was petite and quiet. She looked like a child standing next to her cop-husband who was more chubby than tall.

Officer Klump rolled down his window two inches. Shine and Moondog could hear his voice now. Klump looked upset.

"Where you boys headed?" the officer said.

"Away from here," Moondog said.

The officer looked at Moondog and tilted his police hat upward.

"Well, now, you've walked through a crime scene. You think that's right?" he said.

Shine still considered the cold air, unworried.

"We just checking to see if any smoke still there," Moondog said. "That place burned a lot."

"And that's why going past that yellow tape is illegal," Klump said. He lit a long cigarette and blew smoke perfectly through the slit. "I expect you're not going to walk near here again so soon. Am I right?

"We're sorry, Elmer," Shine said. "I just couldn't believe that fire. What it did."

"It did a great deal, son," Klump said. He stared at the fire damage, at two fire department officers who had just arrived to survey it. He rolled down the window a little more. "Fact is, a great deal it did. Or someone might have done."

"You think someone set fire to it?" Shine said.

"You think someone done started that fire?" Moondog said, unwrapping a Hersey's bar.

"Hard to say. That's what we need to do. Look into it."

He rolled up the window, saluted the boys, and drove slowly down the street toward the remains of the Empire and the two fire officers.

A few seconds after officer Klump pulled away, Fremont Jones sped around a corner of Hooper on his bike, in a skittish attempt to follow Klump's cruiser. As soon Fremont Jones biked all the way to the cruiser, he darted away from it, rode down a sidewalk and away from Klump. Shine paid slight attention to Fremont Jones.

"The cops are on to something," Shine said. "Firemen, too. I thought about being a cop when I grow up. They know what's happening. But I don't think I'm up to it."

"You wouldn't want to ride around in that air conditioned car?"

"Naw," Shine said. "You can sit in an air-conditioned house all day."

27

"Think about how cold that car is in the summer."

Shine could tell Moondog was about to offer his dream of becoming a cop only to ride in an air-conditioned car that someone else paid for.

"Man, Shine, it's a real good chance you might not have to come out of that cop car too fast, either," Moondog said. "You could sit in there all day, do it up, do it up Breezy-style, roam the streets up and down, soak up that cold air. Man, that's a cop's life, sitting in that air conditioned car all summer. No one watching you. You by yourself, soaking up that refrigerator air. You hardly see Breezy come out that cruiser. You could just ride around and say hello to everybody, like Breezy."

"Naw," Shine said. "A cop never knows when he might get shot at. Never know about trouble. Not for me."

"I might take a chance on that air conditioning. I wouldn't be worried about some car accident and having to step out and check out the accident and write up a ticket."

"You think sitting in air conditioning is the only thing cops do," Shine said.

***

THEY CAME TO THE WALKING bridge that crossed the Millcreek and began to divide west and north Bedlam, where Shine lived. Shine and Moondog looked down at the creek.

Just when they got comfortable staring at the shallow water cascading over rocks, they heard another voice.

Larry Loomis pulled out a Winston cigarette and lit it, flicking the match off the bridge.

A short guy with an intimidating presence, Larry Loomis was a superb athlete, though he had no inhibitions toward smoking at the most conspicuous times or saying whatever was on his mind. He'd received warnings from his coaches about the smoking, which he'd initiated at age twelve.

Larry Loomis had competed with Shine for a point guard position on the middle school and now soon-to-be freshman basketball teams. Loomis was a step quicker and a better shooter, yet not as skillful a dribbler. Most teams needed scorers more than dribblers at their age, so Larry Loomis typically claimed a second starting role from Shine and played eight to ten minutes more a game than him.

"Doctor L done come by to say hi to you," Larry Loomis said. "Where you two headed?" He blew smoke mostly in Shine's face. "Got something going on?"

"What's going on, L?" Shine said.

Larry Loomis seemed anxious, perturbed. He puffed hard on his Kool. "'Bout to wonder if I should throw you down into that creek, man."

"Why would you say that, man?" Moondog said. He took a step toward Loomis.

"Am I talking to you?" Loomis said, taking a step toward Moondog.

"I can talk for us."

"Why don't you go play somewhere, man? I'm asking Shine. I ain't talkin' to you." Loomis looked again at Shine. "Not so sure I liked how you played me on the court. What you say, Shine?"

He understood Larry Loomis was mad at him. A week ago, Shine grabbed the opportunity to dribble past Larry on the court and flaunt some moves, upon hearing Larry's twisted ankle was still tender. It was a volunteer workout for freshmen. Shine and Larry were on opposite teams. He ran Larry all over the gym, until Larry hailed the coach's attention for a breather. Shine won this battle. He felt antagonized by Larry's success in prior scrimmages, although Shine had improved to a point that he could bounce two balls at the same time.

"Hey, I was just playing ball," Shine said. "I had no idea about your ankle until after the game."

Shine had to at least feign ignorance. He knew Larry was a fighter, another reason the coaches favored him. The coaches tiptoed around Larry Loomis. They tended to side with fighters. Fighters were more formidable competitors. Larry Loomis was not afraid to elbow or knee someone, and this often got him chosen as a starter.

"Good thing we're the same size, the same age, and point guards," Loomis said. "It's a good thing for you."

"It's a good thing," Moondog said.

"I say what he says," Shine said, nodding toward Moondog. He wanted the conversation to end. He wanted no part of Larry Loomis.

"Let me tell you another thing, brother man. I'm on to your sister."

"What do you mean?"

"I know she likes U.S. What's you say, Moondog? He's your brother."

"Nothing," Moondog said.

"What do you mean?" Shine said.

"I mean, that's not cool. Better watch that. Not cool for a white girl to hit on a black boy. You better talk to your sis. The color thang, man."

"Man, you need to find somebody else to rat on," Moondog said. "Ain't nobody listening to your jive. And my brother Ulysses is bigger than you."

Larry Loomis blew his final puffs of smoke toward Moondog.

Larry looked fearless. He flicked his cigarette high in the air, watched it whirligig down into the creek. Larry Loomis stretched out his arms, his non-rebuttal and a show of authority. He was small, very muscular, and unafraid of anyone.

When Loomis spit and got ready to ride away, Shine looked back across the bridge and saw two guys walking toward it that he knew were involved with the Black Panther Party. They had sprouting afros and wore black shirts with red letters that spelled, "Black Power."

"Here come the twins," Moondog said.

He once described to Shine how Troy and Terrence Simms joined the Black Panther Party. "That's what my Dad says. The Panthers are supposed to be looking out for folks like police look out for a city. My Dad said."

"Hasn't Alphonso said something about the Black Panthers?"

"He's interested. He said something about joining up."

"They seem mad when you see them on the news. Like Alphonso."

"Alphonso said the Black Panthers are challenging everything," Moondog said. "He says he likes that attitude. Plus he hangs around with the twins."

The boys hadn't expected to see Troy and Terrence Simms walk this close to them. Or to the bridge or fire department and police station. Maybe they were heading toward Bedlam High School in north Bedlam. It housed the indoor pool. The high school sat a few blocks from Shine's house. The twins had just graduated.

"They live with their mama, grandmamma, and aunt," Moondog had told Shine. "Troy and Terrence watch over the family."

Just to the side of the Bedlam High football stadium, which bordered the creek, Shine saw officer Klump's cruiser emerge from its recent presence in west Bedlam. The cruiser veered to the curb.

Klump motioned for the boys to come over. Shine wondered if the officer intended to put distance between him and the twins.

"Maybe Breezy'll give us a ride to the rec shelter," Moondog said, as they crossed the street. The officer told them to get in the backseat.

"Where you heading?" he said.

"The rec shelter at Garland," Shine said. "I have to do clean-up work."

"I'll give you a lift."

In the cruiser's cold interior, Klump offered no opinion of the twins, the Empire, or the day itself, only saying, "Stay out of trouble." He smiled and put out his cigarette in the ashtray. Shine couldn't determine if the smile was genuine or a sly way of implying that Klump would somehow be aware of their routines, since he was his neighbor.

***

HE DROPPED THEM OFF AT Garland Park's recreation shelter, an open structure with a concrete foundation and shingled roof run by the city for elementary-age children.

Shine worked ten hours a week at the rec shelter. It was three blocks from his house. As soon as they stepped from the officer's cruiser, the two could hear the voices of children.

They saw three boys fling checkers at each other, two girls on the grass playing the game "Twister," several tossing a Frisbee, and two girls simply sitting at a picnic table and watching the others. Cynthia Reynolds sat talking to the two black girls, one whose long straight hair touched her shoulders.

The boys overheard Cynthia consoling one of the girls who talked about her older brother. "He's leaving for Vietnam in two weeks," she said. "My momma is upset. So is my granny."

"How long will he be gone?" Cynthia said.

"I hope not long."

"Why are we fighting in a war?" the other girl asked.

"I don't know," Cyntha said. "The government thinks there are enemies across the ocean trying to hurt people. That's what the news says. The government thinks we should help the people who are getting hurt. I don't know exactly why."

Shine sat next to Cynthia, his friend since first grade. She was the girl with whom he kept in closest touch. Last Valentine's Day, Shine bought her the first gift he had ever purchased for a girl: a heart-shaped pillow. Cynthia lived close to him and always showed concern for his mother, especially when she dealt with a migraine.

"You didn't hop a train, did you?" she asked Shine.

"Not today," Moondog said. Cynthia didn't take her eyes off of Shine.

"Shine Ross?"

"What?"

"Did you hop a train?"

He laughed. He looked at Moondog. "No, we took a day off."

"That's good. You should take a lot of days off."

"We're gonna lose our style if we don't stay up with it," Moondog said.

"I think you hopped a train," she said.

Cynthia walked over to the Frisbee-throwing group. For Shine, sitting in the shade of the rec shelter lessened the blow of the sun. But, when he saw one of city workers begin to drag baseball field-number-one, he told Moondog to sit tight, that he'd return in a minute.

Two weeks ago this middle-age city worker listened patiently to Shine's questions about dragging the ball fields. The city worker, Baldy Babcock, explained that the square grate fastened to the tractor weighed 300 pounds. The grate lay flat on the ground. It could be angled up or down when Baldy pulled a lever below the steering wheel.

The man said he couldn't drive the tractor around the infield's dirt more than ten miles-per-hour. Otherwise, speeding up would cause the grate to kick up too much dirt, naturally sending it in dust-clouds to the houses at the top of Garland.

The man also promised Shine he could take it for a whirl around the infield.

The time was now.

"I'll get a drink of water up the tool shed while you take her around a few times," Baldy said. "Don't kick up dust. We don't need no irate phone calls from the old ladies up there," he said, pointing to the houses.

He helped Shine climb up to the seat. Shine lowered the lever and positioned the grate on the ground. He was near the edge of the outfield. As he hit the accelerator he felt the ominous power of the tractor and the weight of the grate. He eased up on the accelerator, feathered it, and kept intent on steering in a decent circle around the infield.

Baldy walked toward the tool shed without looking back. Although Shine had listened to the man and wanted to be as cautious as possible, he was seduced by the engine's power as he gained a little speed, accelerating to a point beyond ten miles-per-hour.

Two minutes later, the tractor reached fifteen mph. Shine knew he was in control, steering with the confidence of a farmer. He drove faster. He glanced over his shoulder to see the grate swing from side to side. When he looked back at that smooth layer of dirt, he witnessed dust funneling toward those houses on the edge of the park.

Big problem now.

Shine knew that the worker named Baldy had been right. Those clouds would slice through trees and smear the sides of those houses. If one of the women was in her yard, she'd breathe in even the thinnest remnant of dust.

Shine slowed to a stop.

He'd circled the infield seven times. He waited for Baldy who was walking back across the field, shaking his head.

"You got a lead foot. I hope I don't get no call. I can see that dirt making its way on up. Lord."

"I lost track how fast I was going. Dirt kicked up too fast. Looked like a little storm cloud when I turned around."

SCARTOOTH

CYNTHIA.

Cynthia Reynolds.

She made sure she came to see Shine when he called to tell her about JoJo's escape.

"I thought you'd want to know," he said. "JoJo talked to you a lot. You two clicked."

"Maybe I can help."

"You can go search with me."

As Shine drew a picture of JoJo on his LOST PARROT poster, he remembered first grade. He remembered when the teacher, Miss Mason, paired him with Cynthia as bus and row-buddies on their first field trip to hear the Cincinnati Symphony Orchestra at Music Hall. He remembered Cynthia's frizzy black hair and blue eyes. He remembered that the ice cube he dared to clutch was her hand. He remembered his own sweaty hand in hers at age six.

In class, Miss Mason caught Shine staring at Cynthia and ignoring the letters she put on the blackboard.

She still let Shine act as Milk Boy for the month and carry twenty cartons of milk in a single wire crate from the cafeteria for the class' morning snack time.

Shine could not remember the exact time that he first liked Cynthia, though it could have been settled when he touched her cold hand at Music Hall.

Or it might have been sealed when she wrapped her fingers around his during a Beethoven symphony. Cynthia squeezed Shine's fingers harder when the conductor turned around, scowled at the rows of students from different schools, and reprimanded a group for talking during a song.

Breathing heavily, the conductor blurted, "Music. It, people, is to be respected. Now, quiet." Then he tapped his conductor's stand and pushed the symphony into another song.

Shine remembered his bluntness: "Music. Respect it." The words congealed almost like a bruise. Years later, they strangely inspired him to take his trumpet-playing seriously, especially when Seeing Eye would put his arm around him and say, "You got chops, Shine Ross. Keep it up."

Now, in Shine's dining room, Cynthia studied Shine's patience: he used a green Crayon to add a final green shading to JoJo's wings. It was the last of fifteen small posters he'd created using, as a guide, a photo of a younger JoJo.

He put the batch of green, yellow, and red crayons back in a coffee can filled with crayons he used in first grade.

He was ready to plaster fifteen telephone poles.

Shine's mother handed Cynthia the other fourteen posters. "Hold onto these. He'll lose them."

Shine thought of his and Cynthia's friendship as on-again, off-again. In fifth grade he liked Jackie Lansing. In sixth grade, Donna Taber. In eighth grade, Tina Lynn Noel. Yet he always talked to Cynthia Reynolds, and it was Cynthia that he took to dances. It was to Cynthia that he could tell his train-hopping plans. At some point he wanted to ride a boxcar as far as Dayton, Ohio.

As graceful and likable as she was around other people – and given her knack for getting straight-A's – Cynthia had never been one to rat on anyone, especially Shine. She could get upset, but she wouldn't rat.

***

JUDSON ROSS DROVE HIS SON and Cynthia to certain telephone poles on which they stapled LOST PARROT posters.

Shine's strategy was to post at every fourth pole. His father returned the night before, parking his rig at the end of Monte Avenue. In spite of five hours sleep, Judson seemed as anxious as Shine to find JoJo. Uncle Jerry was his brother, and he told Shine he was determined to help his brother.

Judson Ross rolled up to stop signs in north and east Bedlam. He rolled right through each intersection, hardly coming to a full stop. "I'd like to do this quickly," he said. ""No telling where that bird is. Don't tell anyone I barely stop at intersections."

They saved the last two posters for Hattendorf's Grocery, not far from the Ross house. His father kept the car running. Shine went inside to tape one to the inside of the main door, and Cynthia stapled hers to a telephone pole. When they returned to the car, they saw a north Bedlam resident, whom they didn't recognize, talking to Shine's father. They got in the car. The man was still talking.

"You know they ain't going to give in to police without a fight," the man said.

"Like I said, I haven't heard anything about it yet," Judson Ross said.

"You know we don't need a disruption from over west Bedlam."

"Well, I think you might be blowing it out of proportion."

"I don't. I'm thinking, what could be the worst?"

"I'll probably be on the road, anyway," Shine's father said.

"You might want to have your ammunition ready," the man said. "Can't never tell. I'll stay up til I think it's safe. May be a long night."

"I'll have to talk to Elmer Klump about it. He lives across the street. I'll see what the cops know."

"I don't like it for any of them cops," the man said. He kept nervously rearranging a Cincinnati Reds baseball cap on his head.

"Well, like I said, I haven't heard anything," Judson said. "I've been on the road."

The man pulled away from the window, looked in the backseat, and waved to Shine and Cynthia. "You kids be careful now," he said, and walked away.

"What was that about?" Shine said.

"Just this man named Homer I've known since high school."

"Why'd he seem upset?"

"Who knows? He says some big-named official from the Black Panthers is going to have a rally in west Bedlam soon. Homer thinks this guy might stir up trouble, might stir up something. He's acting like he's preparing."

"He said something about guns," Cynthia said.

"Well, you know," Judson said. He pulled in his driveway.

"What about needing a gun?" Shine said.

"I wouldn't think much about that right now."

***

SHINE PULLED HIS TRUMPET OUT of his case.

The mid-afternoon sunlight filled his bedroom window and desk, and it brightened the pages of his sheet music. Shine adjusted his music stand and practiced. A few wrong notes bounced off the wall. It took little time for him to connect with the phrasing he needed to stir up a rhythm with F-scale, C-scale, and G-scale notes.

Shine had a weird habit: when he hit a wrong note, he muttered, "Wait," to himself. He was aware of repeating "wait," but he couldn't help himself. Shine hit impressive clusters of notes in very smooth rhythms. His playing swayed beautifully between hard and soft notes. He had a natural ear for tone. He steadied his fingers on the valves.

He was trying to learn a new song, "La-La Means I Love You," by the Delfonics. Pop Weasel had passed along the sheet music to him several weeks ago. "It''s not a hard song to learn, especially for you," he said. "Go slow. It's a nice love song.""

Shine ordinarily spent an hour five days a week practicing. The attention complemented the teaching he got once a week from Mr. Erdman, the band teacher. Shine was fifteen and already a candidate to become a first-seat trumpet player in the band. Every time he went to Moondog's house and Pop Weasel was there, they would talk trumpet. Or Pop would outright begin playing in front of the two boys, Ulysses, Alphonso Peace, or whoever happened to be in the room.

Strange that, suddenly, Shine's father knocked on the bedroom door and asked to come in.

He had on his trucker's overalls with a Rodeway company patch sewn to a strap. Shine detected grease on a sleeve of his work shirt. His father's face was red, his eyes bloodshot, perhaps from not enough sleep, or else from the demand of being on the road more than he was home.

Judson Ross was perpetually calm. However, inside that calmness was anxiety – a coal-fire gathering heat – over his wish to be home more. Before school had let out for summer, Shine overheard his father tell his mother that his back was beginning to ache from long distance driving. Yet he was high in demand for delivery-driving.

He often craved the road.

Shine and his sister were used to the absences. They dealt with the moments of solitude when they had something to ask him and he was unavailable.

Apparently, his father would not be around the house long today.

His Rodeway overalls signaled another haul. Shine suspected his father's time in the bedroom would be limited.

"Hey," his father said.

"Hey."

"Sounds good."

"I'm getting better." Shine stood and put his trumpet on the bed. He sat again at his desk chair and propped his feet on a open desk drawer.

"I got a call quicker than I expected. I'm leaving for Kansas City in an hour, then back up to Detroit, to Ford Motor Company. This'll be good money."

"How long will you be on the road?"

"Four days tops."

"That still seems a long time."

"Real sorry that it is."

"I have another freshman scrimmage you'll miss."

"Yeah. I'll call your mother and find out what happened."

Shine sat at his desk and looked away from his father and at his poster of Walt Frazier of the New York Knicks.

"There's a war on in Vietnam and we're busy moving machine parts, truck parts, and whatnot," his father said. "That's what happens with a war. Work stays busy.

Sometimes I just haul and I'm not a hundred percent sure what I'm hauling."

Neither spoke for a few seconds.

"Watch your mother and your sister," his father said. "One more thing. Don't go walking around with Moondog over there in west Bedlam at night. Don't be gung-ho about walking around too late."

"Why's that?"

"Because."

"Because why?"

"Because you're young. Do what I say."

"Why's that something special? Because I'm young?"

"Because I said you're young and your thought process is still shallow. You'll know what I'm talking about when you grow up some."

"Am I in trouble?"

"No. And I want to keep it that way."

His father left the room, shutting the door. He never slammed any door. He once told Shine he wanted no door noise to trigger the onset of any Josephine Ross headache.

There were certain things Shine realized his father couldn't talk about at length. Or wouldn't. One thing was his mother's migraine headaches.

Another thing was her passion for teaching hearing-challenged adults and youth at the church.

Shine walked out of his room toward the kitchen and saw his mother using sign language in front of his father. She crossed, uncrossed, and flapped her arms and hands in front of his face. It was odd. Judson Ross knew very little sign language; he was slowly learning. He likely had no idea what his wife was expressing.

But that was his mother. His father just stood and watched her.

Josephine Ross was literally talking to him in this language of arms, hands, and fingers. She kept at it: contorting her fingers, poking her own chest, her forehead, her chin. She cocked her right arm and whisked it near his father's chin, nearly jabbing him.

Shine had no idea what the signs were. He just knew that she'd been taking advanced lessons and she was good and confident.

His father nodded and walked away. His mother looked at the stove, folding her hands in her apron.

"What did you say to him in that sign language?" Shine said. His mother turned around.

"Nothing."

Shine picked up his basketball lying in the living room.

"Well," his mother said, walking toward the kitchen. "I was signing something about aloneness."

She walked into the kitchen, and as she did the cuckoo clock in the cramped dining room whistled two o'clock.

***

OFFICER KLUMP MET SHINE IN front of his circular, above-ground pool and tossed him a towel. "It's all yours," he said. "Swim as long as you want. Did you invite your friend, Moondog?"

45

"I called him. He said he'd think about it."

"You know he's always been welcome to swim here."

"Thanks."

"The Missus and I are heading out. We'll be back later."

"You got a minute? I got a question."

"Shoot."

"I meant to ask you about something you might not tell me about."

"What's that?"

"I wondered about the Black Panthers. The Black Panther Party. I wondered what's going on. Do you know if they're coming this way?"

The officer scratched his head. He shrugged, an intentional replacement for words. He took out a long cigarette and lit it. "You know about them, do you?"

Shine had not frequently seen Breezy out of uniform. Maybe once every month. He noticed a prominent rash climbing the officer's left arm. Klump put his hand over part of it when he saw Shine staring.

"Poison ivy," Klump said. "Killer stuff when you're neck deep in it and don't know it."

"I heard some people talking," Shine said. "I see them on the news. The Black Panthers. They dangerous?"

"I don't know how dangerous. I know some things that I'm not going to share. Let's just say that."

"Are they coming to Bedlam?"

The officer puffed on his cigarette, shrugging again. With the cigarette dangling between his lips, he adjusted the belt on his Bermuda shorts and tugged his shirt, which seemed to squeeze his large stomach overlapping his belt.

"Coming?

"Coming to Bedlam," Shine said.

"We'll see. I've got other things to worry about."

While Shine swam, knowing he had the pool to himself, the officer followed him to the other side and stood at the rim. When Shine came up for air, he sensed the officer had an unfinished message to deliver. Breezy took two drags to finish off his cigarette before lighting another.

"Let me fill you in on something."

"Ok."

"There's some blanks to fill in," the officer said. "Have you heard of Bobby Hutton? From the t.v. news? He was known as Lil' Bobby Hutton? Very young guy in California."

"No."

"A Mister Bobby Hutton from Oakland, California, was a very young member of the Black Panther Party. Believe just 16. Sixteen when he was shot and killed a few months ago. About a year older than you. Imagine that. He was shot by police, several. Out in Oakland. Out where the Black Panther Party mostly started. Shot multiple times. That's trouble. Reports were that he wasn't armed – no gun, he'd dropped it on the street, I guess. They said he was giving himself up. I probably shouldn't talk too much about it."

Shine watched Klump smoke.

He tried to imagine what it must have felt like for a young man nearly his age, a boy, really, to be struck by not one but a number of bullets. What amount of pain would rush through the body? And did this Little Bobby Hutton die quickly? And why was he even involved with a group called the Black Panther Party?

"And I think young Hutton's death, plus the fact that a Mr. Huey Newton of the Black Panther Party shot and killed a police officer this year – a lot of those facts have helped contribute to the rise of this Black Panther Party. It goes back further. They're pretty well organized."

Klump took a long drag.

The fact that a 16-year old boy died from gunshot wounds startled Shine.

He accidentally knocked his knee against the side of the pool and felt pain. He thought of dead Bobby Hutton from California. Shine only knew California from the photographs in an encyclopedia. Shine imagined the pain in his knee multiplying hundreds of times.

"Do the Black Panthers have you worried?" Shine said, trying to ignore his knee. "Should we — should my family – be worried?"

"I don't know. Don't have that answer."

"I just hear things about needing to watch it," Shine said. "My dad hears this."

"Ok, listen. There's supposed to be some gathering in west Bedlam at old Drake school, at the old school building where black students had to go before the Bedlam district integrated everybody in 1963. It moved every black student and all the teachers into the bigger school down the street, with the white students. That's integration. Big move."

"They moved a school?"

"That's how it went. Only white kids went to the big school before '63."

Shine swam back and forth within range of Klump telling his story. He floated on his back, trying not to think of his knee. He stared at a huge motionless cloud.

The officer didn't hesitate to emphasize that, to his little knowledge, the Black Panther Party wanted to protect and help the black population, help them get better education, medical treatment, better jobs. "This is what I hear," he said.

Klump explained to Shine that, as far as he knew from reading, the Black Panthers were not afraid of police and not afraid of taking a stand for their agenda. They were visible. The pushed. Their business was real serious. They also had guns. They showed their guns. They'd dealt violence, although they favored non-violence, and they didn't care what the government thought.

"When's this?" Shine said. "In west Bedlam at the old school?

"Less than a month," Klump said. "There's a leader coming to speak, stirring up interest. H. Rap Brown. R-A-P. Brown. Mister Brown's a-coming, and I imagine people from Jefferson Heights might come over, too. This isn't a picnic. Make sense?"

"Sure." Shine let his legs float while he held onto the pool rim. "I mean, a little. But someone told Dad he might need a gun."

"No one needs a gun."

"But Dad or grandpa might have to be on the lookout?"

49

The officer tossed down his cigarette and squished it with his shoe.

"No." he said. "It means I, or we – us patrol officers — have to be on the lookout for anything. Per usual. Which means," and the officer pointed a finger at Shine, "people should go on about their business without worrying."

***

SHINE SWAM ALONE FOR AN hour and without Moondog showing up. When he walked back home, Cynthia was sitting on the couch watching a soap opera with his mother.

"I ran into Larry Loomis at the high school pool this afternoon. He said he had a talk with you," Cynthia said.

"He said he owed me for something I did last week," Shine said. "I'm not worried."

"I don't trust him," she said. "He has an ugly stare. I don't think he likes you."

"I'm not around him much. Just basketball."

Shine's sister Allison came out of the kitchen where she'd answered the phone and interrupted her mother when she was about to speak. "You already got a call, Shine. A JoJo sighting," she said. "Let's go."

Shine was surprised that Ulysses Weasel waited for Allison in his car. Shine and Cynthia got in the backseat. U.S. wore his typical sunglasses.

Allison had just returned from driving around with Ulysses and then going into Hattendorf's. The grocery store sat in a curious location. Although it had provided food-buying choices to those living in Bedlam, and especially in north Bedlam, it also catered to Jefferson Heights and even Mount Relling. It was less than a quarter mile from the bordering small city of Jefferson Heights, whose pulse came to initially beat in the 1920s. A few decades later, that pulse had pumped more lifeblood in the form of a city-blessed incorporation. Jefferson Heights was always historical and a festive place. The city was one of the only cities in the country in which a majority of black residents lived.

Hattendorf's, one of a handful of grocery stores in Bedlam, catered to a loyal mix of residents from Bedlam, Jefferson Heights, Mount Relling, and beyond.

Shine knew his sister's routine: Ulysses would enter Hattendorf's first and pretend to shop for soup or bread or fruit, staying a food aisle's distance from Allison, who would enter three minutes later. They wanted to be near each other, although they were revealing little of that closeness in public. At least for now.

Allison and U.S. were cautious. More and more attention was being focused on the Vietnam War. The ground battle with North Vietnamese. The bombing. Gunsmoke over rice paddy fields. Army helicopters dipping down past the fields.

Yet, on another t.v. screen far removed from Vietnam, frantic voices eked out gloom and doom messages and songs and speeches that spread every day across the U.S. The news canned and spilled to the public footage of demonstrations. Some demonstrators lashed out chaos in cities like Detroit, Chicago, Baltimore.

Smoke fanned out from fires swallowing buildings and cars. It drenched the night.

Cops whipped down streets. Fire trucks roared.

People seemed aimless, infuriated.

They wrapped the American flag around baby strollers and store mannequins.

They hung cardboard-painted peace signs outside apartment windows.

They draped a flag from the hands of a statue. They planted a flag-on-a-pole on the edge of a city dump.

Shine realized his sister harbored a quiet wisdom about how to control her fondness for Ulysses: his gentleness, his mellow personality, and his totally similar fondness for Allison. Lately, Shine kept noticing how his sister would not flaunt her beauty or her poise, but only do certain subtle things before moving on to her next task.

Ulysses was reluctant to get out of the car on Shine and Allison's street during the day. Once in awhile he did. Whenever Allison went into the house to change her shoes or clothes, U.S. would sit in his car, baseball cap pulled down, sunglasses high on his nose.

***

ALLISON DROVE ULYSSES' 1966 CHEVY Caprice. He bought the car when he turned seventeen. When he was with Allison, he often let her drive the car.

Shine could tell Allison was infatuated with Ulysses Weasel, Moondog's brother. U.S. had a trim mustache, large hands and long fingers, and he towered over everyone at six-feet-three-inches tall. He spoke softly, measuring his words. His motions were deliberate, and nothing seemed to bother him.

With his height, U.S. had never played basketball, instead directing his athleticism toward running hurdles in track. Even so, he never went all out. He was too laid-back. His coach could do nothing because U.S. was one of the most naturally gifted runners in Bedlam.

U.S. only ran because Pop Weasel said, "Make something of yourself. You want to end up like your cousin Alphonso?"

Shine didn't question why Allison wanted to help him find JoJo. She had originally shown little interest, believing JoJo would never return. He didn't question how long Allison and U.S. had been together today, or question her about their previous night together.

His sister had a take-charge personality.

They stopped next to a park, a hundred yards from the nearest house. The woman who called lived on Emerald Street, not far from Garland.

With U.S. staying in the car, the three traipsed through yards leading to the lady's house. They gazed into trees trying to spot JoJo. They skipped over flower beds, weeds, assorted house junk. They jogged around water sprinklers. They wound up at 530 Emerald Street, a corner house.

The lady who lived in the house pointed to an elm tree that was actually in her neighbor's yard.

"I saw your-all's poster in Hattendorf's," she whispered. "Up there. Midways up. It looks like a parrot to me."

"It is," Allison said.

Cynthia grabbed Shine's arm. "Go easy. Don't rush up there."

For the next twenty minutes they tried to coax JoJo down from the tree.

JoJo squawked. He tilted his head. He flew down several branches. He squawked when Shine called his name. He tilted his head more. He squawked when Allison called his name. It looked optimistic.

JoJo looked like an immaculate bulbous ornament dropped onto that tree by an angel of God.

Shine climbed the lower branches. JoJo squawked louder. The lady who'd called stood next to Allison. "All this morning I saw him go house to house, up and down the street, hanging on bird feeders."

"He's an escaped parrot.

"He's a beauty," the lady said. "He's a he, right?"

"A male Amazon parrot, that's right. A double yellow-headed male."

"Oh my God, it's a beauty. He's a hungry one. He just went up and down to any bird feeder. Up and down. There's lots of them in these backyards. Madge Hawkins saw him. You know Madge? She lives four houses down. You want me to call the police?"

"No, no," said Allison. "Don't call a soul. It has to be quiet. JoJo knows us."

Shine slipped on a branch but held his balance. JoJo hopped up a branch.

He was twenty feet from the parrot; he'd need to climb higher, and the branches were thinner the more he climbed. He had a blanket tied around his waist. If JoJo came to him, he would undo it with one hand, unfurl it, and fling it over the parrot. He would try not to hurt JoJo, although he wouldn't exactly exercise gentleness, either.

The phone rang in the lady's kitchen. She'd left her screened back door open. She finally hurried to answer it on the sixth ring.

Exasperated, Allison and Cynthia looked at each other. With that door wide open, and the phone apparently attached near the backdoor, the ringing had been so obnoxious that it shattered the silence in which Shine worked. He talked calmly to JoJo, certain that the ringing unnerved the parrot. It was as if he was telling JoJo secrets. The parrot occasionally squawked when Shine stopped whispering.

A few minutes later, two neighbor ladies came into the yard and watched Shine attempt to climb higher. When he did, JoJo flew to another neighbor's tree.

When one of the ladies, a very plump woman, sat on the end of a picnic table bench, it tipped enough that she lost her balance. Startled, she got up quickly, shouting about nearly falling, and if she had fallen, she said, she might have broken her damn leg.

When she raised her voice – by the time she'd finished whining about the bench – JoJo had flown off.

JoJo flew down the treeline and disappeared into a canopy of trees. Shine lost track of his green and yellow colors.

Shine climbed down and walked up to the woman. "I'd like to put this blanket over you, lady," he said.

The woman shrugged and apologized for scaring off JoJo. The three walked back to the car. Allison yanked two green apples from a tree. Ulysses was dozing, his elbow out the window, his head resting on his hand.

When he woke he said, "Any luck?"

"Almost," Allison said, starting the car. "And then there was stupid commotion."

MERCY

WHAT MIGHT A YOUNG MAN like Shine Ross be thinking when suddenly there are multiple new twists in his life?

A fire in west Bedlam thought suspicious?

The inexcusable escape of JoJo the parrot?

A young black man in California, a teen named Bobby Hutton, shot after he apparently surrendered in a confrontation with Oakland police? Officer Elmer "Breezy" Klump saying, "We have to be prepared for anything in Bedlam."

A girl, Cynthia Reynolds, who increasingly liked him and wanted to spend more time with him?

A mother who seemed more likely to have headaches than ever?

The growing influence of the Black Panther Party on people Shine knew? A war in which people he knew were fighting?

57

His father working more than ever? The thought that Larry Loomis was out for him? Shine's desire to play his trumpet and basketball more?

A guy like Shine Ross might think, "I gotta know more."

Or a guy like Shine might think, "Should I pay more attention to Cynthia Reynolds than anything else? Is this a good thing?"

He might think, "What would happen if the Black Panthers came to west Bedlam or Jefferson Heights? With guns?"

Or, as a quick aside, he might think and never utter a word to anyone: "Should I, Shine Ross, try smoking a cigarette just one time? Just this once? Who'd catch me if I hid it, just once?"

In a way he couldn't define, Shine was enamored with the kind of cigarette Breezy smoked.

The officer seemed undaunted by any hint of tension bubbling in Bedlam. Breezy's calmness was rooted in the confident way he held a cigarette. Breezy took slow carefree drags, and the smoke eased from his lips and nostrils.

What was a young man to think?

One time at school, Shine walked by Doug Compton, Tommy Lister, and Danny Moscovitch – seniors and great athletes – while they smoked cigs in Compton's car during lunch on a cold winter day. The car's windows were rolled halfway down. Shine was heading home to get the packed lunch he'd forgotten when he passed Compton's car.

Commercial after commercial appeared on t.v. which flashed this handsome cowboy riding horseback, a western guy who lit up a cigarette at the end of a ride on a mountainous stretch of ranch land. It was a Marlboro. And he was the Marlboro Man.

Shine thought that to try a cigarette was not to bond with it forever. It was an act of curiosity made real. Nothing more. A guy like Shine Ross might think, "I have to know more."

***

THIS MORNING HE WALKED TO Garland Park from home. He was an hour early for four hours' work at the rec shelter. The park's silence had not yet been shaken by shouting kids or the work of the city's grass-cutters. Shine admired the denseness of trees, the hiding places.

All he had to do was find a wide tree trunk. And he found one.

He sat against it, facing away from the houses above Garland. No kids. No cars. No city workers.

His first smoke didn't even begin with a brand new cigarette. His parents did not smoke, so he couldn't sneak a family cigarette. Shine had no access to smokes, really. His father had quit years ago, barely into his 20s, when a car accident he was involved in shamed Judson Ross into quitting any private vices he'd acquired.

So, Shine did something he knew would be embarrassing if anyone found out: over the last three weeks, storing them in a metal Band-Aid box, he discreetly collected half-smoked cigarettes at Garland's baseball fields. He was still working up the nerve to go into a gas station and pop thirty-five cents into the machine for a pack of Kools. He saw clusters of half or barely-smoked cigarettes under bleachers and near the concession stand. When no one was looking he would casually pick up one – well, any one without lipstick on the filter – and ease it in his pocket. He saved it for the Band-Aid box. He wiped off filters at home with a damp washcloth and dried them with Kleenex, careful not to get the tobacco wet.

Shine had taken a pack of matches his mother used to light the stove. Wrapped in his handkerchief were two half-smoked cigarettes he'd lifted from the Band-Aid box. He craned his neck looking for anyone or any passing car, even though it was early and anyone in a car could not see him unless they were staring directly at him.

He strained to stay so low that he was nearly lying down, an exposed tree root as his pillow.

Shine lit the cigarette and coughed. He inhaled and blew out smoke. It ran right into his nostrils. He waved the smoke away from his face. There didn't seem to be too much harm in this inhalation, he thought. His lungs didn't fill with smoke. He hadn't become cross-eyed, overcome with tar or nicotine. He coughed only twice. He imagined himself as an adult, an authority figure sitting on a chair at the billiards hall in little downtown Bedlam, and casually puffing, waiting to play the winner of a billiards game. Puffing slowly, watching billiard balls clank against each other. Watching the other men position their cigarettes between their lips as they lined up their shots.

Shine didn't want to waste time in these woods. He only wanted to test smoking.

How did it feel to hold a cigarette? How could he master smoke rings? How did it feel to blow smoke out of his nose?

He coughed when he tried the nose thing. Smoke burned his throat. No more nose smoke.

The first half-cigarette took three minutes to smoke. He crushed it on the ground with his gym shoe. The second cigarette lasted a minute less. Shine did not want to be discovered squatting near that tree. He'd never be able to explain his story on the spot.

He mashed the second half-cigarette against the tree.

AS SHINE WALKED DOWN THE hill leading to the rec shelter, he noticed several cars coming down the access drive.

Two of the cars belonged to rec shelter workers. No sign of Cynthia who would walk. One car belonged to a parent dropping off kids. Shine recognized a white car that resembled an unmarked police car. This distinct car was driven by city administrator Maury Riggs.

Riggs pulled next to Shine, rolled down his window, and asked to speak with him. Shine followed the car to a parking space near the creek.

"Mr. Ross, good to see you," he said.

"You, too."

"How's things going?" Riggs said.

"We're busy."

"You must be. You're putting in the hours. You're even dragging field number one." Riggs nodded toward field number one in the background.

Shine felt himself sweating too early in the morning.

He imagined that Maury Riggs saw his nervousness drain down his face.

Riggs never chatted with a rec worker unless there was a problem.

"I understand you sat in for Baldy Babcock the other day."

"Who?"

Riggs paused as if expecting Shine to respond. "I talked to him about the complaint we got." He paused again, tilted his massive head downward, and squinted at Shine. "Baldy Babcock's gonna be ok. Got that?"

"I'm sorry, Mr. Riggs. I didn't mean to kick up dirt."

"Water under the bridge," Riggs said. "Hey, I was a kid. Now, one of those lady-folks up top stands by a window all day, gawking. Not a blame thing to do but look out a window, I reckon. One of those women is taking mental notes all the live-long day. Know what I mean?"

Shine looked at the ground.

He hoped Riggs couldn't smell cigarette smoke. When Shine lit a cigarette, the prospect of smoke infesting his T-shirt didn't occur to him. On the other hand, Riggs' car smelled like of cigar factory.

A two-way radio kept crackling, offering raspy voices. Shine already knew the homeowner's complaint was about the sheets of ball field dust that rose to the top of the hill.

Shine wondered when Riggs first got that call about ball field number one.

"No more dragging the field," Riggs said. "Legally, son, you're too young to be on a tractor." Riggs paused again. "You know what mercy is?"

"Yes sir."

"There you go. Mercy this time."

"Thanks for that," Shine said.

Riggs rubbed his double-chin and then asked a question that startled Shine. He pointed toward the creek. "You're over there a good bit, over in west Bedlam. Your friend's Moondog Weasel. Am I right? His dad's a good man. Known him for years. A musician."

"Yes sir."

"You know Moondog Weasel?"

"Yes sir."

"Say, you might be hearing any talk about the Empire fire? You know, I was wondering if your friend thinks he might know someone who's looking to start trouble?"

"No sir."

"I believe he's got - Moondog's got - this cousin? His last name? Peace?"

Shine's neck started to sweat. He wiped his ear with his short shirtsleeve. "That's his cousin's name. Alphonso. He in trouble?"

"Not yet. Far as I can tell. But can you do me a favor?"

"What's that?"

"Can you ask your friend Moondog if he's ever heard his cousin talk about fire? If Peace has ever talked about burning things? I'd like to know what your friend thinks."

Riggs pointed a finger directly at Shine. "Remember. Mercy."

He left Shine standing in the shaded lot. Shine was mystified by the fact that Riggs wanted to know more about Alphonso Peace. He was surprised that Alphonso's name even came up. He'd remember this conversation all day and all night, and probably well into the summer.

***

SHINE MET CYNTHIA IN LATE afternoon at the creek, after work and at her request.

He'd finished playing two hours of basketball on the school's lot. He had done his best to avoid Larry Loomis. Because the pick-up games were comprised of four different teams and about twenty-two total players, Shine made it a point to be on a team that never faced Larry Loomis' team.

Cynthia pulled her hair into a ponytail. She wore a sleeveless yellow blouse. She had gone home to change clothes after work at the rec shelter. Shine noticed that this pair of Cynthia's cut-off jean shorts accentuated her tanned legs. He noticed there was not a freckle or blemish on either leg. She took off her sandals. He only untied his gym shoes. She sat cross-legged on a rock.

They sat in silence listening to the creek. Shine kept thinking about Maury Riggs' visit and his inquiry about Alphonso Peace. He jumped down from the rock and scooped up several flat rocks. He gave some to Cynthia.

"Watch this," he said. He flung a flat rock sidearm across the creek, watching it skip three times. "You fling it now. See if you can get three skips.""

"In a minute. You try again."

With the next two rocks, Shine botched his aim and never got the rocks to skip. He skipped his last rock four times across the creek.

Cynthia climbed down from the rock and pitched her flat ones across the creek. Each one skipped four or five times. Amid her laughter and finger-pointing at Shine and her soft-spoken boasting that she had the golden arm for throwing rocks, Shine picked up a huge rock, and with both hands, heaved it, causing water to splash in front of them.

"Show off," he said. "But I give it to you. I lose."

"All luck," she said. "I win."

They climbed back on the rock. This time Shine took off his shoes. Cynthia leaned toward him without touching him. Before Shine could react, Cynthia smelled his shirt.

"Your shirt smells a little like cigarette smoke."

"Sweat. It's sweaty from playing ball. I can smell it, too. Sweat and smoke. They smell alike. Sorry I didn't shower." He wanted to change the subject, and fast, yet he had no clue what to bring up.

"I think I can tell sweat from smoke."

"I did take my shirt off after the third game. I don't know, maybe I left it on top of somebody's smoky shirt. Some of those guys smoke, you know?"

"Sometimes I wonder."

Shine expected her to launch into a sermon about cigarettes. Cynthia had no clue he'd sneaked a smoke. But, the more she leaned in, the more she smiled. In an attempt to veer the topic away from smoke, Shine leaned in and put his head on her shoulder. Anything to divert her attention from his shirt.

"I like that," she said.

"That's why I did it."

"You can do that."

"Here?"

"Anywhere."

He lifted his head. "I just saw a rat swim on the other side," he said. "The size of a big shoe. It's already gone."

Cynthia acted as if she didn't hear him. She reciprocated by putting her head on his shoulder and guided his arm around her shoulder.

"Let's think like this, Shine. Let's just be us this way. Can't we?"

"I guess."

"You guess?"

"We're just fine, ok?"

"Fine is all?" she said.

He had no other immediate answer and he wasn't sure if Cynthia was expecting him to answer with more passion. Shine thought he was doing the best he could in the affection department. This was more than a half-hearted commitment. Sitting here on this rock with Cynthia Reynolds only validated what he believed: he did like her.

And he was confident he could put his arm around her anytime.

Cynthia turned her face so that she could quickly peck Shine on the lips with a kiss. "There. That's for you."

***

ANOTHER SET OF RAILROAD TRACKS
divided Bedlam and its neighbor, Mount Relling.

The entire landscape of Relling occupied both the part of the valley to which Bedlam and Jefferson Heights belonged and a steep, quarter-mile hill that merged with a few other sub-divisions above the valley's factories and interstate.

At the bottom of that hill, on Frost Avenue, were a box-shaped shoe store, a playground, a Texaco station, and, on another corner, Edward's Pony Keg. A store like Hattendorf's, it featured six, red stools at a lunch counter. A patron had to be careful not to let the bouncy swivel of a stool agitate the eating motion. Behind the counter were the wildly popular twenty flavors of ice cream inside a vat. To see that vat from outside, you stared through a gaudy "E" painted in the window.

Allison parked Ulysses' Caprice toward the back of the store. It was early evening.

She went in and bought two cups of chocolate. By the time she made it back, the tops of the mountainous scoops were melting. She handed Ulysses his cup. He clutched it with his thumb and three fingers. With his pinkie, he spun the radio dial to WSAI. He licked the melting ice cream off a finger.

They sat silent for awhile, listening to "Ooh Ooh Child" and "Since You've Been Gone - Sweet, Sweet Baby." Allison watched each car coming into and leaving Edward's lot. A gray-haired man and woman who pulled into the slot next to the Caprice glanced their way. Allison noticed they tilted their heads in unison to get a better look at Ulysses. Allison stared at the woman. The couple got out with the woman continuing to eye the front of the car. They shuffled through the Pony Keg's door.

"They haven't seen a black me before."

"They haven't seen us before."

"When do they get to see a black man hanging out in Mount Relling?" Ulysses said. "What they see is what they get."

"You mean what they see is this beautiful car?"

"Yeah, that's right. They get to see this beautiful car and this beautiful driver."

"Mister, I would tone it down. Eat your ice cream. I don't want you to get Mount Relling all up in arms. It's like you're the first black person to ever appear in this parking lot."

"Maybe I am."

"Maybe you're not."

Ulysses licked more ice cream off a finger.

"I hope those old folks don't think they need to call a cop. They didn't hear me scream," Allison said.

"She was just giving us the eye. You blame her? Look who you're with."

U.S. put his hand on Allison's arm. She put her cup on the dashboard. She scooted down a few inches in the driver's seat. She touched his hand.

"Here's my finger. It's sticky," she said. U.S. took it and wiped it on a napkin.

"It's dark in here," Ulysses said. "They see a dark man." He laughed. "Hey, I'm testifying. I'm the goodness of darkness. I think I want to sing real loud now."

"Don't sing. You'll wake up the dead in that cemetery."

Ulysses craned his neck to see the edge of Mount Relling cemetery, which sat a few hundred feet from Edward's and stretched several blocks and out of sight until a fence divided it from a little league field.

"Wait here," Allison said.

She got out of the car and went into the Pony Keg. While Ulysses savored the remaining spoonfuls of his ice cream, Allison circled the candy rack near the cash register. At the end of the short check-out line was the gray-haired couple.

Allison walked near the woman and stood not behind her, but next to her, an arm's length away. Wearing her floppy, pink summer hat, she flipped up the front of the brim and glanced at the woman.

The woman looked at her. Neither said a word. Allison smiled.

The woman elbowed her husband who seemed oblivious to anything except the cashier, a boy wearing a dirty meat-cutter's apron who didn't seem too quick about counting change. The boy mumbled to the customer in front of the elderly couple, paused, and started counting all over again. He fumbled opening a bag and ripped the bottom. He looked out the front window and muttered, "Why me at this register? Always me."

Allison flipped down the brim and walked out.

Ulysses had crumpled both cups into a ball and was licking the tips of his fingers.

"I just wanted that couple to see me once more. Since they've already formed an impression."

"I know they're fond of you even more."

The drive back to Bedlam would take only a few minutes. Evening arrived and streetlights clarified the roads. Still, Allison had barely pulled out of Edward's before she realized a car behind the Caprice had inched closer to the back of it.

Allison pulled over. She didn't turn off the engine. The car behind her pulled over.

She waited twenty seconds with the Caprice curbside. Ulysses peered through the back window, trying to determine who was in the car. Allison pulled away. The trailing car, a long sedan, pulled away with even more speed, its right front tire rubbing the curb.

In an attempt to widen the distance between them, Allison mashed the accelerator as the Caprice came closer to the railroad tracks separating Relling and Bedlam. The sedan lost no speed. The driver kept with Allison. When she was within twenty feet of the tracks, she slowed down because the tracks were old and grooved, parts of the pavement sunken. The tracks' unevenness jarred a car.

It was when the Caprice slowed that she and Ulysses flinched and ducked.

They heard a thud: an object hit the car's roof.

Allison steadied the steering wheel enough to turn and look behind the Caprice.

Another thud. Another launch jolted them: a second rock - something large enough to get their attention.

70

A third object, smaller, struck the roof. Allison pulled over.

The sedan swerved and pulled next to her. A rider lowered the passenger's window halfway.

"Stay in the car," Ulysses said. "Stay cool. This could get crazy."

With her window down, Allison cursed in their direction, but they didn't hear it. Music from the car stereo swept out of the window.

The sedan was filled with four black guys. Young. Neither Allison nor Ulysses recognized the hunkered down driver or front passenger. Cigarette smoke crept out the window.

Each wore sunglasses, even though it was now darker. Their laughter smothered the music. Then the driver turned down the volume.

"Hey," said the front seat passenger with a hat way too large for his head. "You all got that message? You there, girl." He was laughing so hard he spit. "Hey, you can't be with no brothers," he said, shaking his finger. "Brother over there, hey, you can't be with no white girl, man."

Ulysses leaned over and said, "Go on, man."

He tried to catch a glimpse of the passengers. He couldn't. The guys blended with the dark interior. Only a shiny chain dangling from the rearview mirror was detectable. Allison stared straight ahead at two one-floor buildings. She couldn't identify any of the four. She tried. She was afraid to look over again, fearing another rock. And this time through the window.

71

Ulysses heard the driver shout in his direction: "Man, next time they ain't no warning. Get you a fine black girl. That's what."

The sedan took off in front of the Caprice, coughing exhaust. The tires spun.

Ulysses got out of the Caprice and surveyed the roof: amazingly, one minor dent from three rocks.

As they drove back to Bedlam, Allison and Ulysses believed that the guys had been driving through Mount Relling and, upon slowing at the intersection by Edwards, spotted Ulysses' Caprice. Someone knew his car. Someone pointed it out, and someone saw Allison in the driver's seat. They knew Ulysses had passed the keys to her.

Someone knew a lot. Someone was not guessing.

Allison pulled in front of her house, sliding out without saying much more to Ulysses except for, "See you tomorrow. I'll let you know when. Be safe going back." She put her hand on his cheek and he raised two fingers in a peace sign.

"It'll be ok," he said. "I'm thinking about you and that ice cream."

When she walked inside the house, the Caprice had already spun around the corner, tail lights disappearing into the darkness.

***

SHINE, MOONDOG, AND POP WEASEL went in the back door of The Hot Spot. A tall man stood opening the door for several musicians carrying in instruments and small amplifiers.

The two boys followed Pop who played his trumpet weekly at The Hot Spot in Greendale.

"Don't bring your horn tonight, Shine. Maybe one day," Pop had said.

Moondog carried his father's case into the club.

The set-up went smoothly. Sparse light hung over two billiards tables in a corner. Dim light over a long bar, which was nicked and faded. The lounge, box-shaped and windowless, was dominated by round tables and way too many metal chairs. Ashtrays everywhere. Backless bar stools. Most visible were the towering ceiling fans that kicked out a breeze.

Pop had invited Shine and his son to watch him begin his stint with a new R&B band. When Pop walked through the backdoor, the bartender had yelled, "Say, Pop? How you doin'? And who you got with you?"

Before Pop could answer, the bartender pointed toward the tall man. "You boys, that's Mr. Dog," he said. "You got to stay back here. You underage. You take a piss, you best get Mr. Dog's permission. Run everything by Mr. Dog, you hear?"

"Check that," Moondog said.

THE BACK EXIT DOOR FLOPPED open and shut every few minutes. The boys sat in uncomfortable chairs. They could feel a breeze slip through the door when it opened. Mr. Dog, the tall man beside the door, never once moved. Mr. Dog's sunglasses hid his eyes.

Shine propped his chair back, toothpick in his mouth. Mr. Dog looked down at him. Shine wondered if he'd been staring at him all along. Moondog's stick of licorice hung out of his mouth. He chewed it like he would bubble gum, his arms folded behind his head. In front of the bar, in the corner with the four-piece band, Seeing Eye swung his trumpet. His cheeks ballooned when he belted out the tune, his fingers on trumpet keys.

Seeing Eye played with that one good eye wide open.

Woven in a tight circle were the bass guitarist, sax player, and drummer. Each musician sweat. Shine watched Seeing Eye keep beat with his left foot. He watched his style. It simmered in the corner of instruments. It never cooled off. The heat from the music stretched along the floor, branched out among tables; it rose and touched every dancer in club.

The Hot Spot spun with music. The band plowed its funky rhythm and blues into the party-goers' hands and feet.

They danced. Their bodies twisted on barstools and chairs.

People craned their necks to see a sax solo or a Seeing Eye trumpet riff. The place got crowded. Every chair and table were taken. Shine tried to disregard the fact that he could only see two other white people in the club: two men with shoulder-length hair, wearing chains with peace pendants. Apparently, the men knew others at their table.

Shine saw a waitress squeeze through a group and walk toward them.

"You boys want a ice water?" she said.

"Sounds fine," Shine said.

"Say what?" she said, cupping her ear.

He shouted over the music. "Yes, thanks. Water's good."

"You need help carrying anything?" Moondog asked her. "I got to get out of this chair." Mr. Dog stepped one foot closer to Moondog, as if to caution him.

"You want a ice water or not?" she asked Moondog.

"I'll take that, and thanks," he said, gnawing the end of his licorice. He pulled another stick out of his pocket.

The waitress had long drooping eyelashes and silver hoop earrings. Her hair was a perfect dark mound. The density of her perfect hair gave her the appearance of being tall. The waitress didn't hurry. She side-stepped the dancing bodies, steadying the drinks tray on the palm of her hand.

She shuffled past tables. Several people cornered her, wanting refills. When she leaned forward to take orders, Shine noticed the sequins bordering the bottom of the waitress' short skirt. Although the skirt was tight, she took long strides. When she walked, the fancy sequins glowed.

About the time Pop Weasel's set ended, the waitress returned with two mugs of ice water.

"You all got mugs, now," she said. "Somebody must think you're special." She wiped her forehead with a finger. "I'm seeing that outdoor breeze would be good for me."

The ceiling fans blew more hot air than cool. Empty drink glasses filled every table. In the time the band played two sets, Shine grew hungry. Two mugs of ice water over three hours didn't strengthen his numb legs.

The boys stood and sat, stood and sat every ten minutes. Some people dancing pointed in the boys' direction and waved to them. Dancers, unnerved, whirled on the crammed dance floor, every bodily limb in motion.

Now, Mr. Dog moved cat-quick from the back door to the entrance of the club. Minutes earlier, when the set ended, Seeing Eye and the band headed to the parking lot to get some air.

Shine and Moondog heard noise louder than any voices inside The Hot Spot.

Mr. Dog hurried back, as if he'd forgotten something. Shine and Moondog stood again, but the tall man stood next to them. He cleared his throat. Shine turned to look and Mr. Dog shook his head "no." He lifted his finger to his lips signaling, "Be quiet."

An altercation of some sort was occurring outside.

Mr. Dog got an "ok" sign from the bartender and, finally, he lead the boys outside through the front door where people gathered. He forced a path to get the boys fully outdoors.

Shine saw Moondog's father sitting in a lawn chair, holding the side of his face, his head down. Four or five people hovered around him. Moondog had learned to stay calm. He rarely saw his father roused. Shine stayed calm, standing next to his friend.

Another man with an abundant, wiry afro, who was held back by a few party-goers, shouted first at Seeing Eye and then at the sky.

A tipsy woman elbowed her way next to Mr. Dog. The woman, obviously drunk, said to Shine, "You know that trumpet player?"

"That's my friend's dad," he said.

"That so?"

"Did my friend's dad get in a fight?"

"He ain't fought nobody," said the drunk woman. "Somebody came at him. Sneaky. I heard it. That trumpet player said, 'Don't talk nasty about my little white friend like that. He's a youngster. Great little horn player. That's my boy's school friend.' That crazy man over there cold-cocked the trumpet player, just like that." The drunk woman gazed at Mr. Dog who stared at her. She walked away, grumbling.

Moondog went over to his father. He knelt and looked at his face.

The man who cold-cocked Seeing Eye had a feathery afro. His hair seemed to hang in the air as he yelled at the sky. He yelled directly at someone's car tires. He yelled at the ground. "Ain't no underage white folk allowed in my bar."

"It ain't your bar," said the waitress who'd served Shine and Moondog. She put her face a few inches from the man's. "It ain't your bar. It's my bar. I work it. Hear me?"

"You bring that one boy in here again, guess what?" the man yelled to Pop Weasel, who ignored him. "I don't like the way he look at women."

Mr. Dog stepped toward the belligerent man. "What you gonna do?" Mr. Dog said. "A couple white folk in here already."

"Not young," the man said, "And I ain't talkin' to you."

"Whatever you do got to get past me. That ain't happening."

Moondog and a few others walked with Pop Weasel back into The Hot Spot. A man with a red fedora walked the drunk man to his car and insisted he sit in it.

The waitress wadded up a bar towel full of ice cubes. She held it on Pop Weasel's cheek before he took it over, patting his cheek with the icy towel. When he took it off, Shine and Moondog noticed the bump.

"It's alright, son," Pop said. "You never know people. I don't know that cat, but he has a real problem with color. He'll be what he is."

"He doesn't even know me," Shine said. "I'm by the back exit."

"He just knows what he sees," Pop said. "Which is messed up."

"We going home soon?" Shine said.

"Wait it out," Moondog said.

"We'll be home in two hours flat," Pop said.

"That'll be a long two," Shine said. "I like this place, But, Pop, you can't get hurt anymore."

The trumpet player planted a few more handfuls of ice in the towel and put it on his cheek, under his blind eye. His trumpet sat upright on its stand in front of the drums, the horn gleaming under the corner light.

PROPHET

THE SUNOCO STATION ON THE corner of Woodard and Densing had the only cigarette machine in north Bedlam, except for the Touchdown Grill, a bar in the center of Bedlam's shopping district. Two blocks of family-owned stores lined the district.

The back sides of those stores on one side of the street came within two hundred feet of train tracks, with Mount Relling technically on the other side of the tracks.

Shine walked to the side of the gas station. He suspected the chubby car mechanic was inside the garage laboring over a brake job, a radiator, or a water pump. Shine heard him rev up a drill. He scooted along the outside wall. It was important he do this quietly and quickly. The wall led to the side glass door, the cigarette machine right inside it, within eyesight.

In his mind, Shine rehearsed being quick to pump in a quarter and dime for a pack. A puny thirty-five cents. He had to dig through the pennies in his glass jar at home for the dime. The last thing he wanted was the hefty mechanic to wobble into the lobby and discover him with his hand on a pull lever. It was early in the morning and no one yet pulled in to get gas.

Shine scanned two rows of cigarette options. Winston, Pall Mall, Salem, Chesterfield, Kent, Marlboro, Kool. A few more.

Shine felt like a man coming home after a day's work at the factory. This man he imagined: he had run out of cigarettes during his work shift; he needed to bulk up on a new pack; and so before he went home to his wife's delicious cooking, he was going to open a new pack of menthols and enjoy a smoke before dinner. The man he imagined: his wife's cooking would taste so much better after he smoked one cigarette, and he could relax far more if he had a smoke before dinner.

One problem: Shine was a teen.

Buying this pack of Kools was a big risk, although he was no slouch. The half-smoked cigs in his rusty band-aid box were stale. He'd be 16-years old in ten more months. He'd be ready to drive. Besides, he knew that his father used to smoke from time to time. And cigarettes were prevalent on t.v. So, why not this machine? Why not the Sunoco station?

Shine's effort to insert thirty five cents, grip the lever, and begin to pull it was graceful. So graceful as one sweeping gesture that it reminded him of catching a basketball under a basket so smoothly that all he had to do was toss the ball off the backboard, sink it, and score. One movement, one motion that resulted in not one misfire.

Except the pull lever stuck.

He could feel his face burn with frustration.

Shine tried easing the lever outward. He turned around. No mechanic yet. He jerked the lever. He jerked it again, harder. He kicked the bottom. He tapped the glass at the point of the cigarette pack's image. He tapped the glass again and again. He tapped it hard with four knuckles.

"You got to really jiggle that handle. I mean, really jiggle it."

Shine turned around and saw the fat mechanic wiping his big hands on a dirty towel. "Jiggle it big. Jiggle. You getting those for your Dad?"

"Yeah. He just got back from a long trip," Shine said. His father was on the road, truck-driving, and he'd quit smoking many years ago.

"I'll let it go this time," the mechanic said. He held out his right arm and with that right hand poking at air, he imitated the correct way Shine should jiggle the lever. Then he walked back into the garage. Shine heard a metal tool strike the floor.

He jiggled the lever hard, again, and the pack of Kools dropped into the tray. Shine looked outside and fled out the door. He stashed his Kools a sock. He preferred not to have a pants pocket reveal a rectangular bulge throughout the day.

***

AFTER HE PICKED UP MOONDOG, the boys headed past a far edge of Garland Park where they waited at their favorite train-hopping spot.

Most every train coming through Bedlam had to stop near the factories, unload material, and pack and haul new equipment. It took several miles after a Bedlam stop before a train picked up decent speed. Trains nearing this spot just past the park crept slowly.

Easy to hop a boxcar.

Shine felt the rickety movement of the train rolling forward. The boxcar rattled. The boys sat straight and braced their backs The wheels churned. Sweltering heat rose from the tracks. Shine imagined how much concentration it must have taken to build train tracks on which fifty box cars moved fluidly for hundreds of miles.

Moondog tossed a mashed bag of potato chips to Shine. He let it lay on the floor. "Brought two bags," Moondog said. "They're still good, even though I had them crammed in my pockets."

Shine was so busy settling himself and daydreaming that minutes passed before he or Moondog detected a lumpy blanket in the corner. An impressive lump. More like a grotesque hump. Shine caught a whiff of onions and gasoline coming from that direction. The blanket moved. Moondog scooted closer to Shine. "What you think?" he said.

"Not now. Quiet," Shine said.

They watched the blanket. Shine stiffened when a head abruptly rose from it. A man whose oily hair was matted against his eyebrows peered at them. He squinted. He uttered words that were unclear. Shine's first thought was that this was, in fact, a living, breathing hobo that legend affirms will ride boxcars all over the country, roaming from city to city.

This is the scavenger. This is the ghost-like person he and his friends talked about.

His second thought frightened him: Are he and Moondog in danger? Would they even survive the trip to Hamilton and back?

Shine had a third thought: Did he make a really bad mistake hopping this boxcar?

The man threw off a corner of his blanket. He kept his legs covered. His shirt was unbuttoned. One arm sported a tattoo of an arrow wide as a belt. It went from his elbow to his shoulder.

The onions-gasoline smell remained.

"Where you headed?" the man said.

"Hamilton," Shine said.

"Where you headed?" Moondog said.

The man stared, saying nothing. When he kept tilting his head, as if he had trouble seeing the boys, Shine thought that to say little would be their best defense, until the train slowed enough - slowed to maybe ten miles-per-hour - for him and Moondog to leap out, hit the ground, and run for it. At least run several hundred yards without looking back.

Shine remembered he once heard that a hobo would steal anything.

"We don't have anything," Shine said.

"I didn't ask," the man said, breaking his silence. He mumbled something else undetectable.

"Where you going?" Moondog said again. The man just looked at him. He lit a cigarette he pulled from underneath the blanket. The blanket had a base of pink tarnished by a grimy sheen that turned it yellowish.

"I may have something for you's," the man said.

"You got something?" Shine said. His hands sweat. He realized Moondog had a small screwdriver a little larger than a toothpick. Moondog poked his leg with it so Shine would know.

"You's comin' from Bedlam?"

"Yeah," Shine said.

"You know what?"

"What?"

"Here's the thing," the man said. "You got a candy bar?"

"Nope," Moondog said. "We ate it."

The man snickered. It was as if he heard a joke yet sought permission to laugh at it. A harsh chuckle.

"Damn. I ain't ate yet. Oh, well."

"Here's chips," Shine said. He flung his crumpled bag of chips on the man's blanket, and he opened it immediately.

"You's don't know I'm like a seer of things," the man said. "I kind of see things differently, you could say. Like in dreams. Or like when I'm looking at something really, really carefully. Eyeballing it."

Shine had no idea where the conversation was going. The man finished the chips before he spoke anymore. The boys were captivated. In Shine's colorful imagining, the man could have leaped from the blanket and held a knife to his throat. Yet this man just sat under a blanket in real summer heat. The arrow tattoo seemed larger than his whole body.

"See, I reckon I just know things. I reckon I'm just like one of them prophets. You's want something to know while we're aboard this here train?"

"What's that?" Shine said.

"Let me tell," the man said. "How about that fire, that big old fire that burned down that factory back in Bedlam? One a few weeks ago? Flames blazin' all over heaven."

"We saw that fire," Shine said. "It happened just about in my friend's backyard." He nodded to Moondog. "What about it?"

"Well," the man said, "I done saw in my mind someone starting that fire. I don't believe it started by itself, and I ain't believing it was something exploded in there. I got something else in my mind."

Shine's thinking encompassed so much territory now, even to the point of his wondering whether this man set the fire. How could Shine know? The man stayed silent as he finished his cigarette. He lifted his legs under the blanket and repositioned himself. Moondog wadded his empty chips bag.

The constant clang of train cars disrupted Shine's thinking.

"Way I see's it," the man said, "was that someone young set that-there fire. I'd say like in high school. That age. You's know a lot of kids in high school. I don't. I done quit when I was 14. I up and left. They never come looking for me, neither."

"Someone set that fire?" Shine said.

"Someone in his neighborhood." The man pointed to Moondog. "Sir," he said to Moondog, "I hate to spell that out about your neck of woods. But, sir, I got clarity. You might even know a person who set it - that-there fire. Yep.

85

You might even know a person. I'm just real glad it wasn't you. You're too busy hoppin' trains."

"I wasn't around, anyway," Moondog said. "Who'd want to burn down a job place like the Empire? People worked there."

"Someone done did," the man said, lighting another cigarette.

As the train slowed, Shine could see the outskirts of the sprawling General Motors factory in Hamilton.

"You's know what else?" the man said. "That's a good campground fire me and my friends make back in the park in Bedlam, ain't it? You's like those campfires, huh?"

During the few seconds Shine turned and looked at Moondog, the man had mashed out his cigarette, rolled up his blanket, and said goodbye. He leaped out of the boxcar. Shine got up and peered outside, watching the hobo roll on the ground and then stand up and shake his stiff legs one at a time.

***

SHINE COULDN'T SHAKE THE DAY that he and Moondog encountered the hobo.

The hobo had persuaded Shine to think much more about how the Empire fire started.

"It didn't start itself," the hobo said.

These words alone triggered a new notion that someone could have ignited it at a calculated moment - on a day the Empire was closed and on a day when no employees were around. On a lazy Sunday.

Was the hobo a liar? Was he a real bum? He seemed smart even though he talked crazy. His clothes stunk. His blanket stunk. Is this how prophets smelled? How could this guy know about the fire?

Shine pulled out his trumpet and wiped fingerprints off the bell with his shirt. He oiled the valves. He fiddled with the spit valve. He practiced chords. He got his lips comfortable on the mouthpiece. When he heard a dog barking outside, he looked out his bedroom window and watched a neighbor's beagle chase a squirrel. The dog paced back and forth.

Shine practiced the song, "Grazing in the Grass." Pop had written the notes for him on music-liner paper. The song was new, arriving as a single record in late spring and soaring on the summer pop music charts. It had been performed and recorded in the spring by a great South African trumpeter named Hugh Masekela.

An up-tempo song, it required nimble fingering. Shine played certain notes at certain times. He loved the song because in his mind he could hear Pop strike riffs both at home and at The Hot Spot that his own fingers could not stick. Shine could hear Pop's feverish high notes, and he felt the shift to a slower tempo, soft and distant.

Shine sat on a desk chair and played. He set a fan a few feet away, its old spinning blades tick-tick-ticking, cutting into the silence between songs.

The early afternoon dragged on. Bedroom door shut. Jeans, short pants, and clean underwear lying in a pile on the unmade bed. Seeing Eye told him, "Practice now, or never do it at all."

"Grazing in the Grass." Because Hugh Masekela was from South Africa, Shine thought of tall jungle grass in Africa. He imagined a trumpet player holding his trumpet high and bellowing notes toward the grass.

He heard a knock on his door. When he stood, with his short pants all bunched up, he grimaced as his sweaty legs stuck to the chair.

He let in his mother, who examined that pile on his bed.

"Where you going to sleep tonight?"

"On top of those clothes," Shine said.

"Any way you can tone it down a notch or two? Or practice in the garage?"

Shine hadn't seen his mother all day. But he knew from the washcloth that she was battling a new headache. She rubbed the washcloth in circles on her neck.

"I'll be two more minutes, no more."

When he finished one last part, he played "Taps" softly and put away his horn.

Josephine Ross sat at the dining room table writing a letter. Shine stood a few feet behind her peering over her shoulder.

In the time that his mother left his room, she put on white gloves. Shine watched his mother hold her pen in the air. Her posture suggested she was preparing to conduct an orchestra.

Shine took another step forward.

"I'm writing to Mrs. Ruth Lyons," his mother said.

"You writing her directly?"

"She reads all her mail."

"Ruth Lyons is really famous," Shine said. "I'm not sure she reads all her mail."

"Ruth Lyons always says she reads all her fan mail. But, I'm writing her directly to ask her for a ticket to the show," his mother said. She brandished her pen in the air before starting another sentence.

Shine watched her. The wet washcloth hung around her neck. She held out one hand, admiring a white glove. Her penmanship was perfect. She formed large letters and underlined the words "please" and "thank you" and the entire sentence, "I help support all your accomplishments, especially The Ruth Lyons Fund which helps children in hospitals receive Christmas gifts."

Ruth Lyons was one of the most famous, daytime, t.v. talk show hosts in the country. Her show, The 50-50 Club, was easily the most charming show on daytime t.v. The show in Cincinnati dominated television at noon on weekdays. In a motherly manner, Ruth Lyons chatted with other national entertainers. She joked, questioned, chided. She wore white gloves. During intermissions, she directed her cameramen to pan the audience and capture her white-gloved women, sitting in rows, who waved in unison at cameras.

"I've been trying to get a ticket for a year," his mother said. "I think it'll work this time. I underlined her lovely Children's Fund. I forgot to do that before."

"Maybe a couple of your letters got lost in all the mail she gets," Shine said.

"No, she reads all her mail," his mother said. "She might forget to give some letters to the ticket people."

As she took off the gloves and licked the envelope, the doorbell rang.

The woman at the door used sign language in front of Josephine. The woman was deaf, and it appeared she knew Shine's mother. Maybe from church. She could have been a deaf church-goer who saw Josephine every Sunday.

"Shine, Miss Louise needs your help changing a flat tire," his mother said. "Spare tire is there. Her car's out in front. The tire blew out next to Hattendorf's, but she felt more comfortable driving here on a flat."

"I'll try," he said. He'd never changed a tire in his life.

After he struggled to fit the car-jack underneath the driver's side front end, his hands slipped jacking up the car.

He clinched the tire iron tighter. He grunted. He could only loosen two lug nuts. He exerted rubbery arm strength on the other four. The deaf woman stood over him. Shine heard her muffled attempt to speak undetectable words, though he didn't look back at her.

When he got up to stretch, he saw movement by the corner shrubs. Standing half-hidden by the shrubs was Ulysses. Shine waved him over.

Adjusting his sunglasses, his hands deep in his pockets, Ulysses glanced up and down the street. He walked toward the car.

"Were you hiding?" he said to Ulysses.

"Naw. Just dropped off Allison, and I heard noise out here. Checking it out."

"The tire iron," Shine said. "I can't loosen these lug nuts." He handed the tire iron to Ulysses, who, already kneeling, surveyed the car's front.

Shine hesitated introducing Ulysses to the deaf woman; he took at least five minutes to do so. When he did, Ulysses had finished tightening the lug nuts on the spare tire. By that time, Josephine Ross had come back outside, continuing to hold her washcloth at the base of her neck.

"Is Allison with you?" she asked Ulysses.

"She went inside," he said.

"Oh."

The deaf woman signed to Josephine and she signed back. Shine's mother glanced at Ulysses and back at the deaf woman, pointing toward Ulysses.

"Miss Louise thanks both of you," she said. "She also asked who Ulysses is."

"Am I ok here?" Ulysses said.

"I told her you're a friend of the family," Shine's mother said.

The two women continued with their sign language. Shine and Ulysses watched them.

"She also said Ulysses is a strong young man. Very strong to get that tire off." Josephine clutched Shine's shoulder, guiding him to look at her. "Miss Louise said Shine was awfully nice to let Ulysses help with the tire."

"A friend of the family, mom," he said.

***

IT WAS EVENING. A FEW bats flew overhead.

Shine fumbled in his pants pocket for the pack of Kools he bought for thirty-five cents at the gas station. The rusty Band-Aid box was secure in his back pocket. He thought about transferring the new cigarettes to the old box before they got crushed. First, he decided to smoke two.

No quiz from his mother as to where he was headed. He'd gone out the back door. No sight of Allison. She must have been with Ulysses. Moondog had not called him. Cynthia had not called. She was going with friends to eat. No games at Garland tonight. No action. Just the empty ball fields and parking lot.

There were no new messages from his mother about JoJo.

JoJo.

Shine walked down Garland hill and sat just inside the woods. He could still see up the hill. With his first puff, images of JoJo flooded his mind. He imagined JoJo in his cage, crowned with those colors. The majestic feathers.

JoJo swooped from tree to tree amid other night creatures, merging in the deep night with the woods and backyards. JoJo had not the convenience of pretty metal or a square mirror in which to admire himself, or the hands that filled his food and water trays. The bird's new turf must have included fear and confusion: Shine wondered if JoJo was darting around, half-hidden, like some drunk person stumbling in a parking lot in search of his car.

SHINE PULLED THREE POSTCARDS FROM his back pants pocket.

He'd folded and re-folded the postcards so much that they looked like a paper accordion. His father's big loops in his d's and l's looked like o's. Every sentence was abbreviated.

"Shine, good mileage. Weather fine. No roadkill…" His father squeezed in as much detail as possible, using a majority of the postcard space. "No need for worry. Black Panthers talk. Study them. They're educated. They want right things but go overboard. Some want to teach. Some violent. Mixed bag. Talk to Klump if curious." His father always got in a word about Shine's mother: "Wash dishes. Be there. Keep eyes peeled. Your sister too. Love, Dad."

Shine had hardly talked at all with his father about the Black Panther Party. Shine had no idea about this "violence" his father took no time to describe. What violence?

Shine's father wrote on a card: "Hang tough. Practice well - trumpet & basketball."

***

THE GUYS LINED UP AGAINST a concrete wall.

The outdoor basketball court abutted the highway exit ramp into Bedlam. It sat on a lower tier of ground below two tennis courts. There were enough guys to form two teams of five players.

Two seniors, who supervised this volunteer scrimmage, picked the teams. They separated Shine and Larry Loomis forcing them to guard each other.

What blue was left in the sky invited another push of gray smoke from Fox Paper, Inc. Another factory across the highway made bedding material like mattresses and batting for quilts.

The heavy air hovered over the court. The guys had to play below the tennis courts today, because a new gym floor was being installed in the high school gym.

Shine picked up Larry Loomis who was dribbling. He pressured him, jabbing at the ball, trying to upset Larry's dribbling and passing. Shine was quick. He felt he could wrest the ball from Larry, who seemed to dribble endlessly.

For the most part, over fifteen minutes, Shine outplayed Larry Loomis.

Among the upperclassmen, Shine scored four points on fast-break layups, bettering Larry's two points on a fluke jump shot. The scrimmage heated up. It was a man's game played by boys underneath the canopy of factory exhaust.

After the second three-minute break, both teams faced off again. Shine claimed an even greater burst of energy than Larry Loomis. Twice, the basketball bounced off Larry's foot and out of bounds. When he missed a layup, he bent over, his hands on his knees.

Shine dished his passes to the two tallest seniors. Looking insecure, Larry telegraphed his passes to the hulking forward, who missed shot after shot.

When Shine sped down court on a fast break, he realized Larry Loomis had abruptly met him as Shine neared the basket. Shine caught the pass and barely had a chance to shoot it.

Shine felt the force of Larry's body against his. Unexpected force.

Shine landed against that wall rising up to the tennis courts.

Was it an intentional shove, Shine wondered. What's up with Larry Loomis?

He didn't know. He knelt on one knee, holding his head. It happened far too quickly. A trickle of blood formed.

None of the other players saw the action. Nor did anyone see Larry Loomis throw an elbow. Both teams just played until a senior spotted Shine on a knee. He had definitely been on the receiving end of a blatant foul. The game stopped for a minute.

Shine's forehead had grazed concrete. He could've jarred a tooth completely loose. All these thoughts were circling his mind. Head, face, teeth. Cheek, nose, chin. Only his head ached.

He had felt Larry Loomis' left leg come down first, shoving him enough to upset his balance. And then, watching his shot arc toward the basket, he felt a forearm. He saw Larry out of the corner of his eye. Shine struggled to regain his balance, yet tripped and slammed into the wall.

Shine's forehead took the brunt of the impact. Only five feet away from the concrete, his body picked up such speed that he couldn't stop.

As Shine replayed the action before he was shoved, he believed Larry Loomis was glaring at him coming down the court. Larry seemed frustrated that he had not yet blocked Shine's shots or stolen the ball from Shine.

The sunlight faded, so the game was called. Two seniors, who realized the cut might need stitches, wrapped a towel around Shine's forehead and helped him into a car.

They rushed him to Good Samaritan Hospital before Shine could ask Larry why he threw a leg and elbow.

When his mother met him in the Emergency Room at Good Samaritan, Shine was stitched up. The doctor told him to sleep sitting up. "Just kidding," the doctor said. "You just need to sleep and not tilt your head. And no pillow fights."

Josephine Ross ran two fingers over the head gauze wrapped around her son's head.

"Hold your head still when you walk," she said. "Don't jerk it. Don't bend down. At least for the next few days."

It must have been the pain medication that helped Shine partially sleep in the car on the way home. There were no speedy dreams. No scene of Larry Loomis coming toward him on the court, denying his shot, and coercing him into the wall. No replay. No dream at all.

There was only a sense of comfort, in between spurts of a throbbing headache.

***

SHINE CAME TO WORK AT the Garland recreation shelter with white gauze taped around his head.

Cynthia and another girl, a co-worker, were busy wiping boxes of checkers, chess sets, games, and playing cards. The co-worker soon hurled a water hose across the floor, turned on the faucet, and sprayed muddy footprints off a swingset.

Three girls sat around Cynthia and the co-worker. Two of the girls were from north Bedlam and one was from west Bedlam.

"My mama let me stay all night with my friend from school, "the girl from west Bedlam said, pausing. "She can come stay at my house in west Bedlam anytime. That's what my mama said." She pointed to her friend. "Her name's Becky. Mine's Lacey. They rhyme. We're like sisters, only she's white. My mama said that's just color. That's not the heart. I don't know what my mama means."

The girl Becky set up her friend's jumbo-size red checkers and waited patiently for her to start the game.

"Can your friend talk?" Cynthia said.

"Yep," Becky said, kicking her legs under the table. "I can talk."

A piece of gauze came loose from Shine's head and flopped over an ear. He got tape from the crayon box and asked Cynthia to wrap the tape around the gauze. Shine thought of his friendship with Moondog. A black friend. He would tell Moondog things he wouldn't tell his sister or his father. Moondog's father, Seeing Eye, a man who was kinder to Shine than any teacher, shared his music with the same passion Judson Ross talked trucking and wrote Shine postcards from different cities.

"Did you have a good time staying all night with your friend here?" Cynthia asked the girl Lacey.

"We played house," the girl said. "I kept thinking of my house and my daddy."

"Your daddy?"

"He lost his job. He's sad. It burned down. He said his job burned up. You know that fire? That building?"

Shine sat across from the three girls. "You mean the fire that burned down the warehouse?"

"That's the one." She and her friend Becky moved checkers across the jumbo board.

"Does he think he knows what happened?" Shine got up and walked to a wood railing. The previously loose piece of gauze dangled again. He pressed the tape back on it.

"No. My daddy just thinks it caught fire. My daddy said it could be somebody started it, too, but he don't think about that. He's sad. So, I come over to my friend Becky's. Our names rhyme."

The female co-worker chimed in: "I wouldn't doubt that fire was set."

"How would you know?" Shine said.

"My dad's a volunteer fireman. He was there."

"I think she might know more than you," Cynthia said.

Away from the table now, she watched other kids come down the hill to the rec shelter. She jokingly jerked Shine's arm, which caused him to lose his balance as he tried walking the wood railing from one shelter corner to another. Losing balance, he had to jump down.

"Does he think the fire was set maybe on purpose?" Shine said.

"He thinks you can't rule it out. Who knows? Arson?" the co-worker said. "Dad said there's some suspicion to the whole thing. Weird."

"That's wild." Shine hopped on the wood railing pretending to use it as a surfboard, before kids swarmed the shelter. "I'd sure like to know who did it, if it was done."

Shine stared at a wall to maintain his balance.

Silence. A white car pulled up to the shelter. Shine was unaware that Maury Riggs rolled down his window and was waving him over. Not until Cynthia shouted, "Shine."

He jumped down and jogged over to Maury Riggs, feeling his gauze to make sure his forehead was still covered.

"Yes sir."

"I heard about your head. Just wanted to check in with you," Maury Riggs said. He flicked an ash off his cigar and lit it again.

"I'm fine, Mr. Riggs. No headache today."

"You look spiffy. Tell me, have you heard anything from your friend Moondog?" He was now whispering to Shine. "You know, because I know your father and your father's hauled some bricks and whatnot to my house before, and not even charged me, not even one red cent. Because of that, I want to give you a leg up on a few things. Your father's a hard worker. He's to be trusted."

"I think so, too." Shine had no one idea what Maury Riggs was implying or about to tell him. He had no idea if it was some secret or gossip.

A group of kids passed Shine and the white city car, staring at him as they skipped toward the swingset.

He could feel that loose gauze dangling on his ear.

"You remember my mentioning that cousin of your friend's, Mr. Peace?"

"I remember that." Shine wound the gauze around his ear like a strand of long hair.

"That's right. You might promise me something," Riggs said. "Right now, if you can." He hung his elbow outside his car and hunched closer to Shine, leaning his head partially out the window.

"It's a promise," Shine said.

"Keep this to yourself. Don't you get too close to that Peace fella."

"Right. Ok."

"Be careful in that neighborhood, son. My suggestion."

Shine didn't ask why he should avoid Alphonso Peace. He already made an effort to avoid him. He'd told Moondog to be careful around him. Still, Alphonso Peace basically slept, ate, and worked under Pop Weasel's roof. He rarely spoke to anyone, according to Moondog, and he seemed inhospitable to family.

Maury Riggs sank fully back into the car seat. His large body shape-shifted to consume much of the front seat. Shine turned to look at the kids on the swingset.

Shine stepped back as Riggs flicked another ash from his cigar. He rolled up the window, turned the steering wheel, and sped up Garland hill, leaving a tail of dust in his wake.

**

SHINE LUGGED HIS TRUMPET CASE up the basement stairs.

He'd decided to belt some tunes in the basement, but the space reminded him of a cave. At least his bedroom had a window. He could daydream between songs and at least count treetops.

Shine was determined to memorize the notes to "Grazing in the Grass."

Allison noticed her brother's distraction.

"Shine," she said. "Shine!"

"Say what?" he said, turning to see his mother take a bite of carrot cake she and Allison were sharing.

Shine set down his case and walked toward the cake. His fingers still smelled of valve oil.

"Could you please tell our mother about Ulysses," his sister said.

"What do you mean?" Shine said.

"I mean, let her know who I believe he is." She looked away from her mother and at the doorway leading into the kitchen.

Josephine Ross chewed another bite of cake. She stared at an antique china cabinet. Allison now stared at her mother. Shine stared at Allison. He was speechless.

"He's your good friend?" Shine said.

His mother dabbed at her plate with her fork. Allison rubbed her hands, having pushed her empty plate to the middle of the table.

"I don't think our mother trusts me," she said. "There's something about Ulysses."

"I always call him U.S.," Shine said, trying to change the subject.

"Nothing really bothers me, Allison," Josephine said. "I just don't know a lot about him."

"But you said, mother, that - and I quote - 'He comes from over there.'"

Jeffrey Hillard

"Well, I meant the west side. That's all I meant. I meant that he's not from here."

"You mean, not from white north Bedlam. You mean, he's a black boy. You mean, he's a young guy my age, and he doesn't live in our neighborhood. What you mean, mother, is, I'm white. I should date somebody white."

Shine bit into and swallowed nearly half of his cake. "Can I be excused?" he said.

"Not yet," Allison said. "Stay here. You're a witness."

"I'm not ready to witness anything."

"Is Ulysses a good person, Shine?" she said. "Is he nice to me? Is he nice to you? Does his being black bother you?"

Josephine turned to face Allison, while she could also glance at her son.

"I think he's a good guy," Shine said. "He doesn't play that much basketball, but he's funny. Yeah, he's funny."

"I think I like him, Allison," her mother said. "I do. Let's say I haven't been one hundred percent sure how you have been seeing him. If you were having dating plans. That's all."

"I have good taste, mother."

"I'm not questioning your taste, daughter."

"I think he's a good person," Shine said. "If he played basketball, I'd know more about him He's tall. Moondog always talks about him. He says U.S. is smart. He could drive when he was fourteen."

102

"Be quiet, Shine." Allison looked at the cake. "If I would ever kiss Ulysses, mother, what would you do?"

"Well, Allison, guess I might think about that. Then I'd make it seem like I didn't see anything. Maybe I might think, that's my daughter who says her taste is very good."

"Trust," Allison said. "You got to trust. This is 1968. It's not the 19th century."

***

IT WAS LATE EVENING when Shine went back down to the basement and retrieved his valve oil he forgot.

The door leading into the garage was open. The garage light was on. He heard Allison rummaging in the garage, flipping through one of their father's toolboxes. The sound of her banging one metal object against another grew louder. He walked into the garage.

Ulysses' Caprice was parked in their wide garage. Allison wrestled with a car jack. She tried to fit the jack's latch under the front fender, but it kept sliding off. The metal base of the jack slipped and she kicked it. She hadn't come close to locking the jack into its mount.

"Need some help?" Shine said.

"Dammit," she said.

"I can get that tire off," Shine said. "You got another one?"

"Dammit. Get over here."

Shine's sister flung a hammer against a sack of bird feed. She gripped a screwdriver as if she were planning to jab a rotted garden hose. She stood, took a deep breath, and settled into a moment of poise.

103

"Just help me get this spare tire on."

"What happened?"

"Enough. "Don't ask."

But Shine kept asking. "Did you just now see the flat tire?"

"Look," she said, pointing to a puncture in the tire. "The Caprice was in the driveway. All I can figure is, when the sun went down, someone must've driven by and took a knife to the tire. Nobody saw it. All I can figure."

"That's wild," Shine said. "That was fast."

"Dammit. Don't ask."

Shine surprised even himself with his agility at flat tire-removal. He felt gash. He knew that whoever slashed the tire meant it. The tire had been sliced wide open.

Allison's version of the evening was quick. Shine couldn't sneak in another question. His sister rambled. She had dropped off Ulysses at home and drove back to north Bedlam. After Ulysses complained to her that he suspected several people were suspiciously eying his car and stopping to look at it, Allison thought it best to drive the car back to her family's garage for a few days.

"There are people Ulysses can't trust," she said.

"Like who?"

"I don't know. But I think I might know. Stop it. Don't ask."

"You can't tell your own brother? Who would I tell?"

"Ulysses' own brother, fool. You'd tell Moondog. Everything."

"Never."

"Always," Allison said. "And you wouldn't shut up, either. So, don't ask me."

Shine rode shotgun. It was after 11:00. Allison had called Ulysses from the basement phone and explained the ordeal. He wanted the Caprice returned now. He wanted to look at the slashed tire. He wanted to see the damage. When U.S. drove Allison and Shine back home at 11:30, he kept the radio volume turned up loud enough so that no one could clearly say anything.

Inside his cool demeanor, Ulysses was seething.

***

THE NEXT DAY, MOONDOG RECOUNTED for Shine the entire scenario, how Ulysses dealt with the crime. The two friends waited to hop a train near the Garland fence, their usual spot.

It would take only a short train ride this time for Moondog to describe how his brother U.S. channeled his anger, which kept a certain person's bedroom from being totally upturned. Not a sheet or pillow or person were touched. U.S. channeled his anger by sitting on it, preventing him from turning Alphonso's bedroom into damaged goods.

The two boys hopped out of the musty boxcar and onto dirt ground near West Chester, thirty minutes after the train arrived in Bedlam.

A patch of woods formed the edge of a warehouse district. Sitting on a monstrous fallen log in the middle of the woods, they could still see warehouses. They opened their cans of Mountain Dew. They couldn't wait.

Moondog left out no small detail that his brother had shared with him. Moondog told Shine of the quiet yet menacing way Ulysses knelt by the side of his cousin Alphonso's bed, waiting with a flashlight, as Alphonso slept and snored.

When he'd first seen the slash, Ulysses felt that Alphonso might pull such a stunt - or at least pay someone to do it. He more than wanted to question his cousin. Ulysses, in a way he tried hard to stifle, wanted to hurt him.

Moondog's big brother had waited by Alphonso's bed, more like a Boy Scout cot. Moondog elaborated in colorful detail, and he scrunched his face with every gesture.

"U.S. would have got him good had he woken up. Alphonso's face would've got the blunt end of that flashlight."

U.S. had waited one, two, three hours quietly by Alphonso's bed. The guy who slept with that peace-sign chain necklace never stirred. Only Alphonso's snoring lifted a corner of the bedsheet. Had Alphonso stirred, Moondog told Shine, his brother Ulysses was ready to shove that flashlight in Alphonso's face.

"He would've made Alphonso eat that flashlight."

After three hours, U.S. was seriously thinking about waking Alphonso with blinding light, and then dragging his sorry ass right out of bed. Moondog's brother had planned to at least tie a sock around his mouth.

All for messing with his Caprice. For slashing a tire.

"And here's another thing," Moondog said. "It was possible that Alphonso could have scooted far down in his backseat when those guys threw rocks at Ulysses' car, the night he and Allison went to Edward's Pony Keg for ice cream.

According to Moondog, Ulysses waited for Alphonso's snoring to cease and for him to get up.

U.S. thought his presence on the floor beside Alphonso would rouse him. He preferred not to engage unless absolutely necessary. He felt it necessary. It was about his Caprice. It was about thirty dollars for a new tire. He knew that blade had to be Alphonso's. Alphonso had criticized him recently about seeing Allison. He heard Alphonso's whiny voice in his head.

Moondog told Shine that Alphonso said to his brother: "What you want with that white girl? Man, why you want her?"

Moondog told Shine that Alphonso had laid into U.S at the dinner table. Alphonso knew. He knew Ulysses liked her. Alphonso said he'd not tell anyone that it might really upset. That is, any of his Black Panther brothers.

Ulysses did not trust him.

In Moondog's report to Shine as they sat on that monstrous fallen log in the woods, Ulysses had remained cool and patient, kneeling against Alphonso's bed. Ulysses wanted to find that knife.

He looked around Alphonso's room. His cousin hid the blade, no doubt. He couldn't find it.

Actually, U.S. never got that chance to whip Alphonso, Moondog told Shine on that fallen log.

Ulysses got tired. His eyes began to droop. It was in the middle of the night. Early morning.

What Ulysses did was write a note in pencil and leave the paper flat on his cousin's chest, while he snored:

"You did nothing that I don't know about. Listen up - nothing I don't know about. I pity you."

Sitting on that moldy log in the woods, Shine listened to Moondog without saying one word.

Shine knew he'd been right about characterizing his friend's brother in front of Allison and his mother. Ulysses was smart. He was very smart and patient. He cared about Allison. Shine sensed this each time he was around the couple. Ulysses was the good kind of slick. He knew how to act and when to act.

Shine understood why his sister liked him.

Moondog said to Shine before they jumped off of that fallen log and hopped a train back to Bedlam, "Man, my brother will wait this out. Alphonso gonna slip up. My brother's making a list of everything. There'll be a time."

BRACE

SHINE DID NOT SEE LARRY Loomis step out of the dark alley next to Bettman's Grocery until Larry fell in stride with him.

Larry sidled up as if some stranger had flashed a dark towel next to Shine's face.

With Moondog slumped on the couch listening to his friend and his father play, Shine had just finished a set of songs for trumpet with Seeing Eye. Pop clipped sheet music on a gleaming music stand.

Each time he left Moondog's, Shine walked this route back to his house in north Bedlam.

No way would he cut across the creek's rocks at night. Not with those obese creek rats watchful from dead tree limbs clumped along the banks or from those huge rock slabs.

At first, Shine didn't see the knife Larry Loomis clutched against his floppy t-shirt. Not until Larry Loomis elbowed him, told him, "Look down."

Shine looked down, made out a blade.

109

He said nothing, but he sure picked up his stride. Larry kept pace. Without so much as glancing sideways at Larry, Shine thought about running. He hoped he might run into a friend or someone in a car who knew him and might yell, "Hey, Shine Ross, what's going on? Hey, can I walk with you guys?" Or, better: "Hey, Shine, you need a ride?" At which time Shine would run hard toward that car, jump in, and only then would he beg for help.

Right now, he felt that Larry Loomis could outrun him anywhere.

Even though Larry wore his untied, high-top Converse gym shoes, shoelaces dragging, shoe tongues flipped up, Shine could imagine Larry keeping up. If Shine ran, Larry might even tackle him, forcing that big blade to scrape his leg or, God forbid, his neck.

Shine walked with the destiny of crossing the walking bridge into north Bedlam, by the police station. He imagined his mother yelling at him to do some ungodly chores like sweep the basement, clean the kitchen baseboards, and then clean the whole garage. Imagining his mother's voice, he walked faster: "Shine, get home. You've got to get those cobwebs cleared out of the basement."

At the crosswalk, Larry Loomis grabbed Shine's arm. In a calm voice, he said, "Shine, I got to show you something real cool, man. Over there." He pointed to a vacant building. "Real cool."

Shine didn't resist.

It was a small flat structure with one window. A dim light hung near the side window on a cinderblock wall.

Shine noticed graffiti on the wall with the words, "Black Power," spray-painted in the shape of a heart.

Larry Loomis opened the door, turned on a light. Before Shine could finish scanning the few tools, cabinets, and all-around vacant space, he felt the tip of Loomis' knife at his side.

"Sit in that chair in the middle of the floor," Larry Loomis said. "This is Doctor L talkin' to you. I ain't got a lot of time, man."

"What's going on? Why you got that knife?"

Shine sat in the chair and watched Larry. He weighed his option to run. He felt intimidated by the blade. Larry had absentmindedly set it down. Shine decided that Larry would try to chase him if he ran, so he just sat and watched him unravel a spool of twine.

"Don't try to run," Larry said. "Brace yourself. There's something we got to do here. Just sit and brace yourself."

Shine decided to play along, as Larry Loomis wrapped the twine around his upper body and the back of the chair. Shine had a hard time believing Larry was serious. Loomis could be such a joker that the thought of Loomis detaining him like this was marginally ridiculous.

"Now, who's the better basketball player? Me or you?" Larry Loomis said.

"It's a tie."

"I have one-up on you," Larry said. "Say that. Go on. Say, 'You got one-up on me. You're better.'"

"Why do I have to lie?"

He stayed calm and looked straight ahead. All the sudden he heard the crack of a bullwhip. Larry Loomis had a bullwhip in his hand. He whipped it again, but it hit his own leg. He yelled. He whipped it yet again, and it broke. Loomis threw it against the wall. Shine turned to see Loomis pick up a hubcap. He spun it in his hands. He rolled it a few feet, the hubcap landing near the chair.

Loomis held the hubcap in front of Shine. Already, Shine felt the twine loosening on his hands and back. And he hadn't tried to loosen it. Obviously, Larry's attempt at tying a knot failed. Shine wiggled his arms when Larry looked away.

"How would you like to eat this hubcap?" He held it closer. And then, as if he were launching a Frisbee, he whirled the hubcap across the room. It knocked over a raggedy lampshade. He walked over to a work table and toyed with a ball-peen hammer. The hammer worried Shine.

"How are your knees, man?"

"I can jump," Shine said, still playing along.

"You may not jump after tonight,"

Larry placed three burned out light bulbs side by side on the work table.

"Who's job place is this?" Shine finally asked. He was restless and nervous. "How'd you know to walk me here?"

"It's a cousin's friend's place," Larry said. "He repairs toasters and ovens."

"But the place is pretty empty," Shine said.

"He ain't working now," Loomis said. "But I got a key." And with that he pounded a light bulb into the table. "I love that sound of glass," he said. He flicked broken pieces onto the floor and crunched them with his foot.

112

He arranged a second light bulb on the table. This time Shine could see Larry's hand quivering. The bulb made a pop-sound when Larry struck it. Shine felt he could slip out of the twine and run out of the door. He might have to throw the chair at Larry.

About that time, they heard an abrupt noise. Shine and Larry both looked in the direction of the window, where someone outside pounded on it.

The person kept pounding. Shine squinted. Larry yelled something. He put down his hammer. He kicked a stool out of the way. Shine could see the face of Fremont Jones pressed against the glass. Fremont Jones' nose looked like a small lightbulb. Fremont pounded his fist against the glass again. For Fremont's head to reach the window, the short boy must have been standing on a rock.

Fremont Jones shook his head back and forth frantically.

Larry ran for the door; the door was jammed. By the time Larry yanked it open, Fremont had disappeared.

Shine stood up, the loose twine sliding off his body and down the back of the chair. Larry Loomis, in his own disappearing act, left the door wide open. Shine could guess he was chasing Fremont Jones. When Shine crept outside, he saw neither Loomis nor Fremont Jones. He'd always seen Fremont Jones on his bike, and so Shine imagined Fremont could take off quickly.

Shine never imagined his mother's voice could be so timely. It was in his head, and he jogged with renewed energy toward north Bedlam.

***

113

SHINE AND CYNTHIA PUT LIDS on the board games' boxes at the rec shelter and hosed down the shelter's concrete slab, freeing it of bubble gum and muddy footprints. They were the last workers to leave that afternoon.

Moondog met them at the top of Garland hill. He seemed eager to walk with Shine to the basketball courts and get in some practice.

"Can I come?" Cynthia asked.

"Why not?" Shine said.

"You can stand under the basket and catch my shots as I sink them," Moondog said. "Every one a swish."

"Cynthia, you can catch Moondog's air balls," Shine said. "And I'll get my own rebounds."

Shine had said nothing to Moondog about the incident with Larry Loomis. He'd shared every detail with Cynthia, who had waited for him at his house. She watched "The Beverly Hillbillies" with Josephine and Allison, bowls of popcorn on their laps. Cynthia checked her watch every ten minutes, wondering when Shine would be home. "You shouldn't wait for him so much, Cynthia," Allison said. "Who knows where he is."

Shine still felt a twinge of humiliation. He could've ripped apart the feebly-tied twine; it wasn't tight and the knot was so loose it fell apart. But, he was afraid of the knife. He had no idea whether Larry created his plot as a gag or some message.

That knife held the clue Shine would never know.

The three friends passed the basketball back and forth walking down the sidewalk. Shine attempted to spin the ball on his finger. It bounced off his elbow and landed in a flower bed.

"Nice going," Cynthia said. "Break a rose stem, why don't you?"

Shine spun it again. He used his other hand to whip the ball around and balance it. This attempt lasted three seconds.

Moondog dribbled it between his legs; he couldn't yet keep the ball balanced and spinning on his finger. "This is how Walt Frazier does it," he said. "Walt can take notes. I got him down. The New York Knicks will use me later on, after Frazier retires." The ball ricocheted off his foot when the three stopped at a corner before crossing.

Moondog pulled his Snickers Bar out of his front pocket.

Cynthia tossed the ball in the air, putting a back spin on it so that, when the ball hit sidewalk, it bounced back. Shine taught her the back spin. He passed the ball behind his back to Moondog. Cynthia jumped in and intercepted it.

They neared Bedlam City Hall, where the police and fire stations were also housed. They slowed down. Officer Klump came around the corner of the building before Alphonso Peace, each walking toward the police station. A heavy man, Klump appeared to take really deep breaths.

Klump looked serious and straight ahead. Several steps behind Alphonso Peace walked a police officer who lived in west Bedlam named Watson. No one seemed to know his first name. Shine had once asked Klump what officer Watson's first name was. "No one at school knows," Shine said. "I think we should keep it that way," Klump said. "Officer Watson has a ton of respect."

"Man, what's Breezy doing with my cousin?" Moondog whispered.

The friends now stood in front of Bud's Barber Shop, its red, white, and blue glass barber pole spinning and illuminating the outside of the shop's window.

"I wonder what they're doing," Shine said. Cynthia held the basketball under her arm.

Shine dashed across the street.

"Breezy, what's going on? That's Moondog's cousin," Shine said, receiving a cold stare from Alphonso Peace.

"Tell my cousin to stick with his own business," Alphonso Peace said. "You, too."

Officer Watson said nothing. He poked Alphonso Peace's back with a clipboard. "Man, don't push that thing too hard," Alphonso said.

"You two go inside," Klump said to officer Watson. "I'll be right in." He put his hand on Alphonso's shoulder, and the young man flinched. Klump waited until the two went inside. "All I can say is that we're talking to him right now."

"About what?" Shine said. He flashed the palm of his hand at Cynthia and Moondog, signaling them to stay put.

"There was some rock throwing. A car got hit," Klump said.

"You know I know that. My sister was in the car. Did Alphonso do it?"

"We don't know. Someone - not saying who - called in a tip that this young man might have been talking too loud to someone about rocks. That's all I'll say."

116

"You think Alphonso did that to his own cousin? He lives in the same house."

"Not really," Klump said. "Don't know. I think the person who called is a crank, has a wild imagination."

"Why bring Alphonso to the police station?"

"Keeps us busy." Chuckling, Klump glanced across the street at Moondog and Cynthia and then walked into the station.

The three shot basketball for a half hour without ever mentioning how vague Officer Breezy was.

Cynthia stopped the boys before all of them walked away from the court. "I didn't tell you about Raymond Armantrout, did I?" she said. "You know, Raymond's been hanging around a lot with Wayne deLong. They drag right down the middle of Hooper in the middle of the night. Wayne's in his Mustang, doesn't even have his license."

Raymond Armantrout spent his fifteen-year old waking life working on cars when not in school. His aloofness tended to keep students wondering if he had a close friend. No one messed with Raymond. It was rumored that, well after midnight once, he used a screwdriver to pry open the door of a small grocery store in another part of Bedlam, steal a bag full cat food, and feed a swarm of feral cats on his street.

Raymond Armantrout began driving at age twelve. His step-father owned a stock-racing car, although he'd taught Raymond how to drive in a souped-up Camaro. Raymond drove alone when he turned thirteen. From what Shine learned, Raymond's step-father, usually drunk, would hit the Camaro's horn, announcing to neighbors that

Raymond was about to inspect the streets of Bedlam in his Camaro.

"So," Cynthia said, "I was walking up to the rec shelter, and I saw Raymond with a cop. The cop had Raymond's arm. Neither of them looked at me. But I heard the officer say something like, 'Raymond, with your long hair, you're gonna be in trouble by just looking tough. You don't need trouble. You'd best stop throwing rocks and racing that Camaro. Best cut that hair.'"

"You sure?" Shine said.

"Something like that," Cynthia said. "I swear. That cop was loud, getting right in Raymond's face. Outside."

"But," Moondog interrupted her, "when Ulysses and Allison were in his car, someone threw rocks from another car, and whoever threw them wasn't Raymond Armantrout. It was somebody else. We know that."

"Right," Shine said. "But a cop will ask anyone who's known to throw rocks, like Raymond Armantrout. Were they in Relling? Were they in Bedlam? Were they home?"

When Moondog turned to walk toward his house, Shine said, "Watch your back tonight. You saw your cousin go into the station."

"I always got my own back," Moondog said, and jogged toward the walking bridge.

***

SHINE CUT THREE ROSE STEMS with fully bloomed roses. He wrapped them in aluminum foil and gave them to Moondog.

"Here, you won't get stuck. You want to give my mom roses? It's her garden. These'll do."

Josephine Ross sat on the couch propping a new, orange ice pack on her forehead. She had been lying down for two hours before the boys and Shine's Aunt Ruth arrived. For two days, Shine's mother had a clear head, an alertness to normal house cleaning and to pulling weeds from her garden. For two days, not a trickle of pain. Not a scent of Vick's Vapor Rub coming from her head.

Today, she could actually watch television with her sister. Aunt Ruth sat on the other end of the couch. It was noon and the local t.v. show's host, Ruth Lyons, sang to her audience of mostly women. She danced to a tune played by her house band. A small bouquet of flowers, attached to her microphone, followed Ruth Lyons' hand whenever she moved it. Her dainty white gloves were conspicuous.

On the coffee table lay Josephine Ross' identical white gloves, still untouched this afternoon.

While Shine rummaged in the kitchen for a vase, Moondog presented Shine's mother with the red roses. "I hope you feel better," he said.

Without taking her eyes off Ruth Lyons, who was now dancing with her co-host as women in the audience clapped louder, Shine's mother said, "Thank you, Moondog. Those look nice in my garden, don't they?"

"No other house on the street has such big roses."

"Coming down the street, they do look pretty when you see them," aunt Ruth said.

119

Jeffrey Hillard

"Shine, could you dig up a vase? Under the sink," his mother said. But before she finished the sentence, Shine produced the vase.

"They'll look good right here, by your gloves," he said.

Before the show ended, Moondog refilled Josephine's orange ice pack. He ate the last of his roast beef sandwich. One last time, Ruth Lyons directed her cameraman to focus on the women, and they waved. Row by row, the cameraman caught each woman and man waving one last time as the band played its final song.

Suddenly, everyone in the living room jumped and turned when they heard an object collide with the front window.

"Oh my God. JoJo," aunt Ruth said. "He crashed into the window."

Shine, Moondog, and aunt Ruth pulled back the curtain. Shine's mother stood, dropping the ice pack on the couch. "Good Jesus," she said.

Shine opened the front door, less than anxious to look in the vicinity of the noise. He looked below the window. No JoJo. No green, blue, and orange feathers. No bird lying on its side. He did not see two, pebble-size red eyes on the ground staring at the house. He relaxed.

"Don't tell me what you see, Shine," aunt Ruth said.

"JoJo's not here."

"Oh my God. Good. I'm a nervous wreck." Shine's aunt sat back down on the couch and this time she picked up her sister's ice pack. "I need this a few minutes, Josie."

120

Obvious to Shine now was that the paperboy had been late delivering the *Enquirer* and he hurriedly tossed it toward the window.

JoJo was still out there. Uncle Jerry was searching.

"I've heard noise in places I've never dreamed of," aunt Ruth said. "I think I hear JoJo all the time. Come back, JoJo. You need to just come back."

While the subject turned to loss, the subject also turned to an unattractive scene. Moondog, who turned far more somber in the past half-hour, said: "I saw my cousin Alphonso come out of Bettman's last night. His pockets bulged with candy. I know he's not paying for candy. He doesn't have a job, for one thing," Shine's mother and aunt were in the kitchen, out of earshot.

"What are you talking about?" Shine said.

"He had to be taking it."

"Did he see you?"

"I was around the corner across the street. He couldn't have seen."

"That's crazy."

"He looked happy. Like he just did something," Moondog said. Old man Bettman won't give anybody candy. I heard Alphonso once say, 'Why does old Bettman put it there by the front door like that?'"

***

ON A HOT AND CLOUDY day, after Ulysses picked up Allison in mid-afternoon, and they quenched their thirst with Dr. Pepper from Hattendorf's, Allison drove his Caprice to Mount Relling.

When they approached an intersection near the highway overpass, the couple noticed a man and woman taping to a telephone pole a poster for the Black Panther Party rally in west Bedlam. August 10th.

The rally. The woman wore thick-rimmed sunglasses. She tip-toed, lifting the poster as high as she could, as the man ran tape around the border. Allison and Ulysses could see a photograph of the Black Panther Party member, H. Rap Brown. His face comprised most of it, his large eyes staring toward the highway.

In an arc above his head were words: ON AUGUST 10 AT DRAKE SCHOOL - CEDAR AVENUE - 8:00 PM - H. RAP BROWN.

Allison and Ulysses planned to spend a few hours at Pee Wee Valley amusement park. A suburban monument to leisure, Pee Wee Valley was open only on weekends. It contained a spread of fourteen small rides, especially suited for children. The largest ride, whose two caged cars swung twenty feet in the air and turned in circles, was its most popular.

The parking lot was packed fender to fender.

Allison pulled the Caprice next to a Dodge.

Pee Wee Valley, as small a park as its name suggested, sat on the far northern part of Mount Relling. In its simple square of space, the rides leaped into view as one drove down Rellington Avenue. One strip of tickets costs two dollars. Ulysses put four, crumpled dollar bills in Allison's hand. The girl at the ticket window looked to be Allison's age.

"You go to Mount Relling?" Allison asked her.

Ulysses stood around the corner from the ticket window. He pivoted to see who she was talking to.

"Right," the girl said. "Do I know you?"

"No, we go to Bedlam." Allison tugged on Ulysses' shirt to bring him closer. "He's in my grade. We'll be seniors. I just love Pee Wee Valley." Allison flexed her moxie.

The girl in the ticket booth glanced at Ulysses when she said, "I'm a senior, too. Well, o.k., I hope you guys have a good time riding." As if startled, she quickly looked down at the ticket drawer.

"We'll do that," Allison said.

They heard thunder.

Both looked up at the shifting clouds like large bits of grayish broken plates. They made their way toward the merry-go-round, Allison's favorite. In spite of the threat of rain, the park was crowded and people criss-crossed in front of the couple. In the line for the merry-go-round, kids clung to the chains forming a path to the ride, flipping their bodies against the chains. Parents pulled them back, trying to keep them in line.

Allison and Ulysses' arms touched. She rubbed her fingers on his hand. He rubbed her fingers in return. She wove her fingers inside his hand. He squeezed her hand.

"You want to try this here?" Ulysses said.

"Try what?"

Ulysses whispered in her ear: "Touching my hand?"

"You're touching my hand."

Just then a little girl poked Ulysses in the arm. "Do you live in Mount Relling?" she said, looking up at him.

"No. Bedlam. West Bedlam." He put an emphasis on "west," within earshot of her mother.

"Are you riding this ride?" the girl said, pointing to the merry-go-round. The child's mother spun her around and directed her back in line.

When they got off the ride, they felt light drops of rain, mist-thin. The sky appeared ready to open up.

"What's next?" Ulysses said.

Allison grabbed his arm and they headed for the Go-Cart track. They noticed families darting for the parking lot. The couple ignored the rain. The attendant let them to race their gas-powered cars seven laps, before he held up a finger, signaling one last lap.

The rain overwhelmed the ride attendants. They shut each one down; Allison and Ulysses were about to get into a ferris wheel car. There was no one else in line. The attendant looked tired and bored. He pulled the bill of his Pee Wee Valley ball cap down to keep his face dry. His shirt was soaked, gym shoes muddy from the dirt path to the ferris wheel.

Ulysses noticed a girl about four or five-years old standing by herself between the ferris wheel and the bumper cars. It rained harder. Allison and Ulysses paid no attention to the rain. They were laughing when Ulysses rushed over to the girl.

"Where's your mom?" he said.

"I don't know," she yelled. She covered her face. "I'm getting wetter."

"Let's go," Ulysses said, and lead her by the hand to the ticket booth. The girl was still inside. A huge awning extended from the booth. The three stood under it. Ulysses banged on the door.

"This little girl is lost," he said, after the girl opened the door.

She reached for two big umbrellas. Two people could walk under each one. The cloudburst started to thin. Ulysses and the little girl were under one umbrella, and Allison and the ticket girl under another. Heading to the parking lot, where less than ten cars remained, they saw a woman run toward them. Her rain-soaked hair still bounced.

"I couldn't see you in the rain," the woman said, holding out her arms toward her little girl. "You walked away from the merry-go-round. I ran after your brothers, who ran after your father. It was that cloudburst, honey."

"Mom, I'm wet, but they helped me," the girl said. "I was by the bumper cars."

It was just drizzling now.

"Thank you," the mother said to Ulysses. Jittery from losing sight of her daughter, she looked at Allison and the ticket girl under the other umbrella. "I was looking in the wrong place for her. I couldn't see squat. She's not to go to the bumper cars ever, and there she was." The girl's mother had both arms wrapped around her.

Ulysses folded his umbrella and handed it to the ticket booth girl. He and Allison walked toward the Caprice, though Allison stopped him in the middle of the parking lot. The remaining cars were exiting; Pee Wee Valley had closed.

Allison said, "Come here, Ulysses."

She hugged him. His arms stiffened at first. He'd seen only one black couple in the park, a middle-age man and woman. He wasn't sure Allison should embrace him here, in the absolute middle of a private lot where the few people in the last cars did see them.

She clamped her hands on his head, brought it down gently, and kissed him on the cheek. Her kiss might as well have been planted on his lips for the three times she pecked his cheek.

***

PIANISSIMO

SHINE WAS ASLEEP ON THE COUCH when his mother woke him. She squeezed his shoulder a fifth time.

"Shine, get up. You got a call about JoJo."

Drowsy, he jumped and looked around. His mother seemed to be the last thing he saw in his confusion. "What?"

"A man, Albert, over on Sentry thinks he saw JoJo. Or sees him. I think JoJo's near his house."

Minutes later, Shine was running through backyards on Sentry. The street adjoined another patch of woods. He had to negotiate picnic tables, clotheslines, dog houses, and swingsets.

The backyards were full of unwanted objects to a boy focused on finding an escaped parrot.

He swerved, barely missing a clothesline, and banged his knee against a tricycle, running nearly full-Shine-speed. He leaned against a fence, massaged his kneecap. He didn't feel ready to climb a tree yet.

He waited and scanned the lowest and highest parts of trees. He called out, "JoJo?" He whistled. He called out. He shouted, "Pretty boy? Where you at?"

Shine limped around the front yard of the man named Albert and knocked on his door, but Albert didn't answer. Strangely, no car was in the driveway, yet Albert, within the hour, had just talked to Shine's mother.

He limped around back. The sharp tingling pain in his knee was gone. Shine felt that bounce return.

He hopped Albert's backyard fence and went straight into the woods. Trees were saturated with the greenness of mid-summer. Mosquitoes and birds and squirrels perked up amid the tapestry.

Shine would take a few arm scrapes if it meant he could slash his way closer to JoJo.

It wasn't happening. He didn't see JoJo anywhere.

He thought he heard a familiar parrot call, but soon doubted it. JoJo didn't respond to his calls, and JoJo always responded. The parrot wanted to talk.

Shine wanted to light a cigarette, though he'd left his Band Aid box under a mound of underwear in his dresser.

He was upset at JoJo's absence, and he truly felt he was clumsily making his way through summer.

He daydreamed about JoJo.

He dreamed that the parrot, having just eaten from an overflowing bird feeder, was looking down on him with pity. He daydreamed that JoJo was biding his own sweet time until he decided to fly away toward new territory. Only a matter of time.

The afternoon sun was tailing off.

He saw Albert's car in the driveway when he hopped back over his fence and headed for the street. He chose not to bother the man. In the morning, if he decided to come back before work, he'd ask the man where, exactly, he spotted JoJo. He'd ask the man, "What tree? Did he look at you?"

But not now.

Shine felt a trickle of blood on his head where the bandage had come off and where he'd scraped it on a branch. He'd change the bandage later and think about how far he'd follow a trail next time.

If there was a next time.

***

JUDSON ROSS SAW THE RAT swim near empty soda cans floating on the other side of the Millcreek.

He took aim with his BB rifle. Shine and his father owned the one gun.

His father shuffled between trees to get a more perfect aim.

He steadied the barrel of his Daisy 102-BB gun. Judson Ross fired a BB right into the fat rat's mid-section, alarming it enough that the rat dove under water and resurfaced downstream, not yet dead.

"I missed him mostly," Judson Ross said. "I loosened up some fat."

"Good shot," Shine said. "I saw it twitch."

"You're a better shot. You're steadier."

"Doubt it."

129

"My arms won't hold still like they used to. Too much gear-shifting."

"I guess I'm getting better," Shine said. "I taught Moondog how to aim it pretty straight. But he hates holding a BB gun. He thinks it's trouble."

"What kind of shot is he?"

"It might take him six shots before he hits a tail."

They sat on rocks and waited patiently for another rat. Part of the Bedlam garbage dump site was not far away on the other side of the creek. Old cardboard or mounds of paper seemed to steadily burn.

Shine looked forward to this time with his father.

Although their house was a five minute walk to the creek, Judson packed two peanut butter-and-jelly sandwiches and two bottles of Dr. Pepper. They came down to the creek every couple of months before cold weather swept in and froze chunks of it.

Judson pulled out the sandwiches around noon.

His father drove his truck more and more, logging thousands of miles. If he saw his father twelve days a month, in the last eight months, that might have been a high number. Shine looked forward to any postcard his father sent him. He preferred not to shoot at rats without his father.

Judson Ross took aim and popped another rat in its rear. It swam away and disappeared behind fallen tree branches.

They unwrapped their sandwiches. They heard train whistles and the noon factory whistles, whose noise cut right through the canopy of trees.

"Are you afraid driving through the big cities, the ones where fires break out and people are demonstrating?"

"Not really. You just drive. You keep moving. I've seen some fires in Detroit from the roadside."

"That make you angry? Thinking people will start fires like that?"

"Not really angry."

"Look at the Empire burning down," Shine said. "Moondog and I think somebody might have set it."

"It's a crazy time," his father said. "Vietnam gives us a lot of problems. Look how tense it is here."

Shine saw movement across the creek. He snatched the BB gun out of his father's hand and fired at a shadow. It was only a log drifting downstream.

"I'm trying to be about peace," Judson Ross said. "But it's strange with us here and west Bedlam about to have a Black Panther leader visit. What kind of trouble will that be?"

Shine fired BB's at an old tire across the creek.

"Your grandpa wants us to have a couple of shotguns ready that night," his father said. "I'm sort of against that. Although I see his point. Protection. Hard to say no there."

"You think there'll be trouble?"

"You can't predict anything."

"Pop Weasel doesn't think it'll be trouble," Shine said. "He said H. Rap Brown's coming because he's talking about how important school is and things about work."

"I heard that."

"Pop told me H. Rap Brown is gonna tell people the Black Panthers want to get more people in colleges out

131

from where they are. But, Breezy says Brown might pit people against people. That's his side of it."

When he finished his sandwich, Shine's father took out three new postcards he'd kept folded in his back pocket. He gave them to Shine. Two contained no writing. One captured a serious moment on the road. If this was one of the best ways his father could communicate with him, then Shine would gladly accept the cards. At least he could save them. He filed them in order of the date received and kept them completely to himself. His sister Allison didn't know about the postcards, and Shine wasn't sure if she received the same cards.

He hadn't told Cynthia about them.

Shine read aloud the handwritten card: "Places I drive: trouble. In streets. Vietnam War demonstrations. Hippies clogging up streets. Blacks gathering. Chicago, Detroit, St. Louis. I hope you practice trumpet. Always get better. Be home late next week. You'll get this card by then. Take care of mom. Yours, Dad."

"I forgot to mail it," Judson Ross said.

"Got it now. It must be dangerous where you go."

"I'm safe sitting up high in the truck. When I get out, I'm at truck stops. It's a brotherhood."

It took these few hours at the creek for Shine's allergies to get worked up. His father commented on his red nose; his eyes become watery. He wiped his face on his t-shirt.

Shine heard noise coming from down the creek. Laughter echoed not far away. Small trails wound through Garland and by the creek.

He also heard voices coming from the baseball field. He walked up the bank to look. Neil Nash. Wayne deLong. Nash and deLong were flunkies. They skipped school. They'd each failed a middle school grade. Their fathers worked at the mattress factory. Shine saw Nash's long blond hair. Wayne deLong, whose arms were as skinny as a two fishing poles, wore a ponytail underneath a cap. Both kicked cola and beer bottles around the infield. They acted as if they were trying to break bottles, kicking them into one another.

Neil Nash, wild and daring, was on the verge of dropping out of school when he turned sixteen. Neil picked up a bottle and threw it fifty feet.

Wayne deLong followed Neil Nash anywhere he went.

Shine turned his attention to the other voices emerging from the creek bank. The Simms brothers, Troy and Terrence. They both held walking sticks. Five smaller kids surrounded them playing Tag and being all-around boisterous.

The group, including the Simms brothers, walked toward the field and toward Neil Nash and Wayne deLong.

Shine watched one of the kids pick up a bottle that Neil had thrown near wood bleachers and heave it toward the woods. Another kid skipped a bottle in the direction of Neil Nash.

The two groups looked at each other. Troy and Terrence Simms walked onto the field. Neil and Wayne now stood in the grass outfield. Then, no one really moved.

Allison and Cynthia were walking down the paved drive of Garland Park hill when they also saw the mix of boys. They saw Shine and his father.

"Shine," Cynthia yelled out. She waved.

He waved back and vaguely motioned for her and his sister to hold up, as if to suggest, "Don't come down here." The two girls stopped on the hill.

Shine yelled, "I'll be up. Stay there."

Troy Simms chimed in. He mimicked Cynthia's high-pitched shouting: "Shine. Hey, over here." Troy flailed his raised arms. The group of kids laughed.

Judson Ross walked toward the outfield holding his BB gun.

The only thing Shine could think of was that his father, as the true adult, had a sense of understanding he wanted to establish. His father nestled the Daisy 102-BB gun in his arms, without so much as pointing it at anyone.

Judson walked right into the middle of the two groups. He paused, the BB gun anchored against his chest. Shine could tell he wanted no trouble. The Simms brothers stared at the BB rifle and stepped back.

Judson spoke in a mild-mannered tone directly to Neil Nash, although everyone except the girls on the hill could hear him: "Son, you don't need trouble. It's best you and your friend think about that," he said. "Time you both think about how hard both your dads work. I know both your dads. These aren't easy times."

Neil Nash spit at the ground. He pulled his hair out of eyes. He said, "You don't know him too well. My dad don't talk to me."

Shine heard murmuring between the Simms brothers.

His father instilled calmness. He glanced at all the boys. Wayne deLong picked up four bottles that were not broken, while Neil Nash, in a posture of stubbornness, stared at the outfield fence. Then he, too, picked up bottles, flipping them against the outfield fence.

And then Neil strutted off with Wayne toward another one of Garland's many hills.

***

BURSTS OF SUMMER RAIN WILTED a number of multi-colored JoJo posters that Shine plastered on Bedlam telephone poles. Allison found one decent poster not totally ruined. She and her mother used it as a drawing model.

"This is some of Shine's better work," his mother said.

Allison traced and colored feathers. Her mother drew black borders and wrote the same lettering as before: GREEN BODY. DOUBLE YELLOW-HEADED. AMAZON PARROT. Under the big letters, LOST, she added in smaller letters: Green, Blue, and Yellow feathers in wings and tail. She drew a square border around LOST. Exclamation point.

Since JoJo had been spotted a few times, the family was relieved.

When Josephine and Allison worked together like this, they could do so peacefully. Josephine wouldn't pry into Allison's personal life. Allison didn't gossip. She felt the world was too complex already. She rehashed for her mother that the peace demonstrators - those pinpointing the

135

Vietnam War as their mighty protest - had it right. The demonstrators wanted the government to reduce its deliverance of chaos and torment. The Vietnam War was inflaming everything in America. War stoked the heated actions of leaders and blurred the good intentions of common people living day to day. That's what Allison's civics teacher said, and she liked to quote him. She was quick to memorize.

She and her mother never talked about the dreadful news coming from t.v. reporters on the ground in South Vietnam. The bloody soldiers they saw. The jungle. The young faces.

They watched.

The problems occurred when Allison and her mother would stand in the kitchen alone, waiting for a cake to bake. Just waiting, their hands free and not involved with a project. Josephine asked her daughter what she was up to. She might not have intended to, but the words spilled, branching into a path which Allison snapped apart like twigs, refusing to answer.

Allison felt she was old enough to come and go.

She left notes: "I'll be back at midnight." Or "I'm with Sheila at Tri-County. Shopping." Or, in the last few weeks, ever since Josephine knew that a young man was a part of her daughter's daily concerns, "I'm with Ulysses. Back later. Not sure when. I have door key."

SHINE CAME OUT OF HIS room after practicing his trumpet. Eighth and sixteenth notes. Trills. Two, light, up-tempo songs, including his favorite, "Grazing in the Grass." He went straight to the more staccato-built songs, the quick-tempo ones with fewer rests or pauses. Blowing firmly, he worked on his lip bends.

He played louder.

At times, his mother would knock on the door. In the middle of a song, he'd hear the tat-tat-tat-tat. He didn't open the door because she said not to open it. "When I knock I mean it," she said. "I mean, tone it down. You'll know."

His mother said that his trumpet playing was never the source of her headaches. Mostly, she let him go.

Since Seeing Eye had said to him, "Time is money, and your future depends on your time," Shine thought about his music. Was there a music future? Could he play a bunch of weekends like Seeing Eye? Could he record like Herb Alpert and Al Hirt or Miles Davis? Or play with a symphony? Every time he picked up his horn he saw past a high school band.

This late afternoon, the dining room was quieter than usual.

Shine remembered what his father preached these days, when his mother nursed a migraine: "Walk around this house with a pianissimo touch, Shine," he said. "You know pianissimo? That's a musical term. Means, softly. Don't stomp around and don't take the roof off with your horn."

As Shine studied their new JoJo posters, his mother and sister gazed at the t.v. The local news was running a special segment on the legacy and assassination of Robert Kennedy. Earlier in the month he was killed within hours after giving a speech in a Los Angeles hotel upon winning the California Democratic Presidential primary. After speaking and shaking hands, Robert Kennedy walked through a back way - through the kitchen area - and was shot point-blank by a Palestinian refugee.

Shot near midnight, Kennedy died just after three a.m. the next morning.

His sister's eyes reddened. Shine knew she liked Kennedy.

He glimpsed the gruesome image of Kennedy on the ground, his head visibly bleeding.

Josephine moved into the living room. The flag-draped coffin. Robert Kennedy's children standing in awe. His wife, Ethel, and brother Edward, both stone-faced. The killer, Sirhan Bishara Sirhan, a Palestinian, in handcuffs. Taped footage where two sheriff's deputies, arms locked with those of Sirhan Bishara Sirhan, hustled him out of the Ambassador Hotel in Los Angeles.

Shine, his mother, and his sister listened to the voice-over of Robert Kennedy: "What we need in the United States is not division. What we need in the United States is not violence and lawlessness, but is love and wisdom. And compassion toward one another. And a feeling of justice toward those who still suffer within our country, whether they be white or whether they be black."

SHINE PUT THE NEW POSTERS in the bag and headed out the door.

He'd follow a similar route for hanging them that he used before. If anyone witnessed Shine tacking a poster to a telephone pole, he wanted them to stop and read it.

He tacked posters on poles on Green Avenue, Thelma Drive, Parkside Avenue.

He walked down the street that lead to Garland. No one was playing ball on the main field. Shine walked down the hill to the shed that housed folding chairs and sacks of chalk dust for lining the fields. He thought, "I'll take three minutes." Squatting down in front of the shed, with his back to the street, he pulled a Kool out of his Band-Aid box and lit it. He took two more puffs. The more he pondered JoJo's whereabouts, the more inclined he was to sneak a cigarette. Stress. Larry Loomis.

After Beacon Street, he neared the police station and, down from the station, the walking bridge next to the football stadium. Shine decided to go one more block, as far west as Kroger, one of the valley's largest grocery stores.

When he crossed the street, he also encountered Troy and Terence Simms.

The brothers stepped from behind a parked car on the street next to a telephone pole. Shine hadn't seen them.

Each held a short stack of paper. Shine looked at the pole on which they'd taped a sign: "AUGUST 10 AT DRAKE SCHOOL - CEDAR AVENUE - 8:00 PM - H. RAP BROWN."

The brothers started to get into their car, yet hesitated and walked toward Shine.

"What you got there, man?" asked Troy, the taller and more animated brother.

"Poster about our lost parrot."

"Yeah?" Troy said.

Terrence crossed his arms and blew a bubble with his gum. Evidently, Troy was more talkative.

"He's been gone a while," Shine said.

"A shame, man," Troy said. "Say, how 'bout you use another pole back up there?" He pointed his cigarette toward north Bedlam. His brother's cigarette was tucked above his right ear.

"I covered all over there," Shine said.

"That's cool, but we got this pole covered, man."

Shine watched Terence blow another bubble. By the time he gazed at the street and looked back, Terence was handling a long wooden kitchen match.

"See this?" Terence said, and Shine nodded. He held the long match about a foot from Shine's face. "You want those posters of your bird?" Terrence scraped the match on the sidewalk, igniting a flame. The match burned quickly.

"That's right, man" his brother Troy said. "We only need one poster on it."

SHINE WALKED INTO KROGER, WHICH was about to close. He thumbed through a newspaper full of food coupons. An elderly woman walked up to him. He knew her as Moondog's neighbor, Mrs. Fetters. He knew that, from time to time, Mrs. Fetters also saw Fremont Jones standing outside her kitchen window, peeping inside.

"You're Moondog's friend, right?"

"That's me."

"Pop Weasel talks a lot about you. He says, 'I got this young trumpet player I'm teaching.' You play trumpet, right? What's that on your paper? A bird?" She bent down closer, tilting her glasses. "Would you look at the *color* of those wings? My goodness. It flew off?"

"That's what he did. He kind of escaped."

"Kind of, nothing. He *did* escape. You going around with those posters?"

"I planned to put one on that telephone pole out there," he said, pointing to the street corner, "but I kind of got chased off."

"Chased off? It's a public pole."

"Thanks, Mrs. Fetters."

"You gotta find that bird."

He felt safe walking with the woman. He asked her if he could help stack her groceries in her car trunk. As soon as she opened the trunk, she and Shine both saw Troy and Terrence Simms walking toward her car.

"Let us help you with those groceries," Troy Simms said. "We got this." Shine said goodbye to Moondog's neighbor and walked back into the store lobby.

He waited ten more minutes before he was sure the Simms brothers were gone. Shine didn't see their car next to the telephone pole.

With the speed of a carpenter lining up nails in wood, he tacked the JoJo poster to the pole. He lined up his poster under the "AUGUST 10 AT DRAKE SCHOOL" poster.

The colorful wings of JoJo, lifted the photographic face of a famous person coming to Bedlam.

***

SHINE'S MOTHER HAD CUT UP two watermelons for Shine to take Elmer Klump. She acknowledged his generous offering of his huge pool. Shine always took advantage of it.

141

The least she could do was pass along watermelon.

Some watermelon juice sloshed over the side of the bowl when Shine jogged across the street. He licked his fingers before handing it to the officer whose screen door near the pool was wide open. Klump was hauling sacks of chlorine, dropping them by the pool.

"I'll eat well now," he said. "Tell your mom."

The officer, restless, implied he was in a hurry. The police department required a few hand-picked personnel to look for evidence to gather at the site of the Empire. Klump had been hand-picked.

"You in that big a hurry?" Shine said. "Can I ride over with you?"

"For one, we the department got a fire to deal with. We got to deal with what happened, or who happened, or why. And second, no, you can't."

Shine offered his help. Klump, equally puzzled and amused, craned his neck, implying, "Are you kidding? What? You're fifteen and you know hardly a thing. You're just getting started in life." Yet he kept mostly quiet. He recognized a kid with too much summer time on his hands.

"I'll get Moondog involved, too. Never know. We might hear something. We might talk it up, see what flies."

The officer pointed his finger at Shine. "You never mind. And you stay off that property, bud."

"I'll do what I can."

"Hey, I don't want to get you and your friend for trespassing."

"Hey, you wouldn't do that, would you?"

"In a minute. Sure would."

While the officer poured the last crystals from the chlorine bags into the pool and stirred them, Shine launched into a litany of times he was "sent in the hall" or "sent outside" his sixth grade art classroom, even before he was given the chance to become involved in a project or lesson.

"We had this teacher," he said, "Miss Dudley, terrible art teacher. She came room to room for art. Laid her old lady's bag of colored pencils on the teacher's desk. I must have laughed just once, under my breath, because every time she stepped in the class, she told me and another friend to just sit outside and wait. Not even a chance to do art. Sit out there and wait for the next bell."

"I didn't have the best of luck in school, either," the officer said. "That why I became a cop. I had to prove something."

"Well, I'll bet I can find out something about the Empire."

"You never mind, and that's fair warning. This isn't school. And I'm not a mean teacher."

CHASM

AT BETTMAN'S GROCERY IN WEST Bedlam, it was a known fact that a certain Bedlam police officer liked his Hostess Twinkies. He was so fond of the spongy cream-filled cakes that he bought several twin-packs at one time.

It was a known fact that he liked apple-flavored Jolly Ranchers. The excitable cop was a connoisseur of caramel chews. Each time he came into Bettman's, usually twice a week, he loaded up.

This morning, officer Elmer Klump had broken open a new pack of chews, before he entered Bettman's at lunch time to replenish his stash. His stomach protruded well over his utility belt, nearly burying his gun and flashlight under his blue uniform shirt. The antenna from his police radio was barely visible against his hip. Always talkative and respectful of old man Bettman, Klump rapped on the counter when he arrived.

As one story went, his nickname Breezy originated with a comment by the owner Walter Bettman. "He just breezed right through the store," the owner said. "Breezing up and down the aisles scoping out God know's what. That man can hold some sweets."

With each visit from Klump, the old owner would say, "Breezin' in this direction today?"

Klump paid extra close attention to the little store. It seemed an easy target for a shoplifter. Most of Bettman's candy sat in white buckets next to the entrance. Dip your hand in a bucket and out the door you go. The old man missed bucket-loads at a time.

Old Walter Bettman could not be certain, but he connected a recent episode of half-empty buckets with a young man he never liked in the first place: Larry Loomis.

Larry came into the store three or four times a day. Each time he did, he wavered over something to buy and wound up leaving, buying nothing. Or maybe he bought four cents' worth of Jolly Ranchers, two cents apiece. Here was a young man who showed Walter Bettman he was in no hurry to leave.

The old man suspected Larry of nothing cheery or righteous. He knew Larry's family life had taken a negative turn. Larry's grandmother became ill with some neurological condition in which her arms and legs often went numb. Larry's mother had run off with a black activist who decided to live closer to Washington D.C., and his father remarried and now lived in Georgia. Only Larry's grandfather, an irritable man himself and nearly one hundred percent deaf, took care of his grandson. Or tried to.

When Klump came into the store, after he piled his new stash on the counter, Walter Bettman gave him an earful about Larry Loomis.

"Breezy, I can't have that boy milling around my store any longer," he said.

"What can I do?"

"Here, have this other pack of Twinkies for the road. I'm asking you for a favor. Come by at 4:00. Stand right by this front window and sneak a peak inside. Just peak. The buckets are by the front door. That boy will come in at 4:00. I swear I'm missing my bucket a little while later."

"I can buy those Twinkies, Walter."

"You're a cop. You'd be doing me a favor. Twinkies on the house."

"I'll be back this afternoon. I'll park around the corner and peak in. I'll see if his pockets bulge when he comes out."

Yet, Breezy didn't have to wait until 4:00 and neither did Walter Bettman. Larry Loomis stepped inside the door just as Klump was leaving.

"Hey, officer," Larry said.

"That would be me."

Walter Bettman stood stiffly behind the counter. He glanced at Larry Loomis and then at the officer. Once he realized Larry and Breezy were chatting, he came around the counter and stood next to them, watching the buckets and Larry's every move. One thing for sure: he would never relocate those buckets, no matter what advice anyone gave him. The old man watched Larry play with his afro pick firmly planted in his hair.

"Look, mister officer, I got this reason to tell you something."

Rattling his grocery bag, Klump looked at him.

146

"I know you know Shine Ross and Moondog Weasel. Well, those two lit up that fire at the Empire," Larry said. "I ain't lying. They burnt down that building. I saw Shine Ross and Moondog Weasel around the Empire. It was around that afternoon. Busy over there, you know. You know how it is at places, people working and coming and going from work. But, I seen them on the side. I even seen Wayne deLong drag racing near the Empire. Shine and Moondog and maybe Wayne himself played with matches around all that cardboard."

"I'll make a note of that," Klump said.

"Can you bring them all in? I ain't lying."

"I'll make a note."

Larry Loomis never regarded Walter Bettman while he stood listening to the old man and the officer finish talking. Larry put his fingers on the rim of the big caramel candy bucket, but lifted his fingers, as if he needed to play with his hair. Klump rattled his bag again and scooted past Larry Loomis.

Both of them walked to Klump's police cruiser.

"Thanks for looking into that for me and those boys, Shine and Moondog," Larry said. "Goofing off - that'll get you a burned down building."

Once inside his cruiser, the officer unwrapped a pack of Twinkies and satisfied his growling stomach with the cream-filled cakes. A minute later, he answered a radio call about a broken down, Bedlam garbage truck causing traffic to back up near the high school.

***

147

A SMALLER BANDAGE REPLACED THE gauze. The headaches were mostly gone.

He moved his head more when he practiced. He memorized more difficult scales. He revisited the Hugh Masekala tune.

Shine spent a half-hour in front of his music and another hour dribbling the basketball in his driveway. One hundred times with the right hand; one hundred with the left. Without missing a bounce. He thought about the incidents with Larry Loomis and wondered how he might have upset Larry in the first place. How far back did this rivalry go? Sixth grade? Fifth? They played ball in sixth and fifth grades and both started as guards. They seemed to get along. They fed off each other. Shine noticed that Larry had a bad temper, although he never really directed it at Shine.

The rivalry might have escalated in school this year. Before school let out for summer, their ninth grade history teacher held a mock Presidential election-vote. Would a Republican or Democrat win? Write down a party name on paper, the teacher said. Republican or Democrat. The teacher said the Republican presidential candidate would probably be Richard Nixon; the Democrat candidate, he'd hoped, would be Robert Kennedy. All you do, the teacher told his class, is write "Republican" or "Democrat." Shine's class chose the Democrat party. When students compared write-ins, Shine said he wrote "Democrat."

For some reason, Larry came up to Shine and accused him of lying. "You're a Republican," he said. "It's Republican where you live."

Shine said, "Not so. Not always." He kept backing away from Larry who followed him down the hallway.

It could have been the mock election, or the fact that it became no secret at the school year's end that Allison was hanging with Ulysses, who happened to be Moondog's brother.

No matter. Shine was uncertain about Larry Loomis' outbursts. He still let it eat at him.

He bounced the basketball now against the garage door, until Allison came outside with car keys. She saw his frustration. He threw the ball against the garage door.

She snatched the basketball away from him. "Let's go. We'll be late if you keep this up."

Shine had an appointment with an allergist. Allison drove her mother's car across town to the specialist.

He got in the car blowing his nose. By the time they arrived, Allison had grown annoyed with her brother's faint, whistle-like wheezing.

They waited what seemed like an entire afternoon to see the elderly doctor, a stoop-shouldered man with wire-rim glasses that kept sliding down his nose. When he pushed them up, Shine noticed rivers of veins in his shriveled hand. The doctor limped down the hall and lead them into a small room with wobbly wooden chairs. The room smelled like ammonia.

The doctor fumbled with his stethoscope and tongue depressor, pushing the wooden object so far back in Shine's mouth that he gagged. Allison stared at the seemingly endless number of vials on a shelf. The doctor shuffled to a table. He wrote for five minutes, painfully slowly. Several times he looked up at the ceiling. He wrote.

He looked down again. He mumbled. He chewed the tip of his pen and scratched his head with it.

"I'm going to load you up, now," the old doctor said.

"You're going to load him up?" Allison said.

Shine wiped one eye full of watery drainage.

The doctor rubbed Shine's arm with alcohol and gave him four shots. He explained they would help determine the kind of honest-to-God allergies Shine had. "I'll be back in ten minutes. Don't worry about those bumps up and down your arm. Don't touch them."

During this entire afternoon, and after the slow-moving doctor examined every inch of his arm, neck, eyes, and ears, Shine understood that his allergies required new attention. More shots. Twice-a-month. He hated that word "injection." It meant his arm would throb. His skin would itch. It meant needles and pain. Of the four shots Shine got, only the last one caused him to gasp.

On the way home, he let his stiff arm dangle out the window.

Allison knew her brother needed some kind of break.

She needed to talk to Ulysses. She had a plan.

***

IT WAS ALLISON'S PLAN ALL ALONG.

Ulysses caught himself saying "yes" and "that's right" and "yeah, we can do this."

He had picked up Allison and driven to Edward's Pony Keg in Mount Relling for ice cream. They looked for any sign of a long sedan that might contain four, young men set on trailing them to or from Edward's. They weren't taking chances.

Allison described the kind of stunt that she wanted to pull. In the long run, they wouldn't be cheating. It would be temporarily cheating, just so Ulysses was clear about it. With Shine and Cynthia in tow, safe and snug in the trunk of his car, all four would head to The Swashbuckler Drive-in and watch back-to-back movies. The new John Wayne movie, "The Green Berets," was playing.

"Let's let Shine have some fun. He hasn't found a load of fun this summer - yet. It'll be harmless," Allison said.

"Hold up, girl. You're gonna get everybody in trouble. They got people walking around watching for kids popping out of trunks. Too risky."

"Wrong. We're doing this. But we'll pay for four. It'll be later, when the first movie starts."

"I got questions."

"Never mind them. Once we're inside The Swashbuckler, we pop the trunk, and I'll walk back and pay the ticket-taker at the entrance."

"We'll get busted."

"We're paying, Ulysses. I'll give them a couple extra dollars. I'll say, 'Hey, you forgot to ring up these two in the back seat. They were making out and you missed them.'"

"I'm not there with it."

Allison knew Shine would go along. He was half class-clown anyway, he wanted to play his trumpet at a nearly all-black lounge with Ulysses' father, and he'd already wreaked havoc stirring up a ball field with a tractor. He chased kids around at the rec shelter. But, he seemed sadder than usual.

151

What kind of brother do I have, Allison asked Ulysses. Ulysses said he wasn't quite sure. Allison agreed with him. She wasn't sure either. Except, Shine would consider this hiding-in-the-trunk a strange kind of freedom, a freedom of not having to pay for something.

Allison was also sure that her brother could convince Cynthia. It might be a stretch, but Allison believed Cynthia would hide in a car trunk if it meant being close to her brother.

***

HERE THEY WERE. IN THE car trunk.

Shine felt Cynthia's feet pressing hard into his bent legs. He tried not to actually touch her. He wasn't quite sure how she felt about touching him in the trunk of Ulysses' car, although the placement of her feet was an indicator.

He soon felt an elbow. She jabbed. He lightly jabbed her back. Talk seemed irrelevant. What could one say hiding in a car trunk? He felt conspicuous. He second-guessed his sister and Ulysses' plan.

"This is fun, Shine," she finally said. "I can't believe we went along with this."

"Really? You mean that about it being fun?"

"If we're not at your house, or working, or throwing rocks in the creek, we might as well be in the trunk of a car." When she laughed, she swung an arm, upsetting a box of golf balls. A couple of loose balls rolled against Shine's neck.

"I'm sweating," he said. "I don't want to get caught."

Shine and Cynthia didn't have to touch if they didn't want to.

He shifted an arm and hand so that it touched her shoulder in that dark trunk, more like a pinch than a soft touch. Cynthia's feet were still pressed against his legs. Shine had used his sore arm from the allergy injections. Knowing he still had a patch of redness above the elbow, the throbbing had subsided over the past few days.

They heard voices at the entrance to The Swashbuckler.

Every conceivable sound in the world meant something to them now: keys rattling, cash register clinging, voices rising and falling.

When Shine heard a key turning the trunk latch and then the latch's clicking sound, he was ready to move. The trunk popped open. His sister gazed down at them.

"Don't you two look lost," she said.

Shine let Cynthia maneuver her body out of the trunk first. It was around dusk and they were parked at the very back of the drive-in. No other cars in the the back row yet, not in the corner where the Caprice was parked.

The first feature, "The Green Berets," had begun and people paid such attention to the screen that it was safe for Shine and Cynthia to walk around the Caprice, get their two lawn chairs from the backseat, and put them next to the speakers.

Allison convinced Ulysses to go with her to the front entrance and pay for two movie-goers in their car that the ticket-taker missed. She would create some other story about being too excited for these new movies to even think about who was in the backseat when they arrived. It was a big car, anyway; easy not to see everything from the outside.

Shine and Cynthia were alone.

He looked at Cynthia. He now thought of her as a girlfriend. A could-be girlfriend. Maybe-soon girlfriend, if he didn't mess up. Maybe she could be.

A girlfriend without a ring.

He had no ring to give, and he had no cash. Did the pawn shop carry a ring for a teenager?

Shine usually carried spare change, in a good week. The summer money he made at the rec shelter went to buying school supplies and gym gear. It went to buying a few movie tickets.

That word "girlfriend" entered his vocabulary on the night he joined Cynthia in the trunk of a car.

Maybe he had thought of the word before The Swashbuckler, but the car trunk revived it. That word gave authority to his very being as a possible romantic. Shine felt a new surge of importance. He wondered if Cynthia expected him to buy her things now.

Money, a fleeting thought best kept that way.

The important thing was that he didn't want her to find out about his Kools.

Tonight, amazingly, he did have fifty cents, and he brought her back popcorn and a Barq's rootbeer. He couldn't dismiss Cynthia's eyes, as the actors' voices in the movie seemed to erupt from the speakers hooked onto the car windows.

At some point during the three hours the two couples were at The Swashbuckler, Shine locked his fingers in Cynthia's, and they kissed extremely briefly and twice, right after two easygoing scenes. Shine let her fall asleep with her head on his shoulder, her one arm draped around his neck.

The action in the first movie was a blur to Shine. He replayed the evening in his mind: They'd given each other space in the trunk, in spite of Cynthia's feet. He had jokingly pinched her shoulder, but not aggressively.

Most of all, he had a strange sense that her eyes never veered from him in the darkness of a gigantic car trunk.

***

HE STUMBLED UPON IT AFTER work at the rec shelter.

He and Cynthia were leaving. They walked up Garland's driveway toward the street, and Shine saw the piece of paper on the sidewalk. On the paper he saw photos of H. Rap Brown and Eldridge Cleaver, another Black Panther Party leader, at the top.

The first thing he thought was that any one of the few young girls coming to the rec shelter from west Bedlam could have tacked the flyer to the pole. He imagined that one of their mothers or older sisters, driving them to the shelter, directed one of the girls to punch the tack hard into the wood, so the flyer would stay.

Cynthia read aloud the child-like handwriting: "Come see H. R. Brown live in person from the Panther Party August 10 at 8 on Cedar."

As he pocketed it, a woman standing on her porch shouted down to them. Her house overlooked Garland.

"There's a new one on that pole about everyday," she said. "I come out and take them off. Don't know who's doing it. Some of the kids down there, they up to it?"

Shine knew "some of those kids" meant the girls from west Bedlam who were dropped off in the late morning. There was no rec shelter in west Bedlam; Garland was the closest one of three.

"I've seen a lot of these posters," Shine said. "I've got my lost parrot posters. One's gone from this pole."

"Yeah, I saw that one," the lady said. "You found the parrot yet?"

"Not yet."

"Keep looking. That's a nice-looking bird. Must've cost a lot. I'll keep an eye out."

***

SHINE HAD NEARLY FINISHED SWIMMING in Klump's pool when he saw the officer get out of his Ford truck and hurry toward him.

He waved to get Shine's attention.

"What's the matter, Breezy?"

"You done swimming? Anyway, climb out of there. Pool's closed."

Shine's confusion registered with the officer; he turned back around. "Nothing about you. I just got back from the hospital."

Shine dried off. Klump rambled.

The officer shook his fist. "I'm telling you, that little niece of mine. I knew she couldn't swim. Four-years old. Too big for the kiddie pool. I watched her put a foot on the pool ladder. But I didn't think she had the strength to climb it like a chimpanzee. Just as I turn my back, just as I flip a switch and look away at the kitchen window for one second, there she goes into the pool. Plop. She goes under and bobs up. Up and down a few times with her arms thrashing every which damn way. I know I got to jump in. So I jumped in. Wouldn't anyone? Shorts and t-shirt on. I jump in and get that kid, Tricia. Little thing. She won't get near this pool again for a while."

"Did you have to do CPR?"

"CPR? Of course I did CPR. After a few pumps she spewed it out. Giggled a little but a scared giggle."

"She'll be ok?"

"She's fine. Scared."

Just as Breezy seemed to calm down, he lit a cigarette, changed the subject, and said, "Shine, ride with me. Get in my pick-up truck, go for a ride."

"Where to?"

"West Bedlam."

"Why over there?" Shine said.

"I have to deliver a quick something."

On their way, the officer witnessed Wayne deLong racing on Hooper, heading toward Cedar. He was at least twenty-five miles over the speed limit. Klump was off-duty and in his Ford and without a siren or lights, so he didn't chase deLong. He didn't have his radio either. "I'll catch him real soon," he said. "I definitely will."

Wayne deLong even had the nerve to peel out when a red stop light turned green. And he drove his father's car whenever he got behind a wheel. Wayne sat in the Ford Mustang at the light near Kroger. Klump could not get there fast enough to pull up beside Wayne. He let him speed away.

In less than five minutes, they were inside Bettman's. The officer adjusted his belt and pants getting out of the car. He gave old man Bettman, who was standing by the front door candy buckets, ten H. Rap Brown posters that he'd found laying in the street near City Hall.

"Someone's taking these down," Klump said. "I'll hand them to you. You can take them from here."

"You want some caramel chews to go?" Bettman said.

"Got enough. Still keeping those buckets by the door?"

"I don't change easy," the old man said.

***

SHINE WAS TIRED FOR ONCE.
He ate a late dinner with his mother and Allison. They watched an episode of "Dragnet" and played a guessing game, trying to identify the person responsible for a bank robbery. It turned out to be a middle-aged man who owned a clothing store across the street from the bank. A regular customer, he kept his money at this bank. During intermittent downtime, over six months, he scoped out bank activity and noted any lull in customer service. The clothing store owner was a tailor and concocted the perfect set of old tattered pants, a loose, black long-sleeve shirt, and a rubberized mask to hide his identity. He might have pulled off the caper had he not left shoe prints. The tailor must have stepped in tar on the freshly-paved street outside the bank. The detectives matched his shoes to the tar-prints on the bank floor.

Shine and Allison heard a knock at the door. She jumped up to open it. Ulysses stood outside with a pink carnation in one hand and two JoJo posters in the other.

"I found these two posters on the ground," he said. "Like they'd been torn off. The carnation's for you."

"It's beautiful," Allison said. "I'll put it in water."

Ulysses came in, nodded at Josephine, who never expected Ulysses to knock on the front at this hour, and, secondly, come with a carnation for Allison."

Ulysses shared his discovery that posters for the Black Panther Party rally had been taken down over the past few days.

"Shine told me about those parrot posters," he said, "but I don't see but two or three H. Rap Brown posters anymore. Somebody's been taking them down. That's what we hear."

Shine could never prove that it was not he who took down any Brown poster.

He'd put up at least twenty JoJo posters. He hoped Ulysses wouldn't suspect him of knowing anything about the disappearing H. Rap Brown posters.

"Some are a little upset. Especially that cousin of mine, Alphonso."

Josephine turned on a local special about politics. The reporter stressed the word, "crime." And then the reporter said: "And here in Bedlam, a suburb just north of downtown..." Balancing his reporting with a stream of video and photographs, the reporter described the damage to the Empire. Josephine rubbed the back of her head.

The reporter discussed the recent development that the Bedlam Fire Department considered the Empire fire as arson. "For instance," the reporter said, "police and fire officials in this small community of Bedlam, which sits adjacent to I-75 and is central for regional industry, suspect the fire was intentionally set. They are investigating."

Ulysses mumbled, "I think we know this. What else is new?"

The reporter mentioned the mayor and how he considers his community an entirely safe place to live. Ulysses remained focused on the t.v. Allison put her hand on his arm.

She didn't move her hand even after the special ended.

SKYDOG

BEFORE THEY HOPPED ONTO A boxcar this morning, Shine and Moondog were still talking about a new campfire.

They discovered it in the vicinity of the fence. This hobo camp, down the slope near the tracks, was littered with shoestrings without shoes and aluminum foil without sandwiches. Crushed drink cups sat on top of the ashes.

Moondog was hungry as soon as the train arrived. He pulled out a half-eaten bag of licorice and shared sticks with Shine. They nearly mis-timed their footing hopping on the rail ladder. Once they hopped in and braced themselves, they heard someone grab the ladder and climb up to the car's opening. They had seen no one behind them. They'd heard only the train.

He was a familiar figure.

The man with whom they previously rode, whose old blanket smelled like onions and gasoline, crawled to a corner. Shine sensed the man saw them climb into this one.

A bonafide hobo: tattered shoes, dirty hands, craggy face, body odor. He had a high-pitched voice. Any word with an 's' triggered a whistle sound.

"You's going up to Hamilton again?" the man said. "Been awhile since you's been there?"

"We've rode up there plenty," Shine said.

"How you like ridin'?"

"It's ok," Moondog said. "Gives us time to think."

"What you's thinking about?"

"About who's up for President in November. We talked about it in school."

"You's can't even vote."

"We had a mock vote in school," Shine said. "It came out Democrat. It came out Humphrey won."

"Never heard of him. It don't matter. This country ain't doing no better. Look at me. Look at you's - riding a train. You should be reading books in a liberry. If we're gonna fight in some stinking war, in some place we don't even know, then I'm safer riding trains so's I can keep moving."

"You ride all over the country?" Shine asked.

The man offered them a cigarette. "You's smoke? You's can split this."

"Nope," said Moondog. "We're in sports. And he plays the trumpet with my dad." Shine said nothing about smoking.

"I ride in the warm places, mostly," the man said. "California. Arizona. California has a lot of them Kennedy signs. I know Kennedy's name. You don't see no Nixon signs. I know his name. Yep, I keep up."

The boys acted unafraid of the man. He didn't take his eyes off of them. Shine didn't know whether to show more or less friendliness. He couldn't tell if the man had a weapon. The train was moving and he and his best friend were cornered. Two young guys against one man. The numbers gave Shine some comfort.

The man soon laid down. He'd come with a newer-looking, rolled-up blanket and spread it over his legs.

The man soon fell asleep, still smoking. His cigarette fell out of his fingers and onto a smattering of sawdust. In his boldest move yet, Shine slid over, found the cigarette, picked it up, crushed it against the side.

Shine stood by the opening of the boxcar and watched the sky. In the thick cloud formations, he saw them arranged to suggest dogs were chasing one another. He imagined the sky as an infinite place for dogs to roam. Sky dogs. "Look at those sky dogs up there," he said.

What dogs, man?"

"All these dogs in the sky, just running. Running around in the sky. Not know where they're headed."

"What dogs?" Moondog got up and joined him.

"Those dogs. Call them sky dogs. Those clouds look like dogs. Sky dogs making a run for it. They'll never stop. Like us. They're going places."

"I guess I can see a dog or two. That one there's a German Shepherd."

"Poodle over there," Shine said.

"That's what that hobo's doing," Moondog said. "He's making a run for it. Listen to him snore."

"There's a dog chasing his tail." Shine pointed to a cloud that looked like a Dachshund.

When the train slowed down near another stretch of factories, the boys sat back inside the boxcar so they wouldn't be discovered. By then, the sky dog-clouds had broken into shapeless wisps, flakes in the sky's blueness.

***

WHEN THE TWO LATER RETURNED to Bedlam, Shine could still not get over the fact that they'd met the same hobo they rode with a few weeks ago. The chances of meeting him again were slim.

"I can't believe that was the same hobo," Moondog said.

"I thought he'd bring up the Empire again," Shine said. "I would've asked him if he knew more. I didn't think about it until now."

The two had each bought a bag of candy at Bettman's.

"I wasn't afraid of him this time," Moondog said. "He must've seen us in the woods and followed us. I'll bet you that's his campsite."

"Maybe he wanted to talk some more, but he was too tired," Shine said. "How do you sleep all the time in the woods without a tent? He must keep one eye open."

***

SHINE HELD HIS OWN TRUMPET on Pop Weasel's front porch. Early evening. He waited for Pop to bring out his trumpet. Shine played softly, tooting barely a sound.

He and Moondog waited for Pop to find his sweater. Unnaturally cool, end-of-July air. In their t-shirts, ignoring the coolness, the boys grabbed Pop's offer of a dinner of hotdogs.

When Pop returned, Shine put down his trumpet and listened. Pop began right in, blowing a tune he'd heard on the radio. He looked at Shine as he played. With his left hand, he pointed to his right hand finger movement, urging Shine to watch it.

Alphonso Peace opened the window by the porch. He hung his head outside. "You all make the craziest-ass noise. I was about to sleep," he said.

Pop stopped playing. "This is the wake up call you need." He lifted his trumpet high, like he would a trophy, so Alphonso could see it. "Wrap a pillow around your ears, son."

Alphonso tossed his toothpick, slammed the window enough that it rattled.

"He must've brushed his teeth with that toothpick," Pop said. "Boy will sleep all day."

"I don't trust where he goes during the day," Moondog said. "He ain't sleeping. I see him with the Simms brothers."

"I got my eye on him," Pop said.

"How come Alphonso hasn't gotten new work since the Empire burned down?" Shine said, digging into a new bag of Husman's Potato Chips.

"He stopped working before that fire," Pop said. "He was done tardy one too many times, coming in too late. Can't hold a job that way."

Pop blew part of a song he'd recently played at The Hot Spot. Pop kept saying he needed to brush up on the song's shifting tone, but to Shine he already played with near perfection. He held notes and chipped away at others with a whiz-bang rhythm that could turn heads.

An hour later, Shine admitted he needed a sweatshirt. It was late. He accepted Pop's offer to drive him back to north Bedlam. With Moondog in the backseat, Pop confessed that he wasn't entirely sure he could trust Alphonso Peace around the house. Especially when Alphonso was alone.

"If I lose another dollar bill laying on my kitchen table… I'm wondering."

"I told you about Ulysses missing change," Moondog said. "And you already know about his tire."

"Keep this to yourself, son," his father said. "Not a word. Ulysses either."

"I hear you, Pop. Ulysses gonna take him apart, anyway."

"This isn't news," Pop said, "but we are - he is -family. Alphonso is, and I got to watch that deal."

***

SHINE WAS TWENTY MINUTES LATE for work at the rec shelter. He'd overslept.

Then, too, he remembered he had one Kool in his pants pocket. He snuck that one smoke deep in Garland woods. He sat on the tree-filled hillside with the path on which he and his friends rode sleds in winter.

He popped three sticks of gum in his mouth.

It had been a long several days of trumpet practice with Pop Weasel. Shine could still feel his mouthpiece's impression on his lips from all the playing.

Pop reinforced this new discipline in Shine. It needed to be shaped. Shine ignored the fact that his allergy medicine made him drowsy. Lethargic. He stayed in his seat and played along with Pop. He listened to him talk about Al Hirt, the famous New Orleans trumpeter, a frequent guest on Ruth Lyons' 50-50 Club.

"Al Hirt tilts it this way," Pop said. "Check out Al's fingering. That cat can smoke a song and make your eyes tear up."

When Pop went to get two glasses of ice water, Shine never took his eyes off the sheet music. Pop said, "Play this page. I'll be right back," and soon Shine heard the rattle of ice cubes. He played one page of music two or three times if it meant not stopping until Pop returned.

Before Shine had left for the rec shelter this morning, his mother told him that Cynthia had come by the night before while he practiced with Pop Weasel.

"She wanted to leave you a brand new mouth piece for you trumpet," his mother said. "She did. She put it your room."

"I didn't see it," he said.

"That's because she took it right back."

"Why? Did she say?"

That's when his mother described the confused look on Cynthia's face: "She told me nothing. She marched out the front door. With your mouth piece."

Shine approached Cynthia at the rec shelter. She'd avoided him for awhile, until he mustered the nerve to step in front of her.

"Is something wrong?" he said.

"Not now," Cynthia said.

"Why not?"

"Come around here." She nearly dragged him behind the shelter. He looked at her while she looked into the woods.

"I found cigarettes, Shine."

"How many?"

"It's not funny. Don't make it be."

"You rooting around in my bedroom?"

"I was putting a new mouth piece I bought for you in the top drawer. Hiding it just a little. I wanted it to be a special discovery for you. A surprise. I put a red bow on it. I was going to tell you, 'Look in that top drawer when you get a chance.' There was a rusty metal Band-Aid box staring at me. I thought it was bizarre. I just, well, just opened it. Not to nose around. Look, it was strange. And Shine, you got cigarettes in it."

"I'm sorry."

"Like that matters."

He was quiet. He was overly embarrassed. He didn't know where to tread next with any remark. He was better off kneading his t-shirt while she talked, while eventually she gave him only another chance to quit smoking.

"I hear everything you're saying."

"Shine Ross, don't mess this up."

The rest of the day, Shine could not win one game of checkers, even against kids who were four and five years younger than he was. He was to blame, and only to blame, for the Band-Aid box. For now, because he wasn't quite sure about completely halting something that intrigued him more than anything, he decided he would have to hide the Band-Aid box behind certain books on a shelf. He'd pinpoint a secretive place behind some books that he would never read.

***

SHINE AND MOONDOG RAN THE basketball court. After a half-hour, sweat streamed into Shine's eyes. He got another player to take his place.

It was his hair. Shine's floppy hair swished around his forehead. It flung sweat into his eyes. Shine was forever brushing back the wet strands.

In two different pick-up games, they had been teammates but lost both five-on-five games. Shine scored miserably. Four points in one game; six in the second game. Moondog scored ten points in one game, two in the second game, and most of his points came from lay-ups. On the outdoor court sat next to the highway, the grind of semi-trucks, made it nearly impossible to hear play-calls. Day and night. The trucks' loads. Machinery, paper, textiles. Trucks exited I-75 next to the basketball court.

Shine's head was still tender from his clash with Larry Loomis. He'd felt dizzy every few minutes but didn't say a word. He admitted to Moondog he wasn't game-ready.

Moondog tossed Shine his own shirt after he wiped his face, seeing that Shine's shirt was soaking wet.

"Yeah, but you can't keep using your hard head as an excuse for not hitting the rim," Moondog joked. "Those stitches are gone."

169

Soon, they were munching hamburgers at Golden Point restaurant, across from Kroger and less than a fifty yards downhill from the football field.

They'd cooled off and were halfway through eating a bag of fries when Shine noticed Troy and Terence Simms and Alphonso Peace heading into Golden Point.

Moondog insisted they hurry out of the parking lot. "I don't want to get mixed up with Alphonso right now."

Where to, Shine thought. Head into Kroger? Wander up and down the candy aisle?

Head to the Post Office and act like they were buying stamps?

Yet, the two just stood there. It was as if they decided to have a staring contest at the flag hanging above the Post Office. They finished their fries.

They weren't yet out of the parking lot when Troy Simms came up behind them. Terence Simms soon followed. And Alphonso Peace, struggling to balance a large chocolate shake, double-burger, and fries.

"What's you got going, Moonman?" Troy Simms said to Moondog.

Moondog didn't answer. He and Shine decided to start walking. The Simms brothers and Alphonso kept pace.

"Hey, man, can I ask you something?" said Troy Simms. His brother Terence, the smoker, lit a cigarette and flicked his kitchen match by Moondog's foot. Shine knew Troy Simms was talking to him. "One question, man."

"What?" Shine said.

"You two hanging out a lot over by the old Empire. You go all around and climb over that yellow cop tape and sifting for things. What's you two looking for, man?"

170

"How do you know?"

"We live near there," Terence Simms said. "We see."

"We're just snooping around," Moondog said.

"You know something we don't, little one?" Alphonso Peace said to his cousin. He planted himself between the Simms brothers and Shine and Moondog, imposing himself in the conversation. Again, Shine and Moondog started walking. Troy Simms leveled a few accusations at the two. Terence Simms smoked.

Shine decided to stop. He whisked Moondog around, too.

"Time we stop this nonsense," Shine said. "Do you guys know something about that fire?"

"Who? Us?" Alphonso said. "You talking to us?"

"You talking to us?" Troy said. "Now, *that's* nonsense."

"Look," Shine said, "would anyone want to burn down the Empire?"

The three guys glared at Shine and Moondog. Terence Simms blew a sequence of smoke rings, before tossing his cigarette down.

"You know what we're looking for?" Shine said. "A gas can. Something that will help the fire department and cops."

The Simms brothers and Alphonso Peace, who'd finally finished eating, started laughing. They broke up; they lost it. Troy Simms grabbed his chest. Alphonso wedged a toothpick between his lips.

"If you suggesting we know anything, you go ahead. Tell that cop friend of yours," Troy said.

"You got cop friends, right?" Alphonso Peace said.

"My officer friend is my neighbor," Shine said.

"Right. Neighbor," Troy said.

"I swim in his pool."

"He's a friend," Moondog said. "We gotta go. Come on, Shine, man, we gotta go."

"Moonman, I can see you trying to torch a place," Alphonso said. "You almost blow up the house lighting a gas stove." He belted out a sinister laugh.

"I know what my cop neighbor says," said Shine. "He said he thinks someone set fire to it. I didn't say that. I wish I knew. My uncle worked there. The fire department thinks it. Klump said it's obvious."

"Better check out your uncle," Troy said. "Bad place to work. Bad times. Hard, unfair work, I hear. He might have got mad. I know upset dudes there."

Before Shine and Moondog headed up the street, out of nowhere came Fremont Jones, who cranked his bike pedals with such force that his legs quivered and his feet slipped. He skidded to a stop not far from the Simms brothers and Alphonso. Although it looked as if Fremont Jones was shouting, they could hear only a guttural sound.

Fremont waved and pointed his finger randomly.

Shine felt Fremont was worried about something greater than the words he could not form. In one motion, he swung his bike around and sped off toward west Bedlam.

"Boy can't talk," Troy Simms said.

"He's a mute," Alphonso said. "Little man can't hear, neither. Fool kid."

Everyone watched Fremont blaze across the street by Kroger and climb the hill.

No one knew what he'd tried to say.

It wasn't until Maury Riggs slowed his car to a crawl and motioned toward the two guys that Shine guessed Fremont may have wanted to interfere. He'd looked out for Shine and Moondog. He was capable of disrupting or blending invisibly into a scene. His deafness gave him an unique nature: his in-the-background demeanor itself floated unpredictably in and out of whatever flavor a moment posed. Here, past Golden Point and the beautiful smell of greasy food, Fremont allowed the boys to keep walking.

Maury Riggs invited Shine and Moondog to get in the backseat. Because Riggs was his ultimate boss, Shine wasn't going to to turn down the ride. In the car's quietness, at first, Shine stared at Riggs' casual handling of his cigar. He savored that aroma.

"I'll drop you boys off at the Garland rec shelter," Riggs said. "You can find your way around from there."

In that time of three minutes, Riggs spelled out why the city was soon closing the rec shelter two weeks early. "Saving us money," he said. "It'll give you more vacation time."

Riggs changed the subject to Golden Point.

"Anything you two know that I need to know?" Riggs said, his cigar enormous between his fingers.

Shine and Moondog peered out their windows, saying "not really" almost in unison, not glancing at Riggs who kept eying them in the rearview mirror.

"Those guys back there say anything that might help me know more about them? Moondog? What do you say?"

Moondog mumbled that his cousin was difficult to live with. "That's who he is," he said.

Shine looked away from Riggs.

Troy and Terence Simms appealed to teenagers in west Bedlam. They bought candy for younger kids from Bettman's and swam with them in the school's pool. Shine kept his insights to himself.

"It's ok," Riggs said. "There's certain things best left unsaid. You guys watch yourselves."

When Riggs pulled away, Shine said, "Remember those clouds from the last train? Sky dog clouds? Like big-eared dogs in the sky, big old bodies?"

"Yeah, I remember. That's what you thought it was."

"Sky dogs," Shine said. "That's us. We got that freedom, you know? Those cloud-dogs did whatever they wanted. We can change shapes in the way we do stuff. Act like we don't know something. But we really know stuff. I think Klump and the others have a good idea who set the fire. I let Simms know what I felt, but I didn't say much. Sky dog."

"You say so," Moondog said.

They walked toward Shine's house, anticipating taking a half-hour swim in Klump's pool. They'd already pulled off their shirts and spied the pool with no one in it, fortunately.

FREIGHT

SHINE WADDED HIS RAINCOAT INTO a tight square. The forecast was rain, but he had a different plan. Rain was only a slight obstacle if it meant searching for JoJo. He enlisted his uncle Jerry who finished drinking a Dr. Pepper and fastened his raincoat around his waist.

Shine got another call about JoJo: a new sighting near an edge of Garland Park. His aunt Ruth was helping her sister Josephine dig weeds in her garden in spite of the threat of rain.

His aunt came in to get a pitcher of iced tea. She hesitated when she saw her husband. "Wait. Really, Jerry?"

He ignored his wife's question and was out the front door.

Shine lead the charge. He promised himself that he would not let a little rain detour him from hunting for JoJo. His uncle seemed prepared. He handed Shine the flashlight as they neared the woods. His uncle's sleepless nights were flooded with images of JoJo hurtling in the foreign territory of Bedlam's green space.

Shine caught up with his uncle. "This way, uncle Jerry."

They high-stepped through tall grass.

The hunt continued. Past supper time. Neither he nor his uncle had eaten. He offered his uncle a last Snickers bar, and Jerry snatched it. They put on their matching yellow raincoats in the light rain. It darkened. It was just after seven, though it seemed past midnight. The sky peeled apart sheets of clouds and it poured. Shine and Jerry were under trees and they weren't returning yet.

They had the one flashlight between them. Shine angled the beam toward treetop after treetop, in the general area where old Mr. Waddle claimed he saw JoJo fly. When Shine talked to him earlier, old Mr. Waddle said, "That's a big old bird, and I know I seen a color or two. I was walking my dog. It wasn't a crow."

Rain moved the leaves. When a branch snapped, Shine ran toward it thinking JoJo might be above it.

He heard a louder noise. A clanking noise. A rambunctious noise. His uncle took the flashlight and shined it across the creek to an open space. That area lead to a part of the city dump. The rain had let up fairly quickly.

They were staring at what the light framed: a soaked Larry Loomis dragging a huge green garbage bag. It was heavy enough to slow down Larry. He stopped in the light.

"Man, what's with that?" Larry hollered across the creek. "That light, man. It's blinding me."

"It's me. Shine. And my uncle." They kept the light on Larry, who shaded his eyes.

When Jerry tilted the beam away from Larry, they could still make him out. He wrestled with the weight of the garbage bag. The noise was glass bottles rattling inside the bag. Larry nonchalantly let the wet bag sag behind him, as he played down the embarrassing weight.

There was silence.

"We're looking for my uncle's Amazon parrot," Shine said. "We got a call it might be here. An old man called thinking he saw it."

"Oh, your bird? Right," Larry said.

"You got bottles in that bag?" They were shouting across the creek now.

"Yeah, man. Collecting. We do it in my family. I do it. Hundred bottles every couple of weeks. I just go through it at night, man. They dump 'em here on one side. Two cent a bottle."

"You need a hand?"

"Naw. I'm heading back. I got twenty bucks here. You need me help you look for that bird?"

"We're ok."

Larry Loomis dropped his bag on top of the hill, anyway. He stepped on several boulders that crossed the creek. Shine kept the flashlight in front of Larry so he could see.

"Let me give you a hand."

It was as if a vocal trap door opened wide. Larry explained he was going to return the empties in his garbage bag for money to buy his grandfather a new pair of glasses. "The man can't see," he said. "Blind as that tree." He described his best days as cramming at least fifty to seventy-five bottles every couple of weeks in a garbage bag.

The more Larry Loomis talked, the more an unexpected ease surged between the two. The night of Larry's futile semi-twine-tying of Shine in a faulty chair in a room filled with cobwebs seemed as distant as ever.

His mind flashed back to Larry's scary gestures that night and his inability to tie a simple knot. Shine literally stepped out of that twine. He wondered if Larry was that inept or if he let a so-called knot remain half-tied on purpose. Shine remembered Fremont Jones' face in that window and his thinking he rescued Shine.

The hunt for JoJo continued until Shine heard several dogs in the woods. There always seemed to be dogs roaming Garland. He ran toward the sound of barking. He thought if JoJo was nearby, the bird could have fallen. Would it have been hungry? Tired? The possibilities flashed through Shine's imagination.

They stopped when the barking faded and they saw three dogs run across the ball field. None of the dogs carried any creature in their mouths. Once the threesome combed a section of the woods one last time, Shine persuaded Larry to let his uncle drive him home.

Shine situated his arms under a ridiculous number of pop bottles, and steadied his legs while lifting the garbage bag. He battled Larry's bag of glass. Shine hated for Larry to see him sweat. Larry's bag was dead weight.

On the other side of the bag, Larry was not grunting. They flipped the bag into Jerry's trunk. Bottles clanged. They'd left the bag on the hill where Larry initially dropped it and crossed the creek. They'd returned in Jerry's cavernous Bonneville with dry towels on the front and back seats. Their pants had gotten soaked even with raincoats. They dragged the bottles back to the Bonneville.

Before long, Jerry pulled in front of Larry's house. An old basketball was covered with mud in the front yard. Larry turned quiet during the three-minute ride to his grandfather's house. He insisted on unloading the bag alone.

That guy is strong, Shine thought.

When Larry stuck his face in the open side window, he patted Jerry on the shoulder while looking right at Shine.

"You'll get your bird," he said. "Oh, remember, stay outta my dump."

***

WHEN SHINE SAW THE TWO figures on the embankment leading up to the train tracks ahead of him, Moondog, and Cynthia, who had insisted she come along, he paused.

Shine had confessed to Cynthia that he and Moondog had nearly mastered the trips to Hamilton and back. He felt it best to be honest with her at this stage in their relationship. Yet he made it clear that no amount of protests from Cynthia would keep him from train-hopping.

He recognized the two figures: Wayne deLong and Neil Nash.

"Hey, you three," Wayne said. "Where you going?"

"Hopping the next train when it comes through," Shine said. "We do it once in a while."

"More than that," Moondog said.

"How much more?" Wayne said, watching Neil drink the last of his Barq's Cream Soda and hurl the bottle toward the woods.

"Just about all summer," Moondog said.

"Then we're going, too. Can't stop us."

"Then so what?" Shine said.

They all started to sit on the embankment when Cynthia pulled Shine aside. She lead him twenty feet away from the others. "We have to talk when you get back. I'm not going along with this."

"Not pressuring you to ride," Shine said.

"I don't like it. You better not get hurt."

"I haven't yet. And I won't."

Cynthia stepped closer. She put her arm around his waist. She felt the Band-Aid box in his back pocket and she knew its contents.

"I thought you said you'd get rid of those."

"I'm going to."

They heard the train whistle two minutes before the train appeared near Garland. It barely chugged, perfect for hopping. It had just departed from the factories on the west side of town. There it lost weight in the unloading of material and gained it back with new loads heading north.

Cynthia disappeared toward a trail in Garland. No doubt upset. Shine wasn't planning to smoke yet in front of Moondog; he just wanted to carry the box, as if it gave him good luck.

Perhaps she'd planned to ride with them, until she saw Wayne deLong and Neil Nash.

Moondog winced. It was incredible to Shine how Moondog could twist his ankle hopping onto a train, when logic held that he should twist it hopping off and landing on hard ground.

FOR MUCH OF THE RIDE, Wayne deLong and Neil Nash ribbed Shine and Moondog, flaunting testy phrases like, "Why don't you Oreos hold each other's hand?" And remarks to Shine like, "You got a thing going with your friends in west Bedlam?" And, "You better not get Cynthia Reynolds pregnant. Her dad'll put a bullet in your head." And a remark to Moondog: "You ought to come live with Shine's family, 'cause you're over there enough?" This caused Moondog to scoot toward Neil Nash. Shine grabbed his shoulder, holding him back.

"Stick it, Neil," Shine said. "Wayne, you got cut from football. What team you trying out for next year? You gonna move to Rellington and flunk out there?"

Wayne deLong sized up Shine. He spit in the middle of the boxcar. Shine ignored it. He felt empowered. Shine knew his own record of train-hopping far overshadowed Wayne deLong's, and for that reason he took ownership of the ride. He stood up so that Wayne deLong and Neil Nash could see him keep his balance as the rickety train rounded a bend.

"You do this often, Wayne?"

"Maybe."

"Well, we're naturals."

"I think it's funny how you keep looking for that parrot," Wayne said. "It's gone. Plus, you keep poking your nose where it don't belong, around the old Empire."

"I know what we're doing," Shine said.

181

"I was over there at the hardware store when it caught fire," Wayne said. "Me and my uncle. Funny how things always catch fire over there."

Wayne spoke about a few other things regarding the Empire and his lack of caring that it burned, but the boxcar jolted, stirring up dust, rattling teeth, jerking around everyone, and obliterating any more strands of conversation.

The train was mysteriously slowing. They were captive in a boxcar in the middle of farmland.

The train and railroad track groaned and wheezed under the merciless halting of so much weight. That sheer bulk weight shifting, seeming unsteady in its pains to stop.

They felt that heaviness. Their bodies shifted and slid. The air was stagnant. They sweat profusely with no breeze penetrating the inside.

Shine hung onto a handle that poked him in the head. In his rear-pocket, the Band-Aid box made it impossible to sit comfortably. He squirmed.

"We gotta get off," Wayne deLong said. Although he was the quieter and the more cunning of the two, Wayne seemed the most rattled. "I can't deal with being holed up in a small space too long. I'm gonna lose it. I'm gonna throw up if I don't hop off."

"Then hop off," Neil Nash said. "I'm hopping with you. We'll sleep in a field tonight. Nobody'll miss us."

They squatted and shuffled toward the door. Neil nudged Wayne with his foot, and Wayne jumped. Nothing but tall grass and cornfields. A battered barn maybe three hundred yards away. No birds. Hot summer wind washing against Wayne's and Neil's faces.

Twenty seconds later, Neil jumped, yelling at the sky, flapping his skinny arms in mid-air.

***

IT GOT DARK FAR TOO soon. He'd lost sense of time.

Cynthia warned them that they likely wouldn't be able to catch a return train too quickly. To Shine, she was a prophetess now.

The moon shoved its roundness into view, showing no favor to the two boys.

Once the train started rolling again, they hopped off ten minutes later. The city of Hamilton must have been nearby. They got to a road ten minutes later, Moondog hobbling behind Shine. They found a pay phone, and to his credit, Moondog had not spent his last couple of quarters on beef jerky and Jolly Ranchers. He couldn't believe he had the quarters. "I thought they were long gone back at Bettman's," he said.

Mostly, they jumped because Moondog began complaining more about his growing ankle pain.

Shine called his mother.

He described the general vicinity and the red brick exterior of furniture and clothing stores, as well as a Texaco gas station on one corner. "Really small, but it's a main street," he said. "Must not be far from downtown Hamilton."

Shine tried to swallow the nervousness in his voice he was sure his mother could detect. He pressed his forehead against the phone booth. Josephine reacted calmly on her

183

end. She didn't raise her voice or demand a single embarrassing explanation for hopping a train which could get one killed in an instant. But, Shine could imagine her fuming. He imagined her clinching her teeth. He could see her put the phone back on its cradle, look at Allison, and utter through those clinched teeth, "Wait until I get him home."

The only real question she asked other than for directions was, "How did you boys have any money left?"

"I used about the last of Moondog's change," Shine said. "I'm broke. And can you bring an ice pack? Moondog hurt his ankle."

WHEN JOSEPHINE ROSS ARRIVED, ALLISON was driving, with his mother sitting straight as humanly possible on the passenger's side. Allison wore her white sun hat.

"I can explain why we got a train up here," Shine said.

"Got a train?" his mother said. "You got a train? You don't have to say anything. You shouldn't." She handed a plastic pouch of ice cubes to Moondog.

Shine slid down in the backseat. "It was just for fun, something to do. We watched out, no trouble."

He decided not to go into detail about how Wayne deLong expressed no regret that the Empire burned down. Wayne flashed a sneaky grin when Shine told him about the so-called hunt to find any clue as to who might have set the fire, if it even was arson. Something too secretive about the fire, Shine had told his family one day, and secrets bothered him.

"I'm about positive somebody set that fire," he'd told Wayne deLong.

"Yeah," Wayne said, "I don't blame someone for setting it." He smirked. "If someone was ticked off, or someone wanted some insurance money, or someone was just plain stupid or drunk, it would've happened. Easily."

Most of all, Wayne spilled information that his mother's third husband, a bookkeeper at the Empire, used to cheat workers out of the full amount they should have earned in their paychecks.

Shine spoke not one word of this knowledge to his mother or sister.

"No, you shouldn't say anything more about train-hopping," his mother repeated. The look she gave Shine suggested she might mention this expedition to his father. Shine didn't want that.

She reached into a picnic basket and handed each boy a peanut butter and jelly sandwich.

"Will you tell Dad?"

"I will," Allison spoke up.

"No, she won't," his mother said.

"You hear that, Allison? You won't."

"We'll see."

Moondog nudged Shine. Shine's talking only worsened things, and Moondog wanted it quiet so he could eat his PB&J. It was bad enough they got busted for leaving too late in the day and hopping a train that had not moved for well over an hour.

Soon, the boys' heads rested against the seats. They'd fallen asleep. The ice pouch slipped from Moondog's hand and dripped water. Barely awake, with his mouth wide open and jelly on his upper lip, Shine stretched one leg across the water and never felt the wetness spread.

***

THE BEDLAM CITY COUNCIL CHAMBER on city hall's second floor was packed early. The overflow consisted of a line of people squeezed into a narrow hallway.

Folding chairs in long rows stretched across the room. Shine, Cynthia, and his mother sat in the back row. Edna Rose from north Bedlam sat with the family of Mookie Bell, a west Bedlam landscaper who kept yard immaculate and drove her once a week to Hattendorf's. Next to Mookie's family were the two Berlson brothers from north Bedlam, who owned Berlson's Hardware in west Bedlam.

On another row, Earl Canton, Bedlam's smiling Clerk of Court offered a string of jokes to Melvin Lawson, whose grandfather built west Bedlam's only funeral home. Sure, there were three half-rows of young black men and women sitting together, and three half-rows of white men and women who established their blocks of chairs. The room's atmosphere contained more mystery than revelation.

Everyone stared at the front of the council chamber. What would the Mayor say? How could he address something like a potential Black Panther Party rally and keep it lowkey?

Council members crossed and uncrossed their legs. They played with their ashtrays and one-page agenda. A few cleared their throats.

It only got tense when Mayor Cecil C. Topper pounded his gavel.

"We want to hold this public meeting with integrity on the coming safety issue regarding a planned outdoor speaking engagement," the Mayor said. "I've asked council to be here in case I miss anything." He was a short man with large glasses occupying his whole face. It looked as if he was speaking to the ceiling. The Mayor's pipe smoke shrouded his table.

After Police Chief Wilbur outlined why the attendees at the rally could not march in west Bedlam, he reminded guests that council adopted a "silence ordinance" two years ago that would be in effect. Chief Wilbur read a passage: "Any public gathering of ten or more people at any time after 10:00 p.m. may not create noise deemed a disturbance to other Bedlam residents, regardless of the location of the gathering." It included rallies, open-air meetings, or very late night picnics especially in the summer and early fall. It included political demonstrations.

"What if H. Rap Brown is long-winded?" said Joe Benson, from west Bedlam. A few people in his row chuckled.

"Once a Black Panther Party official gets going, how you gonna stop him?" said Herman Long, who sat next to Benson. More laughter.

"I won't be holding a stopwatch, Mr. Mayor," Benson said.

The questions continued, seeming not to bother a patient Chief Wilburn. He fielded each question, shuffling his police hat between his hands. He stumbled only once, when Herman Long asked for the third time who might alert H. Rap Brown of the city's time limit for public gatherings.

"We will make sure Mr. Brown or any guests he brings know beforehand," Wilburn said.

"Who is 'we'?" Long said.

"We is 'I'. I will," Chief Wilburn said. "Or officer Watson. Or someone on duty. Depends on who's on duty."

"Well, that clears it up real good," Long said. More laughter in the room. Herman Long elbowed Joe Benson, and Benson elbowed the lady next to him.

"What guests?" Benson said. He lit a cigarette and blew smoke high in the air. "Who these guests?"

"We suspect Mr. Brown would have an entourage," the chief said. "Guests of his tagging along."

"Tagging along?" Benson said. He blew more smoke. "That's a weak word, Chief. Ain't no Black Panther tagging along nowhere."

"There's the municipal time limit of twelve o'clock a.m.," Wilburn said. "There will be noise, of course, and that twelve o'clock is the clear and simple cut off time. City policy. Your elected officials voted on that legislation."

"I ain't elected none of them up there," a man mumbled in the last row. More laughter.

Suddenly, in her attempt to be identified as if she was a student in a Bedlam High classroom, Berlita Johnson stood and raised her hand and changed the talk to the condition of her street. "I need to speak my mind sometimes," she said, looking straight at the Mayor. "There's broken glass along the curb on my street from kids messing around. No one's touched it but my car tires by mistake."

"I'll talk to our Service Director about that," the Mayor said. "Tonight, let's stick to the rally."

"Rap Brown won't sweep any curbs," said Alice Johnson, Berlita's sister. "But he'll know a sad-looking alley if he sees it."

"That's what a rally is about, Mayor," Herman Long piped up again. "It's about action. Far as I know, The Party is also about making sure of fair shares. Cleaned up curbs. Good jobs. Hell, I don't want my boy cuttin' hair. I want him to be a doctor, make some real money."

"I'm sure the city can get that street taken care of quickly," said one of the Berlson brothers.

"We're getting off base here," the Mayor said. "Is everyone clear on the safety issue?"

Council members sat silently. A number of them twirled their pencils on the tabletop. Al Tillman, who represented west Bedlam, seemed to want to say something, but instead scratched his head.

Several people in each row, whispering loudly at once, ushered in a new approach for mayor Topper to take. He slammed his gavel, yanked off his glasses, and rose from his chair, although it was nearly impossible for anyone to see that he was standing. It was a half-hour into the meeting, and the wooden chair pressed hard into Shine's rump.

"Case dismissed," the Mayor said. "I mean, this meeting is adjourned."

He asked Chief Wilburn to escort him back to his office.

No one moved. Not quickly.

Shine's mother got up and walked out the door, down the stairs, and outside, with Shine and Cynthia following. Cynthia grabbed Shine's hand. She held it under a city hall street light. Shine felt like saying, "Wait a little while. You want to be noticed?" But, he stuffed his other hand deep in his pocket.

"Well, that was just fascinating, as futile as it was," his mother said. She took out her pair of white gloves but folded them back and dropped them in her purse. "Not a waste of time, but almost. All this hoopla over a big speech. I don't think emotions are going to boil over. It's a speech. It's education."

"I think people in north Bedlam think people in west Bedlam might get really angry, and who knows what'll happen," Shine said. "I think a lot are on edge."

"I don't think people should get revved up," his mother said. "The Chief made it clear that Elmer Klump and others will be on patrol."

Just then, Shine noticed Wayne deLong being escorted by an officer and Wayne's own mother through a back door of the police station. The officer held one arm and his mother the other. Wayne glanced in Shine's direction. Half of Wayne's t-shirt was tucked into his pants, while the other half hung over his belt as if he'd rushed to put on the shirt.

All Shine could wonder was whether or not Wayne got caught drag racing without a driver's license or shoplifting from Hattendorf's. That was his first thought, and really his only thought. Either way, Wayne deLong faced some sort of questions and at least a frightening late evening sitting on a hard chair, watching the officer stare at him and probably consider letting deLong's mother handle the situation.

That is, unless Wayne had committed some crime that would invite a different punishment.

***

A FEW DAYS LATER, WHEN his father was home just before he left on a new east coast delivery, Shine walked into his bedroom and admired the object on the floor in the middle of his room.

He was thrilled to see his father's truck cab parked at the end of the street and even more surprised to see a new trumpet case.

His father seemed to enjoy himself more on the road. His work ranked high. His travel increased. There was something about driving that lured his father to take on new routes and new deliveries. His father's pay increased, although it was the adventure of long-distance driving that attracted him.

Shine didn't fully know how he felt about his father's spirit of adventure. The idea was still new to him. When he practiced his trumpet, images trickled into his mind of his father in his truck driving through another city. He couldn't prevent those images from appearing.

Shine was wiping the outside of the new case when he heard his father talking to his mother in the kitchen. His father outlined ways to protect the house during the evening of the visit by H. Rap Brown. He stressed locking doors at nine. He insisted that Allison's and Shine's whereabouts be accounted for.

He insisted that Josephine's father, a loyal factory worker, hunter, and gun collector, sit by the front door with his Remington 12-gauge "just in case of an emergency," as Judson put it. Josephine turned her head when he mentioned the gun. "I'm not sold on that, Judson," she said. "He doesn't need to be involved. Or with a shotgun in the house."

In fact, Judson mentioned two guns. "You might want to have two. Just so. He's got two."

"No, and not even one," Josephine said.

Shine could detect the friction. He wasn't about to interrupt his mother and father over a gun discussion. He could see his father's determination upset his mother. She rubbed her eyes and reached for a cold washcloth.

His father the Protector. His father the Road-weary Wanderer. Road junkie. The one with a mania for driving. His father in control while at home, and yet he left Josephine uncertain about when he'd literally return. His schedule turned erratic, undependable, and his return miscalculated by two or three days. This wore on Shine's mother, too.

His father said he missed being home, though was ecstatic to be driving in places with different scenery.

All these contradictory remarks did little to clarify his father's current attitude toward family life.

Maybe, as Shine thought about himself, he was this high school guy - this guy at fifteen-going-on-sixteen - filching cigarettes from his Band-Aid box and smoking in Garland in order to think about who is father really was. He wondered. For instance, his father, often gone, tried to connect with Shine when he was home. Shine could tell it was momentary, a cover, because his father suddenly changed the subject and described things and people he saw on his routes.

But then, Shine stared at that new case. And he knew his father cared.

All was well in the world because of a new case with a blue velvet interior with easy-opening latches and big compartments.

Perhaps it was just that his father was a confused wreck, and the only way he could work out his own self-understanding was to travel, and with a fascination for discovering new towns.

Josephine finally settled the argument with her husband. She gave in.

"Alright, look, Allison knows how to use my father's Remington," she said. "I'll make sure she's here. Not my father. She'll help watch. One gun. It won't be loaded until I determine it to be."

She went into the kitchen and shoved dinner plates back into the kitchen cabinet. "And just so you know," she said to her husband, "there's not going to be trouble. This area is safe."

MEANWHILE, SHINE HADN'T READ THREE postcards addressed to him since he was too busy studying the new case.

His father had not mailed the postcards; instead, he tucked them in one of the cushioned compartments.

Shine read the first postcard: "Saw coyotes running in Pennsylvania. You don't want to break down in hill country PA. Never. Wide state with nothing in the center."

The second postcard: "Ran into a group of Vietnam protesters. One woman barely wore any clothes. She had ink covering her body. It said, 'Peace Not War' and 'Ban the Government.' Guys with hair down to their shoulders. They shouted into megaphones. Flashed signs. Weird signs. Guess they don't work like we do."

Shine read the final postcard his father hadn't bothered to send: "Riots up in Baltimore. Not too worried. I keep movin'. Always watch your back, Shine. Helped a man change a tire in a lot where I slept. Older black fella. He helped me. No surprise there. He gave me a quart of melting ice cream. We shared. I gave him bubblegum. We talked. He was irate people torched cars. He's leaving Baltimore. Said cars are the lifeblood of a country. I told him trucks are. He said, who'd torch cars? He said in compassionate way, keep moving, sir."

And Shine felt he knew why his father didn't send the third card, especially: the hint of violence. Judson Ross, family protector; don't let the family know there's rough stuff happening in the rest of the country. Don't whisper a word about Baltimore to your mother. Or to your sister. Say nothing about torched cars. About dopeheads in rainbow, tie-dyed shirts, with hair down to a man's chest. Not a word about the drug "acid." Don't let them know protests are causing upheaval, and in some cases cars are being sucked into fire.

Shine read his father's last handwriting that crawled up the side of the card: "The freight's heavy. Life's that way, too. It's what I make of myself when handling the burden of freight. What anyone makes of himself."

Shine closed his case and tossed the small lock and key somewhere toward the bottom of his closet.

He slid the postcards under his mattress.

SOULFRUIT

WITH A FINGER, SHINE SWIRLED the ice in his cup of water at The Hot Spot.

Moondog had gulped most of his ice water.

Shine held his trumpet on his lap, waiting for Seeing Eye to summon him to the inner circle.

Pop called it the inner circle because the live music buzzing inside The Hot Spot was generated by the three or four musicians playing in the middle of that cramped area. The musicians showered the dancers with R&B, soul, and pop rock. The Hot Spot's power came from that half-circle of horns, guitar, and percussion in a fifteen-by-fifteen square-foot area. Dancers were so close they could touch the amps.

The Hot Spot hadn't yet opened tonight. No one was dancing at six o'clock.

Shine embarked on his try-out. Pop had brought his trumpet and one of the band members plugged in a guitar. It was time for a low-pressure, harmless audition. Pop was prepared to let Shine join in with the band in the evening, if he could hit the proper notes. No riffs. No high-maintenance challenge. Just stand and play along. Look at your music when necessary. No prancing, no toe-tapping, no swinging the horn. Follow the leader.

The deal was that Shine would blend in with the band. He could go solo another time. He'd work his way up.

Once Seeing Eye and his bandmate heard Shine's accompaniment on "Dance to the Music" and "Spooky," they were satisfied that he could team with them later.

"You got Sly Stone's horn part down on 'Dance to the Music,'" Pop said, shoulder-hugging Shine. "You worked those chops."

Moondog echoed his father's enthusiasm: "Shine, you got it."

Pop chimed in more, telling Shine that a pro saxophonist, Mike Sharpe, who created and first played 'Spooky' the year before as an instrumental, would be proud of the way a fifteen-year old trumpet player handled his song.

***

BEFORE THE HOT SPOT OPENED that evening, Shine, Moondog, and Pop returned to Bedlam, changed clothes and ate. In the car, the conversation turned to a proposed set list. "We'll do four songs, and then we'll turn you loose," Seeing Eye said to Shine. "I'll introduce you, as in 'We have a young guest tonight to do a couple of numbers with us. Welcome Shine Ross.' Then you come over with your horn. I'll say something like, 'I've worked with this youngster a lot.' Then we'll start with 'Dance to the Music.' Gollow with 'Spooky.' Got that?"

"Got it."

He and Moondog were soon sitting near the usual back door.

It was around ten when Seeing Eye called Shine to the stage. "Won't you help me welcome a young trumpet player we've practiced with," Pop informed the small crowd. "Shine Ross. Well, we call him by his nickname, Shine." People flicked cigarette ashes into ashtrays, chuckled, and clapped; people drank from bottles and wine glasses. Those on the dance floor gazed at Shine. One person shouted, "You got it, young man."

Shine took his place to the side of Seeing Eye.

They never dawdled. Their playing turned up the dance floor heat. Shine looked down a few times and observed people twirling, swinging their arms to the rhythm. Time passed in musical measures. To Shine, he played hours. It was only fifteen minutes. Two songs.

The waitress patted Shine on the back and said, "You're full of soul. Call you soul fruit. Your new nickname."

SHINE WAS ECSTATIC WHEN HE walked outside The Hot Spot. The band finished its first set.

He towel-dried his face and flung the towel to Moondog. He glanced at all the cars in the lot and discovered his father sitting in his Ford Falcon in one of the lot's corners. He was alone.

Shine walked over. Questions ransacked his mind: Why was his father here? What did he want? Was he spying on me? Was he here to cause trouble? How did he know I was here? Cynthia or Allison could have told him. Shine had been far too excited to keep the breakthrough gig a secret.

All these questions, and to think that his father had surprised him with a sparkling new case for his horn.

"You o.k., dad? How'd you know I was here?"

"Just fine. Just wanted to see where you're working. Cynthia told me the news." Judson Ross rolled down his window all the way now, enticing Shine to come closer. "Watch yourself in these parts. Hear me?"

"These parts?"

"These parts. You get my drift."

"I watch myself." He noticed his father's BB gun on the floor in the backseat. He knew his father would never adequately explain why the gun was on the floor. Shine had never known him to tote it in his car. He always carried it in a gun bag for target practice with rats.

"You coming in?"

"I'll pass this time."

"Next set I'll join the band on the same two songs we did before. You ought to see us."

"I'll take a rain check. There'll be a next time."

Shine knew he'd get nowhere with these noncommittal answers.

"You'll want to hear me in action."

"I know you're good."

"Better when I play with someone, when there's a band."

Shine noticed that grease marks creasing his father's fingers.

"Why are your hands so dirty?" Shine said.

"Well, when you were inside, I helped a fella replace a flat over there," Judson said, pointing to a slot near the front of The Hot Spot. "Took us a while."

Shine figured that his father had been in the parking lot at least an hour. He'd helped a man in a relatively black neighborhood with a minor repair. He wasn't complaining. Perhaps his father was going to keep it to himself.

"That's pretty great you helped out."

"Sure is," Moondog said. He'd come over to the Ford Falcon.

"The man helped me, too," Judson Ross said. "He gave me some fresh fish. Got it on ice in the trunk. I said no thanks, but he kept insisting."

He wiped his hands on his shirt.

"You boys be careful over here," he said again. "Moondog, watch my son. Stay away from those drinks. Don't let anything get out of hand." He winked and shook his finger jokingly. "We're only midway through '68. Crazy stuff is happening at nighttime in America."

Before he pulled away, he said, "Oh, one more thing. I had a talk with Maury Riggs today. He said he's talked to you a few times. You give him any information that he's asked you for. If you can."

"I've talked to him, dad."

"It'll be good for you. And me."

Judson Ross drove away. Shine watched the Ford merge with the darkness. It seemed to him that the only life on this street came from the pulsating music inside the club.

Two hours later, he closed and opened his eyes in the backseat of Pop's car, dodging sleep as best he could. Pop complimented his performance. He was young. He was so underage, in the real sense, even though the manager of The Hot Spot agreed to let Shine play two songs. It happened without incident. Shine cranked out his two songs, and afterward he reclaimed his place by the back door with Moondog.

Drowsy, never more ready for some shut-eye, Shine recalled the way the waitress with the big afro joked with him, calling him "soul fruit." In her loud voice, before the club opened, she'd said, "That white boy got soul. Seeing Eye got him some soul fruit in the band. Keep playing, soul fruit."

Before Pop pulled up to his house, Shine felt under the seats, grabbing around for his trumpet case. All he felt were seat springs and carpet. He lifted Moondog's leg as his friend snored. He reached as far as he could under both sides and felt nothing but burger wrappers. He felt dizzy. He was embarrassed. His own trumpet was missing.

His face tightened. Did he lose the trumpet? Did he forget it? Did he or Moondog leave it in the parking lot?

"Pop, did I give my trumpet to you to put in the trunk?"

"Nope, Nothing in the trunk, young man. What's you need?"

"My trumpet. It's not here."

"You leave it?"

"I don't know. I got caught up talking. I don't know."

201

"You don't remember having it?"

"I don't remember what I did."

"Take yourself back in your mind. Retrace your last steps."

"I did. I can't retrace. They're fuzzy. That was my dad's new case he got me."

Pop worked hard to reassure him that the trumpet would more than likely be safe. He promised Shine he'd call The Hot Spot the next afternoon when it opened, and see if the waitress or manager found it. He might even drive over.

Shine fumbled for his house key and could barely open the door without bending the key. He found his way to his bedroom in the hideous dark. He was so distraught, without his trumpet to set in the middle of his floor, that he forgot to turn on the lights. He just lay down in the middle of the floor with his clothes and shoes still on, and on that vacant floor he went right to sleep, where his horn would ordinarily be within reach.

***

THE BRIGHT STAGE LIGHTS APPEARED, soon followed by the droll famous lady wearing a fluffy pink dress.

The famous lady, a television diva, held a long microphone decorated with a red corsage.

She was famous for hustling cleaning and food products, the Pure Oil Company which serviced gas stations, a national Children's Fund, and more.

Parading the microphone and corsage everywhere she stepped in the Crosley T.V. Station recording studio, Ruth Lyons held the rapt attention of each woman fortunate enough today to be in her "50-50 Club" audience.

Women sat in bleachers and waved at a camera when a cameraman turned his gigantic equipment to face them, usually before commercials.

Josephine, Allison, and Miss Louise sat in the second row.

In spite of Miss Louise's deafness, Josephine ordered her a ticket anyway. She believed that the good vibes Ruth Lyons sent out replaced any need to *hear* Ruth talk or *hear* her sing. Just *being* with Ruth mattered.

Josephine could almost touch Ruth Lyons when she walked by. The three sat behind a very large woman in the first row who breathed heavily and whose white, nylon stretch gloves appeared way too small and not to fit. A few times, Josephine had to lean either way around the large woman to see Ruth.

Ruth's celebrities today were Jimmy Durante and Eva Gabor. Ruth sang. She tried a two-step dance move with a man she invited down from the fourth row, the only man among women in the audience.

"Your name's Fred, am I right?" Ruth said, tapping his shoulder with the microphone. "Fred, try this. Gimme a G-chord, Cliff," she said to her band leader, Cliff Lash, who plunked several piano keys and set the rhythm for the guitar and clarinet. Letting Ruth play the lead, Fred shuffled and stumbled, two-stepping his way with Ruth Lyons across the floor and back to the bleachers. Fred sat stone-faced, out of breath, and only a few rows behind

203

Josephine. Women nudged each other amazed at Ruth's spontaneity.

"That wasn't scripted, ladies," Ruth said, rolling her eyes. "We like it when a man tries to dance."

Howling laughter from row to row. Ruth siphoned every chuckle.

"Fred, you'll do nicely at home practicing those dance steps. You need a good woman to teach you."

During the show's ninety minutes, Ruth flaunted her Hollywood guests. Her motherly tone filled the studio. She persuaded the older comic, Jimmy Durante, to tap dance. He'd rarely tap danced in his life. He was older and his gimmick as a piano-playing comic suited his gruffness. He grumbled and acted put out when Ruth ordered him to get off the piano bench.

Ruth persuaded a zookeeper, Henry, to let out the leash on a baby leopard, allowing it to slink closer to the audience.

Long ago, Ruth won the hearts of women in southern Ohio, Indiana, and northern Kentucky with her saintly way of pledging kindness to others and an understanding that music and laughter were keys to combat the ruts of life.

She was also about selling products.

Each audience guest left with a gift bag of soap, shampoo, cleanser, and snacks, most of them made locally. Each left feeling entertained, as if each lady mattered to Ruth.

Her main agenda was chatting. Ruth walked along the studio stage shaking hands with guests. They were her daytime family. They sat waiting for affirmation. They wanted to be thrilled. They waited for Ruth to scold them for using the wrong dish soap.

"Don't do it, mother. Don't wave your arm at Ruth Lyons," Allison said. "Just sit straight, watch for the blinking *APPLAUSE* light before commercials. Clap when you see the big letters *APPLAUSE*."

Josephine wanted Ruth Lyons to notice *her*. Ruth already noticed the large woman in front of her in the first row. Allison lowered her arm across her mother's lap, knowing she'd be audacious enough to wave at Ruth. Josephine squeezed her hands. When Ruth came closer to the woman in the first row, Josephine blurted, "Hi Ruth, it's Josephine Ross. I wrote you the fan letters."

Allison blushed, putting her hands over her eyes. "Mom, no. Stop."

Ruth glanced up at Josephine. All eyes were on Ruth. She must have noticed more that the large woman wore only one glove. Ruth huddled by the large woman and struck up a conversation. The woman was by herself, no family around, and for this Ruth sympathized.

The talk-show diva asked the large woman where she was from. The woman shouted, "Covington, Kentucky." The audience cheered. Ruth said, "Well, I actually go across the Ohio River once in awhile. I'm pretty sure there's a state over there. I promise." The women's laughter, feverish, hung between the ceiling lights.

Those stage lights were bright and they aggravated Josephine.

In her ever-affectionate way, Ruth joked about the large woman's neighboring state. The women devoured every word. They clapped for the woman who was now trying hard to hide her fat gloved hand.

Ruth's joking with the woman preceded a break by mere seconds.

Her punchlines attracted an unruly amount of stage light on the Kentucky woman. Ruth looked right into her eyes, and said, "You're such a good sport, dear, and I do love Kentucky, and especially love that Kentucky Derby, all those dresses I could wear." The Kentucky woman shook and clapped.

Then, the lights dimmed. The *APPLAUSE* sign blinked. The large woman became tipsy, unbalanced, and as Ruth walked away and over toward Cliff and the band, the large woman leaned backward and passed out, her upper body toppling and pinning Josephine's legs to the bleacher row.

***

ALLISON HAD ALREADY DELUGED HER mother with her flurry of comments after she climbed into the driver's side of the family car.

"I told you I'd do it, Allison. I made it onto Ruth's show. I knew she'd read my letters. She even gave me the knowing eye."

"It was the evil eye, by the way. How's your leg, mom?"

"Just fine. I survived, right?"

"Put ice on your leg when we get home."

"Imagine, Ruth didn't even have to get ice to put on it. I was brave."

Allison typically drove fast and ignored speed limits, and this late afternoon was no exception. The taping of this edition of the "50-50 Club" would air soon, though no definitive date was given.

Allison turned the conversation away from Ruth Lyons by using her last resort, the inclusion of Ulysses, her now-boyfriend. Allison revealed that she and U.S. would go to PeeWee Valley a second time.

"I didn't know there was a first time," Josephine said.

"I told you a while ago."

While Allison drove, in the front seat Josephine relied on sign language for Miss Louise, who angled herself so that she could see Josephine's hands. They were on their way to pick up Ulysses, who had finished work at the car wash station.

Miss Louise signed so that Josephine could interpret for Allison: "Allison's friend Ulysses is a good young man as far as I can tell," Josephine repeated.

"Yes, he is," Allison said, and asked her mother to sign that remark to Miss Louise.

In twenty minutes, Ulysses was riding with Miss Louise in the backseat. Allison would drop off her mother and Miss Louise, and she'd take her time dropping off Ulysses. They might take a ride north on I-75, first, so that Allison could revisit the events of the "50-50 Club."

"Is everything alright, U.S.?" Josephine asked. "I mean, on the west side of town? Everything o.k.?"

"Oh. Probably. Things are heating up over there, Mrs. Ross. From what I see. We got a big rally in a few days. Never had a rally like this one."

"Ulysses, I hope this works out. I hope people stay safe," Josephine said, signing for Miss Louise.

Josephine took a question from Miss Louise and signed it for Ulysses: "Do you think people in north Bedlam should be afraid enough to have guns by their front door? That's what I'm hearing at Hattendorf's. People at the counter, getting groceries, talking about whether they should be afraid. They don't know. Nothing like this has happened before."

"I don't think anyone should be afraid," Ulysses said. "Most everyone's cool."

"And I agree with him," Allison said. "Sign that, mom. Sign that for Miss Louise. We're not afraid. Everyone is cool."

Josephine signed in fragments: "No one. Afraid. Not these two. Not people that Ulysses knows."

Josephine asked Ulysses: "Is anyone toting guns in their homes that your family knows of?"

"No, Mrs. Ross. Not that I know of."

"You know, my father - Allison's grandfather - is a gun collector."

"I don't know anyone, no," Ulysses said.

"Sometimes I worry," Josephine said. "Look at how weird stores are getting already, and we're not much longer away from that speech."

"How's that?" Allison said.

"You know. You see it," her mother said. "Just weird. The Health Department building has been closing late afternoon. No reason. They're always open until dark. Hattendorf's said they're going to begin closing earlier. No reason. Just look around, Allison. You see a few more police milling around Kroger and downtown Bedlam in the afternoon. You never see that. Not in summer. I think how strange it got in that City Hall meeting. The Mayor didn't help things, bolting out of there like that."

Josephine kept signing for Miss Louise. Allison shook her head. She knew U.S. was embarrassed to even engage in the talk of guns or, at this stage, a level of suspicion as described by her mother.

Still, Josephine persisted. "Stop it, mom," Allison said. "Ulysses is a peace-lover."

"Peace-lover, Mrs. Ross," U.S. said. He flashed the peace sign, especially so that Miss Louise could see it.

"I hope that's all of us," Josephine said. "Can you relay that to people you know? I hope all of us are peace-lovers. Think about that."

***

AT THE REC SHELTER, MOONDOG stacked a set of board games on Shine's outstretched arms. He'd come to help. Shine forgot to meet Cynthia the day before at the shelter, so it was his job to finish clearing the grounds of equipment.

There were not many other toys and games to gather since the shelter had been one of several tagged to close two weeks early.

Cynthia and a few other workers cleaned a back room, boxing up tennis rackets, balls, kickballs, horseshoes, ping pong paddles, and tools. The boys used empty boxes for marbles, chess sets, tubes of glue, paper, crayons, pencils, and the board games.

On their walk to the City Hall storage room, they wound up juggling the boxes most of the way. They struggled to hang onto their awkward weight.

The two didn't realize they forgot to seal one box. When they set down the boxes and ran to a water fountain, they didn't see a handful of marbles slide out of a box they'd dropped.

They stopped short of chasing the fugitive marbles. They watched officer Watson escort the Simms brothers from his police car to the front door of the station. It was a curious sight. Officer Watson walked alongside a handcuffed Troy Simms, while Terence, the smoker, quieter, and less peppy of the two brothers, walked casually, with an air of defiance, a short distance behind the officer.

It seemed that Terence Simms could make a break for it and run, he trailed so far behind the officer and his brother. The officer even turned around once and waited for Terence. He just walked far slower and forced the officer to wait for him at the door.

Troy Simms was the one handcuffed, and he stood oblivious to the marbles and to Shine and Moondog. He looked upset. He stared at the ground, kicking it with the toe of his shoe.

"What do you think happened?" Moondog said.

"They did something. No telling."

"I wonder if anyone else knows."

"I don't want to say anything yet. I don't even want them to remember us."

They talked more about the prospect of Troy Simms sitting in a police interview room. They talked about the way the Bedlam cops were patrolling the city more than usual, now that an official of the Black Panther Party had an appointment to speak in an open-air pavilion.

They talked about the odd way several stores closed earlier than usual. There were rarely signs on the doors. By early evening, store lights were out in the shoe store, hardware store, and Bettman's - stores in both north and west Bedlam.

The boys talked about the debris still untouched around the burned-down Empire.

***

THEY HAD NO IDEA WHOSE basketball it was. It lay against the curb near a sewer grate.

Someone either lost it or let it roll downhill from the courts and forgot about it. It looked new.

Shine passed it to Moondog. They cherished this moment when the ball in flight cured their boredom.

The boys jogged. They attempted impossible passes. Behind-the-back flips which floundered; between-their-legs-flips. It was as if the sewer ball hypnotized them.

Until they came to the street with burned debris on one side.

The smell of smoke still lingered in the space: the charred grounds of the Empire.

Moondog held the basketball.

They crept further to make sure they were agreed about the person they recognized on the sidewalk. The person concentrated on something the boys couldn't see.

Shine grabbed Moondog and, to stay hidden, they walked backward several steps, without talking.

Alphonso Peace sat on his bike in front of the debris. The way he stared, he could have been counting shards of broken bricks.

Before eating fries at Golden Point, finding the basketball, and joking around, they'd watched officer Watson escort the Simms brothers into the station. Now, they peeked around the side of a flowery shrub and watched Alphonso Peace eat potato chips. He crumpled the bag and tossed it into a pile of coils.

"Is he in a trance?" Moondog said. "Look, he just spit whatever he's drinking."

"Why do you think he's just sitting there and staring?"

"He worked there. Maybe he's remembering. He was mad when they fired him."

Shine nudged Moondog and pointed toward the corner house. A woman known as Miss Billie, a blind woman, rocked on her porch. The boys didn't know if 'Billie' was her first or last name or even a nickname. She was only Miss Billie, and she was nearing one hundred years old. One of the oldest women in west Bedlam to live well into her nineties, Miss Billie had a housekeeper from north Bedlam named Lilly. Lilly brought Miss Billie church programs. She sometimes cooked her dinner. She dusted the living room, and she did Miss Billie's laundry. Lilly lived on Shine's street and knew Klump and his wife extremely well.

At the time of the fire, Miss Billie, mostly deaf, rocked on her porch, smiling as the smoke-fumes passed by. Lilly stood next to her and patted her hand.

"She can't even see what's going on, much less hear," Shine said.

"Anyone else would yell over at Alphonso and ask what he's looking at," Moondog said. "Weird."

"Right. And she just has that big smile."

"She'll be in that rocking chair all day, or til her fat-ass grandson gets her inside. Woman rocks all day," Moondog said.

The silence of the whole moment split apart. Someone sneezed, and sneezed again. Hard.

The boys surfaced from behind the shrub and peered down Miss Billie's side of the street. They saw Alphonso Peace turn toward the sneezing noise. They saw him whip his bike around and peddle across the street.

They spotted Fremont Jones still sneezing, his fit slow to end. He struggled to balance himself on his own bike. Obviously spying on Alphonso Peace, Fremont had been hiding behind a tree across from the Empire grounds. His sneezing jolted Alphonso from his daydream.

Alphonso lifted Fremont off his bike and dragged him toward a front yard. Fremont waved his handkerchief. The boys hustled down the sidewalk past Miss Billie. They saw Alphonso throw two punches. They heard Fremont Jones squeal. The sound barely rose above the grass. Before Alphonso tried to pin him with his long legs, Fremont squirmed loose and dropped his handkerchief on a branch.

Alphonso grabbed him by the neck and dragged him back to the yard. Fremont's bike lay against the curb. Miss Billie sat on her porch, rocking and smiling.

"Hey, Alphonso, let him go," Moondog said. "Let him go. He ain't did nothing to you."

"Get outta here, boy," Alphonso said. He stopped twisting Fremont's arm to look at both Shine and Moondog.

"He's just a kid," Shine said. "He can't hear."

"He ain't gonna live long, neither," Alphonso said. He suddenly let go of Fremont Jones' arm, pushed himself off the ground, kicked Fremont's leg, grabbed his own bike, and spit in the street, as if nothing happened. With an urgency and a sudden calmness, Alphonso Peace said hardly anything to Fremont except, "I'll make this up, little brother," and he sped off.

JUST

WAS IT CEREAL, GREEN BEANS, or a can of corn that his mother asked him to fetch from downstairs? Shine couldn't remember.

When he had barely opened the basement door, he absolutely forgot.

Shine heard a voice. It was Ulysses' deep melodic voice. Soft, relaxed. Shine paused so quickly, without forcing the door hinges to squeak, that he was certain no one downstairs heard him. He amazed himself by not elbowing the broom and dust pan, ruining an sensitive moment for his sister and Ulysses.

With the door inched open, he listened.

Shine heard his sister's voice. He made out three words: "you," "need," "quiet." The lights were turned off. The washer and dryer weren't running. He was sure his mother didn't know where Allison was at this particular time.

Shine heard Ulysses again, and this time his sister joined in with more to say. He held his breath,

215

exhaling after he counted to thirty. He shut the door a few more inches, but never jeopardized missing the two voices. Shine put his ear in the door space.

He heard Ulysses say: "What do you think now? Are they soft?"

"What's soft?" Shine's sister said.

"My lips."

"I guess," Allison said. "Well, yeah. Softer than what I expected."

"What did you expect?"

"I don't know."

"Did you expect this?"

And Shine heard nothing for awhile. He listened, his ear plastered into the open space. He maintained his slow breathing.

He heard Ulysses say: "What about now?"

"Yeah," his sister said.

"Yeah, what?"

"Yeah, soft."

"I knew you'd think that," Ulysses said.

"You know a lot."

Silence, again.

Shine heard his sister say, "This reminds me of a soap opera. 'Days of Our Lives.' Mom's favorite. When two people kiss, like they can't turn loose."

"That's good," Ulysses said. "Can't turn loose."

Shine had forgotten about any request to bring up beans, corn, or cereal.

He felt an obligation to see his sister in a new light. He considered her real mature now. A woman. No way around it. Summer of 1968: his sister became an adult.

Downstairs in the basement with Ulysses, who charmed her with two tender hands. She handled something that Shine had little clue about: love.

He grabbed his wallet with three dollars in it and, hustling out the door, said to his mother, "I'll get the cans later. Soon. Be back soon."

His new perspective of Allison and Ulysses opened a new way for him to think about Cynthia. Now, it was about Cynthia. There were odd parallels. He hadn't kissed Cynthia, of course, but he knew Allison and Ulysses had landed on a wildly romantic tier. He thought it wise to follow their model: take it easily yet confidently. Shine was fifteen and dramatic.

Enough thinking. He knew a good risk when it smacked him of possibility.

He decided this new approach to Cynthia was more likable.

Shine wanted to show her he did care. He might better accomplish this if, first, he could keep his Band-Aid box of cigarettes far enough out of sight.

***

SHINE WORMED HIS WAY AROUND shoppers scrambling to find rock-bottom bargains inside Ben Franklin's 5 & 10 Cents store.

Lightbulbs: twenty cents for a package of two. Toothpaste: twenty cents. Thirty cents for one bath towel. Bubblegum: a penny.

Cars lining the street outside the dime store crowded one short block of downtown Bedlam.

Shine whisked past the toothpaste and towels until he spied the costume jewelry. He surveyed the chain necklaces with a plastic heart. The plastic hearts glimmered as he handled them. Behind the plastic hearts were weightier necklaces. The best in costume jewelry. It beat the real prices in a jewelry store, which translated into money he did not have.

He hurried to find the least gaudy necklace. It would be unfortunate if one of his friends found him deep in thought over two dime store necklaces. They'd never let him down.

Shine had taste: The plastic heart it was.

He could see Cynthia modeling his nice dollar necklace in front of her mirror, twirling with the radiance of a princess, not withholding her glee. Shine would help fasten the microscopic clasp at the base of her neck.

On the way home, he grappled with his recent whims. He wanted to kiss Cynthia nearly every night. He thought about her especially when she was upset with his train-hopping. He remembered their nudging each other in the trunk of Ulysses' Caprice. The foot-touching. Brush of elbows and fingers. That lovely entrapment in the trunk had been a moment of truth. Their bodies that close, confined, with nowhere else to go. Shine certainly didn't consider it inconvenient, and Cynthia didn't complain.

Shine would think about nearly anything to take his mind off losing his trumpet.

He tried to gauge the amount of time he would spend with Cynthia. They would be sophomores, and she'd show off this new necklace. He'd walk her home.

Once back in school, he would be linked to Cynthia in a most visible way: the necklace. Just shy of the coveted class ring. Or a sterling silver friendship ring.

Ring. A ring was really permanent.

Cynthia's birthday would arrive in a few weeks. In the meantime, Shine stashed the dollar necklace in a drawer with some of his music and a half-pack of Kools.

He couldn't plan substantial dates past the day of her birthday. Pop now expected him to play "upon sudden weekend notice," in Pop's words, and he needed to be ready to jump in Pop's car and head to The Hot Spot.

Pop promised to slip Shine a small cut of the band's pay for a night's work.

Money was becoming more than an object, if Shine expected to impress Cynthia.

A bond could be established, but a large part of it resorted to cash. There were ice cream floats to buy at the Root Beer Stand; burgers and fries at Golden Point; a flower or two every month. That friendship ring.

He also needed to budget thirty-five cents for a pack of cigarettes, although he struggled over whether or not to keep sneaking. Cynthia knew about it, and this was a problem.

Before he lay down to rest in his room, Shine thought that Cynthia might be so enamored with the necklace that she'd forget about his Kools. Maybe he made the right move here. Then, again, maybe he should ditch the Kools. Goodbye, Band-Aid box. No, not yet. Yes, no, possibly, never. Shine couldn't make a decision this close to a nap, and not without his trumpet.

In his daydream, the gleam his trumpet gave off blinded him peacefully.

It was horrible enough that his safeguard, the trumpet, wasn't in his bedroom.

In his daydream, his horn was never stolen. The trumpet and case were lost. Like a lost kid. Like a kid waiting for a parent to show up. Shine's trumpet and case were waiting for their owner to find them.

He wished the horn had a voice so it could call out his name. He wished he could hear a riff, and he really wished the trumpet would just appear in the middle of his bedroom floor, safe and protected.

***

THERE WAS LITTLE ACTION IN Bedlam late at night, except for factory workers running machines. Forklift drivers hauling crates. Machinists cutting metal. Midnight whistles announcing break time.

Smokestacks belched their columns of exhaust as faithfully during third shift as they did during first shift.

Shine got a whiff lying under a picnic table he'd dragged to the middle of his backyard.

Often during the summer he slept outside. He used the picnic table as a tent. He draped two bedsheets over the top and sides. He anchored the corners to the ground with bricks. He anchored the sheets on top with a bike tire. He threw his sleeping bag under the table and propped a flashlight and transistor radio in the corner.

It was a good place for him to listen to hits on WSAI-1360 AM. Low volume.

Shine got antsy and decided to walk from Bedlam across railroad tracks to Mount Relling and then Angilo's Pizza. He craved the store's garlic bread.

There was a variety of store windows for Shine to look in on his way to Angilo's.

He took small bites, savoring the taste of the bread on the way home. He felt better staring at books in the window of the Valley Branch Library in Mount Relling. He didn't think about sneaking a quick smoke in one of Bedlam's alleys, not with garlic on his tongue. He was trying to rid himself of the pull of the Band-Aid box.

Shine crossed back over the tracks, which ran parallel to downtown Bedlam, and sat under the sign, "Where Friends Meet." He walked across the I-75 overpass next to the mattress factory.

Before he came to the tennis and basketball courts, he noticed someone leaning into a garbage can. It was so late and dark; the figure was short and muscular, but child-like. Shine noticed a familiar garbage bag. Larry Loomis' bag. Larry reached into the can and pulled out several empty pop bottles.

Shine filled him in on his night time venture to Angilo's and pulled off a slice of garlic bread to give him. They gazed at the stars and factory smoke for awhile, and it gave Shine a moment to let Larry know how alone he felt having left his trumpet at a club, where he had played in front of a real audience.

"I can't believe they let you in," Larry said.

"I play. I'm working up, and I don't think I'm too bad. Pop Weasel doesn't think so."

"You might have a future."

Shine was still lamenting the loss and it registered with Larry Loomis, but only to a cut-off point. He got up from the bench. "Time to head back, man."

Shine grabbed one side of the garbage bag with about thirty bottles, a small load considering Larry's previous searches. Larry gripped the other side with a gloved hand, and they toted the bag smoothly, without so much as disturbing one bottle.

"I feel like my trumpet's lost forever."

"How you think I feel when I can't find enough pop bottles sometimes," Larry said. "I feel like I done lost the game. Like I got killed on the court and my team's the laughingstock."

***

SHINE AND MOONDOG WERE MIDWAY through their third game of checkers when they heard the muffler rattling under Seeing Eye's old Dodge. It had been his mother's car. Only recently had the Dodge started to mechanically fail him.

"Look who's coming," Moondog said. He munched the last of a cheese sandwich.

"Who?"

"Pop. He's got something."

"What?"

"Looks like your trumpet case."

Shine bounded for the front window. He watched Seeing Eye close the trunk and tote his case up the front walkway. When Shine opened the front door, Seeing Eye dangled it in front of Shine. "Here you go, forgetful. You're a lucky boy."

"That's wild," Moondog said. "You got it back, Pop."

"Thank you, Pop," Shine said. "I can't believe it. I haven't even slept."

"Well, then, here, hold it. And get some sleep."

Before the two trumpeters rummaged through sheets of music, Pop described his trip. He leveled his good eye even with Shine's face to stress the fact that this was a miracle. Shine looked into that eye. The other one angled outward.

"Your fan the waitress saw it wedged under your seat by the back door," Pop said. "She just scooped it up and locked it in the manager's office. She told me, 'I ain't calling nobody at first. Youngster got to learn a lesson some way.' But, I got that call anyway a few days ago, and I said, 'Just hold it under lock and key. I'll be over in a day or two.' They must have felt good about you, because they didn't sell the horn out from under you." Seeing Eye, wiping his forehead, paused to laugh. "You'd been in such a zone playing that night that you flew right out the back door with the sheet music and microphone stand, but not your trumpet, and I didn't even think about it. Moondog missed it, too, sleepy-eyed as he was. I wanted to get on home. Imagine that. Underage trumpet player in a band, and you walked off a job leaving your best tool."

Seeing Eye had known about the trumpet these past few days, but let Shine stew over it. He kept the good news from Moondog. Shine didn't seethe with sadness any longer. He convinced himself *not* to blame Seeing Eye for not calling him immediately. The crisis was over. He looked at his horn with awe. It was about his gripping it again.

They began with fingering exercises and scales. The notes they played climbed. They mastered easier songs, "(Sittin' on) The Dock of the Bay" and "Dance to the Music." Pop favored Sly and the Family Stone. He had a soft spot for Aretha Franklin and Smokey Robinson.

"Let me get something to drink," Pop said.

He came back with two Pepsi's. Moondog brought his saxophone into the room. He'd decided to start taking lessons. Seeing Eye kept an older sax in the basement.

Seeing Eye opened and closed his good eye regularly with each song. Sometimes he kept it closed during short riffs.

The two flipped through more sheets of music, most of which Pop had charted. He'd write out major notes on graph paper after listening to a song over and over.

He taught Shine to feel the rhythm of a song. "Get the major notes down," he said, "and then go off a little bit, like this."

The teaching worked.

While Pop scribbled notes, Shine listened to Moondog pinch out notes in his squeaky effort. Moondog inhaled dramatically. Shine's attention wandered.

Moondog and Pop were concentrating too much on their instruments to notice the figure Shine saw swaying at the side of the house.

Fremont Jones peered through the side window. Only his nose, eyes, and forehead were visible. His fingers gripped the window ledge. Shine easily recognized those features. He suspected Fremont must be standing on a garbage can.

Shine nodded at Fremont and placed his finger to the lips, his suggestion for him to stay down and noiseless. Shine wouldn't spoil what weird curiosity Fremont tried to satisfy. The boy was peeping; he'd learn differently some other day.

He started followed Pop again on a song. He turned his head toward the window, and sure enough, he saw the boy's head bop from side to side. It was as if the music was penetrating Fremont Jones' deafness, massaging his inner ear bones, and firing up the sensory membranes, so that he could actually hear the music in the living room.

HEAT

A PANEL OF LIGHT SWIVELED among the grayer clouds like a wagging finger.

Soon the finger-light pushed most of those clouds aside. The threat of rain let up, but only briefly. A few clouds reared up again dishing out the gray.

Any remaining sunlight was useful. No one had a flashlight. The group of people circling below the Amazon parrot, JoJo, needed every minute. It would be dark in less than a few hours. No telling how long it might take for anyone to coax JoJo from his branch or scare him again into the sneaky tangle of woods.

JoJo was out there, within sight.

Shine had received the call from a woman named Ethel. She had to repeat herself several times because her voice cracked. She had a heavy smoker's shaky hoarseness.

"I said, my name's Ethel, and I seen that bird, the parrot on the poster. This the right number?"

"Yes, m'am. It's the right number."

"Thought so. Who are you?"

"We'll be over in not much longer. I'm the one looking for JoJo. That's my parents' number on the poster."

"Oh. You go to Bedlam?"

"I'll be a sophomore."

"You will, huh?" Ethel gave her crackling laugh. "You a athlete?"

"Basketball mostly. A little baseball."

"You're gonna need to be. You're gonna need to run to keep up with that bird."

"I hope not."

"You don't have no reward out, do you?"

"I'm pretty sure not. Other people have spotted JoJo."

"Thought so," Ethel growled. "I'll keep an eye on it. It's just sitting. I'm looking out my window. If it flies off, I'll try to watch in what direction it goes."

"Please don't make any noise or try to go out and get too close to JoJo."

In her raspy, manly tone, she said, "None of my business to go near it."

When Shine arrived, he saw an older, red brick home that showed its wear in faded streaks of brown gutter paint. It was the result of a painter either spilling paint or brushing the brick with paint, altogether missing the gutter. Ethel's house, at one edge of Garland, sat on the north side of Bedlam like other yards Shine had tromped across searching for JoJo. He was confident the parrot kept to Garland. Kept to his turf, north Bedlam. Close to bird baths.

Maybe JoJo kept watch over the hobos when they believed no one could see them.

Maybe JoJo slept on a branch near camp while they slept.

Shine begged his uncle to remain several yards in back of him, while he took charge. His uncle agreed but to a point. Jerry said his patience was running thin, and he wanted a shot at getting back his parrot. The woman named Ethel gawked out her wide open kitchen window. With her hand cupped over a phone mouthpiece, she was talking to someone in a throaty whisper. The two moved into full view of JoJo. The parrot looked down at them.

Uncle Jerry urged the neighbors to step back into Ethel's yard, or beyond, and not make noise. "That means," he said, "no sighing, no whistling, no chatting, heavy whispering, tongue-clucking, clapping - no clapping ever - sneezing, and blowing noses, if possible. Pinch your nose. We've watched the parrot fly off this summer, so don't muck it up for us. It's my parrot."

JoJo squawked.

JoJo knew who'd come for him.

Shine inched toward the bird. He felt at ease. His muscles relaxed, and he felt like he was gliding along instead of tip-toeing.

"Come on, pretty boy," Shine said. "Come on down. Come on, let's go eat. Wanna eat? Go see Jerry?"

He created as many niceties as he could: sweetie pie, hey good lookin', bud, buddy, buddy-boy, buddy-buddy, sweet JoJo, pretty boy-JoJo. If he could just remember to ramble through the ten or so.

Shine started up the tree on which JoJo perched and squawked. High enough for Shine to worry about him, JoJo hopped down one branch. Big victory. Major step: down a branch, not up one. JoJo hopped down a branch. Second victory. Shine felt the pressure of needed success. He let ten seconds go between each greeting: "Pretty boy." Ten seconds. "Come on, sweetie." Ten. "Buddy-boy." Ten. "Come on, let's eat. Pretty boy."

Shine's arm pits were wet. Each minute counted.

"Ha-row." It was JoJo. "Ha-Row. Pretty boy. Pretty boy," the bird spoke.

"He's saying 'hello,'" Shine shouted down to Jerry.

"Ha-row," JoJo spoke again. "Pretty boy."

"Ha-row," Shine said back.

Shine climbed one more branch. He took a cloth napkin bulging in his pocket, unwrapped it, and offered apple slices to JoJo. The parrot moved only his head back and forth. He studied the food. At least he didn't fly away. "Here, pretty boy," Shine said. "Apple? Here you go." JoJo stared at Shine's hand. He loved food and especially sliced apples.

Shine moved patiently, not looking behind him. He heard whispers. He kept his balance, but he did look over his shoulder once to find his uncle walking back to Ethel's house. The woman was now growling into the phone, giving a play by play of the rescue, a cigarette dangling from her fingers.

Shine held the apple slices higher, pointing it toward JoJo. "Here, eat."

"Ha-row," JoJo spoke. "Pretty boy."

"Ha-row," Shine said. "Buddy boy."

One of uncle Jerry's friends backed a pick-up truck to the end of Ethel's driveway and eased it onto the grass, as close to the woods as possible. He got out and turned on a gigantic reel-to-reel tape player roped to the truck bed. Skittish parrot-talk rose from the speakers. Jerry's friend had offered a solution: let JoJo listen to his own kind, and maybe the parrot-talk would lure him down. Jerry's friend turned up the volume.

Neighbors filed into Ethel's backyard.

Jerry walked back and forth, holding them to a distance. They shifted their facial movements from watching Shine work in the tree to the spinning reel-to-reel player. Neighbors were transfixed. In front of the gathering, uncle Jerry and his friend kept an eye out for any roving kid who might rush the tree.

JoJo came down one more branch.

Shine was about ten feet away.

From the corner of Ethel's house, completely unanticipated given the quiet bodies that had gathered in Ethel's backyard, a boy about six or seven came running hard toward the tree Shine was in. He not only ran, but he shouted. Shine could hear him. And if he could hear the kid, JoJo could hear him, and JoJo would freak out.

The neighbors turned to look. Jerry looked stunned, confused. The voice drowned out the tape player. Someone's kid had gotten loose from a nearby house, or the kid had squirmed out of a parked car.

It was an ax thrown into the silence, ripping apart any possibility for Shine to snatch JoJo and take him back home.

"Shine," the boy shouted. "Hey, Shine. Shine. Whatcha doin' up there? Hey, Shine."

The boy knew Shine. His voice pierced the woods. Shine looked down and recognized the boy.

"Go back, Frankie. You got to go back."

"Hey, Shine."

"Go back. Now."

Jerry rushed over and tried to grab the boy, but it was too late. People began to talk. Shine, who hadn't moved greatly, in regaining his balance, jiggled limbs in regaining his balance. It was way too late now. JoJo must have processed everything, and everything turned into new-found fear and trembling.

And it now seemed so much darker. All the sudden.

Leaves fluttered, a whole large branch of them. And then more leaves. JoJo expanded his wings. JoJo was out of there. Shine watched him fly out of the tree and so quickly that he didn't move.

"Hey, Shine. Bird. Bird," the boy Frankie said.

JoJo had disappeared.

People scattered looking for him in another tree. Shine climbed down. For a moment, the gatherers halted. They watched Shine.

He dashed toward the boy Frankie and shoved him on the ground and climbed on top of him as though positioning himself to throw a series of punches. Jerry pulled him off. Shine ran down the fence-line. Two other teens ran with him.

"JoJo," Shine called out. "Here, pretty boy. Don't do this. Don't do it. Come here."

He could see JoJo in another tree. Past other yards. JoJo flew from tree to tree. He had been seriously spooked by Frankie's ruckus.

Shine and the two or three others tried to keep pace. They were winded.

They ran more. They weren't stopping. JoJo flew more. They spotted the bird weaving his way down the fence line. It looked as if JoJo was speeding toward a final exit. Shine and the others were at the end of the long block of houses, and way past Ethel's street now, and it was getting seriously dark.

He saw JoJo's wings one more time. Barely. It was this last time.

JoJo had flown way off. The parrot was now likely far from the woods. Vanished. The entire sky seemed depleted. The galaxy, to Shine, had collapsed. All the stars had been subtracted to one, little wet spot, like a wadded dishrag. The world was reduced so much that it swallowed JoJo. It carried JoJo somewhere foreign. It carried JoJo to a place that neither Shine nor his uncle Jerry would ever find.

This last time JoJo had surely flown away. Forever.

***

IT WOULD BE VERY HARD and nearly impossible, for a long time, for Shine to get over the western flight of JoJo.

The bird was gone.

The sparkling yellow and green bird, Shine realized, had been pushed out of the woods.

Yet, this sad forcing out gave JoJo the parrot that ultimate option, scared as the bird must have been. JoJo probably opted to take a journey that would bring him in touch with other parrots, after hundreds of miles of travel. Uncle Jerry told him the true story of a population of parrots that gathered in the west. This population of parrots

232

were part of a pattern of migration in which hordes of lost or wild parrots sought the warm areas of Arizona - to realize one state, for sure. This was a story Jerry had read and shared with Shine.

By flying swiftly out of Garland and out of Bedlam, JoJo declared to the crowd parading below him that he'd find another home.

Shine tried to comfort himself by thinking this. He blamed himself for not offering, months ago, to help his uncle clip JoJo's wings, the natural and cautionary trait of caring for a parrot. On the other hand, his uncle was inconsolable. Hours after JoJo flew off, Jerry sat on a couch with his head in his hands and face buried in a towel.

It became the most traumatic bird-watching time ever in Garland woods involving any bird living there.

Shine kept his head under his pillow longer than he'd planned. As difficult as JoJo's loss was, he tried even harder not to think of his uncle Jerry and aunt Ruth. It was as if they'd lost a child. They had no kids. Shine knew it would take Jerry weeks or months to recover. The rest of the summer, his uncle continued to blame himself for unlatching the cage too early and clumsily banging it, triggering the bottom to fling open and giving JoJo an escape route.

As soon as Shine's images of JoJo blurred, he thought of Cynthia. He froze that thought. But Cynthia faded, too, and replacing her were his convictions that someone he actually knew set fire to the Empire and that tension was mounting over the coming Black Panther Party rally. With every pleasant thought, like the dime store necklace he bought Cynthia, a drastic thought slipped into his sleep.

There seemed no limit to problems.

He wanted more than ever to know *if*, in fact, someone he knew burned down the Empire. Could it have happened that way? Could it have been someone from high school? He became more convinced it was.

Arson, the t.v. news suggested, appeared to be a culprit.

SHINE WAS NOT YET READY to ditch his cigarettes.

He considered one more. Two. No more than two. Well, three. No. Two. Out of respect for Cynthia. No more than two. Get rid of the Band-Aid box. Throw it into the creek. He'd hung onto the box too long, like it was some rabbit's foot or four-leaf clover.

He'd get rid of the Band-Aid box and hope to keep her. She was watching his back pockets, and she knew his breath. Still, he decided to light up and send a tribute to a long gone JoJo. He'd send up his own version of menthol smoke signals.

Sitting against a tree stump in one of his special places in Garland, with a view through the chain-link fence of left field, he lit up. He spit on the match tip and buried it under a tuft of grass. In the humid-less afternoon, he didn't yet feel the twinge of a sneezing fit coming on. The more Shine sneaked his smoking in the woods, the more accessible he was to the wild leafy growth he was allergic to. He tried not to think about it. He stared at the closed concession stand. He stared at the empty rows of bleachers on the third base side. He stared at the infield where he once kicked up dust dragging the field.

Shine wondered about his father. He was driving the truck through Illinois by now, on route to Wisconsin for a parts delivery. Shine wondered whether or not his father needed to make this deadline delivery. Was it a real deadline? Who'd know but him? Did his father prefer not to be in Bedlam when he knew the Black Panther rally might stir up trouble? Did he take H. Rap Brown seriously, or think of him as this passerby who couldn't possibly care that much for a town as small as Bedlam? Did his father think that his family - and mostly his own wife - could handle any problems because the Bedlam police were promising safety? Or was Shine's father so prophetic that he believed nothing big would come from H. Rap Brown's speech?

What was it? Shine wondered.

He met Moondog at the tracks twenty minutes late, only because he kept thinking about his father. He could've added another ten to the twenty, but he only had one cigarette left. He would save it.

The train was fortunately late.

They heard its whistle five minutes before the front crept by. Shine waved at one of the conductors, pretending he was exercising his pitching arm by throwing rocks at a tree. The conductor waved. Two minutes later, Moondog was the first to hop and grab a boxcar ladder-bar and pull himself up and into the open car, with Shine right behind him.

"You stink, man," Moondog said.

"Stink how?"

"You smell. You smoke?"

Shine hesitated. "What?"

"Cigarettes?"

"How so?"

"You can smell it. It ain't on me."

"It's on me?"

"Come on, man. You ducking the question," Moondog said.

"Why you want to know?"

"Cynthia caught you yet?"

"I guess I can't keep it from you forever. I'm about to quit."

"You ain't answered. Cynthia know?"

"I'm about to quit."

"About to. Come on." Moondog was laughing now. "I tried it once, man. Alphonso smokes. He smokes a lot. He'll blow smoke out the bedroom window. He sprays Lysol all the time. Pop don't want smoke in his house. He's downstairs. He can't smell a thing."

"You tried it?" Shine said.

"Once. When Alphonso was gone. He had a pack on his bed. Plain in sight. Then I heard Ulysses walking around and I flung my lit one out the window. I'd just lit it, so it didn't stink up his room. I hid in the closet."

Moondog opened a box of Milk Duds and dumped in a mouthful until his jaws bulged.

The train rolled north. It was Friday. Train traffic was prolific on Friday. The boys decided to make it a fast afternoon. They would hop off near Hamilton and the car plant where the trains came to a crawl, and they'd hop right back on a southbound. It inevitably ran through Bedlam.

Moondog seemed more solemn and not his joking self. Minutes passed when he didn't talk, and that wasn't the norm for Moondog.

"What's going on? You seem out of it," Shine said. "I'm the one who's not feeling great. My dad took off with his new truck load."

Moondog stared out the open boxcar, without looking at his friend. "Nothing, man. Well, maybe. I'm thinking of your bird, JoJo. Maybe he wanted to come back but messed up. Got scared. I know you hate not catching that bird."

"Probably why I smoked today," Shine said. "I know he's long gone."

"Naw, you smoke because you're hooked. You been at it before you had JoJo."

"Think so?"

"Know so. You saw someone smoke - like me with Alphonso - and you got into it. I quit. I cough a lot," Moondog said. "Plus, it's hard enough to learn the sax with my lungs."

A few more minutes lapsed before it appeared the two would keep arguing about cigarettes in general.

"Man, everything's closing down in Bedlam. You see that? Everything," Moondog said.

"What do you mean, 'closing up?'"

"Everything. Everything closing early. The pool closed early yesterday. The Sunoco station. Bettman's closed early, and doing it again today. Old man Bettman said he's closing early to get people used to it."

237

"Get used to what?"

"To when the Black Panthers come in."

"Why's he worried? He lives in west Bedlam."

"Old man said he ain't taking chances when the Black Panthers start hollering and stirring it up. He don't want trouble. So he's closing early right now. He told Pop he's closing down at four on August Tenth, when the Panthers hit the west side."

Other places, curiously, were also closing early: the Health Department, a tiny, circular brick building across from the mattress factory; it looked like a miniature brick fortress. Hodge's Gas Station diagonally across from the Health Department and on the other side of the highway bridge. Even Hattendorf's. It was as if businesses were aiming to secure their places days well before H. Rap Brown's appearance.

The last twenty minutes of the train ride back was hideously gut-wrenching. For some reason, their boxcar bucked and swayed down the track. It shook. The train lurched and hammered Shine and Moondog against a side. Shine's back pinched against a wheel-shaped handle that opened and closed the door.

"The train gods hate us now," Moondog said, holding his stomach.

"Hold on," Shine said. "We might break an ankle jumping off this time. It's not slowing down much."

When they did time their jump and somersaulted down the embankment, they dragged themselves to Garland and lay against a tree near one of the earlier hobo camps. The shade was necessary. Their throats were crusty.

The boys had felt the summer heat churn the inside of the boxcar.

That part of the woods was clear of any camp. They investigated. No campfires. No burning tin cans. The boys knew hobos changed camps frequently and just set down where they wanted.

Walking up to Hattendorf's to buy two bottles of Mountain Dew, they made a plan. Moondog invited Shine to come to his house on the night of the Black Panther rally, although Shine discouraged it at first.

"Your dad want you to stay home on August tenth?" Moondog said.

"Maybe, but he's not here and he won't be."

"You'll be in trouble."

"He had my grandpa leave a shotgun. Allison can deal with it."

"That's crazy. I hope it won't get all heated up. Then you'll have to spend the night. That means Alphonso's around, and that might not end good."

They'd already downed the Mountain Dew, talking about stores and gas stations and offices closing early these days. They had just enough change between them, totaling thirty-five cents, to buy a large order of French fries at Golden Point. But, when they crossed the street, they saw the sign: "Store Hours Changed. Open Tomorrow at 11:00." The restaurant's doors were locked, and it wasn't yet six o'clock.

"I'm not worrying about H. Rap Brown," Shine said. "Everybody's all worked up."

"If you come over on the tenth," Moondog said, "just get there before dark."

***

ALLISON SHUT HER EYES AND rolled up the
Life Magazine to use as a hard pillow.

She got steadily sleepy in the waiting room at Good
Samaritan Hospital. On the t.v. perched on a wobbly table
in front of her, a magician pulled an endless paper chain
out of an end of his coat sleeve on "The 50-50 Club" show.

The night before, Allison sat with her mother who'd
had trouble sleeping. Josephine had dealt with a headache
most of the day. Allison exchanged the memory of her
mother groaning in the kitchen at two a.m. for the
magician's mischievous laugh. She marveled at the length
of the paper chain, how Ruth Lyons' own eyes followed
the chain across the floor. Allison knew that floor well. She
guessed the chain's length at thirty feet, before her
attention was completely sapped.

Josephine received a new medication for migraines,
a capsule she could either swallow or literally twist apart
and dump the powdery substance into coffee or tea. Her
doctor had made personal phone calls to a neurologist-
friend to arrange the appointment. His neurologist-friend,
surrendering to the blunt plea of Josephine's doctor, wrote
and circled Josephine's name on a piece of paper and
advanced the name of Josephine Ross to the top of his
lengthy list. The months she might have waited for the new
medicine turned into only a few days.

Gone over two hours inside a web of neurology
rooms, Josephine returned finally and woke Allison, whose
neck hung well over the *Life*. Josephine was drowsy after

receiving a shot and taking a pill. The neurologist had her wait in a dark room before releasing her to the waiting room and check-out.

On the way home, Josephine wore sunglasses and laid her head back on the seat. With each turn, the sunglasses slid down her nose. She let the frame stay lopsided on her face. Allison swatted at a fly on the dashboard. It roamed the ceiling and steering wheel, and landed back on the dash, performing some fierce jig.

Allison smacked the dashboard, missing the fly which darted toward Josephine.

"Take it easy on the car," Josephine said, raising her head.

"I can't stand this fly," Allison said. "I'll wreck if it keeps flitting by my nose."

Josephine rolled down her window and the fly flew out.

"Go back to sleep, mom. Show-off."

Minutes later, Allison slowed when she saw a line of cars barely moving down one of Bedlam's busier streets. Hooper Avenue ran past the basketball and tennis courts, City Hall, the creek bridge, Golden Point, Kroger, and toward west Bedlam. Allison pulled behind a 1966 Camaro convertible. It appeared the driver was shouting at a tree between a sidewalk and the street. The driver flung his arm at no one in particular in a show of concern.

The Camaro kept rolling. It soon sped away with the few cars in front of it. Allison looked over and saw a young boy lying on the ground by the tree and next to his fallen bike.

"That's Fremont Jones," Allison said. "People must have been asking if he needs help."

"What's he doing? " her mother said. "All I see him doing is shaking his head." She craned her neck to see and took off her sunglasses.

"He's hurt."

"How hurt?"

"I can't tell." Allison pulled in a parking slot near the basketball courts and the highway entry ramp.

"You know him?"

"Ulysses does. Most everyone in west Bedlam does."

She told her mother to stay put. Fremont Jones struggled to sit upright, maneuvering what existed of his skinny weight mostly onto his elbows. He was crying. Well within view of Allison, he pointed to his right foot. Allison knelt and pushed the bike away from Fremont, whose rage could only project the lightness of a whimper. He resorted to a rapid sequence of sign language. Fremont could only utter grunts. He raised his arms, pointing to his ankle and then the bike. He lifted his right leg to emphasize the ankle. He showed her his scratched elbow. He clasped his hands and shoved Allison, suggesting he was pushed.

Allison mimed the letters, H-U-R-T. "Hurt bad?" she asked, pointing to his ankle. "B-A-D?" She couldn't tell, even though Fremont had stopped grunting.

By then, Josephine had walked across the street. She bent to touch Fremont's head. He looked up at her. Allison examined the bike. The front tire spokes were slightly bent although the tire rotated. She straightened the crooked seat.

She determined they wouldn't need to haul the bike in the trunk and escort him home.

Allison saw her mother signing. Fremont signed back. His frantic hand and arm gestures looked serious. Fremont's signing prompted Josephine to nod her head. She let Fremont know she understood. Yes, yes, she signed. No, I don't know, she signed. She spoke aloud to accompany her sign language. Allison listened, watching Fremont's movements more. He wiped his eyes with his dirty shirt.

Josephine signed and talked: "So, this boy rode up behind you right here - almost right across from the police department - and jerked you off your bike? Is that what happened? This boy assaulted you? Is this true?"

"Who attacked him, mom?" Allison said.

"Some boy he knows. Someone who has been after him a while, apparently."

"Did he say who? Ask him about names. Ulysses will know."

Josephine signed to Fremont Jones: "Spell that name again. Who was it that jerked you off the bike and hit you in the head on the ground?"

Josephine signed and spoke: "He's saying to me, Alphonso Peace. That's the name. Do you know him, Allison?"

"I know him. He's Ulysses' cousin. You've heard me say he mostly stayed by himself at school."

Josephine signed Allison's response for Fremont. He signed back, "Yes, yes, that's him. Him. Ulysses Weasel's cousin. Pop's family. He no good. He bad."

Josephine took a tissue out of her pocket and gave it to Fremont to wipe his eyes. He stood up. He seemed to regain some energy. "He wants me to thank you, Allison, for checking the tire and straightening his bike seat. He said he knows you a little and you're good. His words."

When Fremont regained his balance and sat on his bike, he tugged Josephine's arm. "Need tell you more something," he signed. "More."

Josephine leaned against the tree and Allison sat on grass. Fremont lifted the bike's front to prove he'd regained strength.

"What?" Josephine said.

"What did he say? Allison asked.

"He has more to tell about this person Alphonso."

Fremont unleashed a flurry of hand and arm gestures. He grunted occasionally, and Josephine whispered to Allison that he was overly excited, and frightened. "He doesn't know what to do."

"What to do with what?"

"He saw a crime. He's telling me about a big crime."

"What crime?" Allison said. "Where?"

"Wait. More coming."

She got more information. He stared toward the street corner with City Hall in view. He told his version of what he encountered hiding across the street from the Empire warehouse. But, he kept looking at City Hall, not at Josephine. "He might be embarrassed," Josephine said. "He's not looking me in the eye. I believe him. I can read someone deaf who's frightened. Or incredibly nervous."

Fremont Jones signed frantically to Josephine. She signed back to him. She interpreted his description for

Allison: "He's saying that, on the day of the fire, he saw someone sneaking around near the back corner of the building. It was before the fire. Not long. Someone sneaking, he says. He watched, hiding across the street. Fremont says he likes to watch people all the time, even in their houses. He says he's good at seeing what people do, where they go. He watches people all day. He'll watch someone a whole afternoon. Sometimes at night. He says his sight is sensitive because he can't hear and talk. He sees. He likes to watch. He rides his bike, watches stuff."

Fremont kept signing to Josephine. She signed back. "Allison," she said, "he says that he's sure that the person he saw was Alphonso. He knows Alphonso a mile away. He saw Alphonso sprinkle some gas, which looked like water to Fremont, and lit some matches and tossed them on a pile of wood back in the corner of the Empire. He did everything fast. Real fast. On the shaded side. That's where workers pile their junk, too."

"Is he sure?" said Allison.

"Are you sure?" Josephine signed to Fremont. "You have to be really sure."

He signed back that he was almost one hundred percent sure. He would swear to it. As Fremont saw it, it was Alphonso, holding a rag, who ran out of the shadows on that one side. It was a long rag, as Josephine interpreted.

Fremont seemed to lose energy in his hand motions and told Josephine that he had to go home. He was afraid. He waved to the two and sped off toward the creek bridge.

"What do you think, mom?" Allison said.

"Well, I have a theory. I think he's been holding in this knowledge of the fire, or what he thinks he saw, for a lot of the summer. I think he's not been sure what he can do with what he saw. I can feel that in his emotional state, the way he talked to me. You can sense that even through sign language. He hasn't had anyone to tell it to, anyone who he feels would believe him. It's about trust. It's like there's no one he could trust with the information. If he told someone in his family, he's thinking they'd just shoo him away. They might laugh it off. And he didn't know if he'd ever get in trouble or not for telling. He's a boy, Allison. He's deaf. He's wondering who would ever take him seriously."

***

SHINE'S MOTHER INSISTED SHE FINISH her toast and coffee before they left the house. Shine jingled her car keys. Cynthia clamped her hand over the keys.

Josephine sipped the hot coffee first from a spoon. She wiped her mouth and downplayed the agenda forming their morning. Cynthia stacked dishes in the sink.

None of the three said a word during the two minute drive to City Hall. No game plan. No questions from Shine. No car radio.

Cynthia was along for the ride. She might even sit on the bench outside the police station, avoiding lists, notes, or tape recordings that a police officer might bring up in the meeting.

The paper mill's whistle cut through the air.

The hissing of presses and fabric cutters inside the mattress factory outlived the whistle.

Shine had no idea how his mother would approach the police. He wanted to do some of the talking, based on the information Fremont Jones provided his mother and Allison. They soothed him and helped the deaf boy back on his bike after his scuffle with Alphonso Peace.

Either Fremont had fabricated the most outlandish story imaginable about Alphonso as a possible suspect in setting fire to the Empire, or else he was telling some shred of truth. Either Fremont had stumbled upon Alphonso tossing gas on a junk-heaped side of the warehouse, or else he was far more audacious than Shine could imagine.

Either Fremont had seen Alphonso ignite the blaze, or else his imagination was unmatched by any other young kid. Either Fremont hid across the street from the Empire and watched Alphonso sprint out of the shadows holding a rag, or else his imagination had conjured a crippling story, one that, if false, could land him in juvenile detention. Or worse.

SHINE AND HIS MOTHER SAT across from officer Klump who happened to be on duty.

Mother and son looked at their bubbly neighbor shuffling paper reports as if he was searching for a certain sentence. Shine watched the officer slip his cigarette onto an ashtray. He was amazed at its length.

The room was musty and sparse. Downright ugly. An air conditioner rattled. A framed photo of the mayor hung lopsided on a wall. Four chairs and a metal table were the only furniture. One ashtray. For a department that reviewed crucial data here, it made sure an interviewee felt unwelcome.

Klump came across as unprepared yet sympathetic. He listened to Josephine describe meeting Fremont Jones for the first time.

"He just lay on the ground, Elmer, looking lost." Her hands never left her purse. She relayed Fremont's stories about the bike mishap, Alphonso's lurking around the Empire one afternoon not long after the school's summer recess, his matches, the sparks engulfing some wood, and the way Alphonso ran out from the shadows holding a nasty rag.

"Every word comes from him," she said.

After several minutes in which the officer scribbled on a clipboard, he looked up to see Shine staring at his cigarette. "You don't want a cigarette, do you, Shine?" The officer laughed.

"No." Shine twisted in his chair. "Uh, nothing."

"The boy, Fremont, hid his bike in bushes," Josephine said. "He lay squat on the ground, curled up against the bushes so he couldn't be seen."

"Let's talk about this older juvenile," Klump said. "This Alphonso Peace who we've watched for a time. And I shouldn't be telling you this, but I trust you won't tell anyone else." The officer winked at Shine, exclusively. "This young man been put on alert by his boss at the Empire for threatening another worker. Believe that? Apparently, he said he'd throw a gas rag in his boss' car at night. Unlit. When the boss, who shall remain nameless, reported this to my Chief, we put it in a top file drawer. Easy access. The boss at the Empire is an upstanding citizen. Not a complainer. The man in question, Mr. Peace, caused just one problem there, but it was a big enough one. Enough to ruffle feathers." Klump shuffled the papers even more. He seemed to lose his place.

"Why do we need that information, Elmer?" Josephine said. "What can I do about a threatened boss?"

"I don't know."

"This is an instance where a young man named Fremont claimed to Allison and me that, number one, he was tackled and pulled off his bike. Number two, he saw the person possibly set fire. This is why I'm here."

"I hear you. I'm taking a statement."

"Fremont's arm is bandaged. I'm a witness to the scraped arm. I didn't see Peace. I saw blood. I saw an eye swelling."

"I'm taking note."

"Now, I don't know about the warehouse. Don't get us confused with that story."

Shine interrupted his mother. His timing seemed off but he persisted: "Call Moondog right now. Knowing him, he's probably practicing his saxophone. He'll tell you his dad doesn't have good things to say about Alphonso, and that's his father's sister's oldest boy."

Klump scribbled. "None of this is evidence. But I'm noting it."

"Another thing," Shine said. "You want me to go over there now? If Ulysses is there, he can get his cousin to come over. He has a way."

"Not necessary."

"Ulysses is sure that Alphonso or someone he paid slashed one of his tires. He's holding that against

Alphonso. He's been walking on egg shells around Ulysses."

"Not necessary."

Klump took drags from his cigarette. He blew smoke at the ceiling, away from Josephine who sat directly across from him.

"Now," he said, "in light of this information, I'm taking it seriously. My Chief is probably going to send officer Watson and a county detective to check it out."

Klump took a gentle drag and scratched his head. "Josephine, if our department needs you, say, to help with sign language if we speak with Jones, is this agreeable?"

"I'll do it if you have no one else."

"Who else talks to deaf people around here?" he said.

"I do."

"I'll note that."

"Are we going to be safe now that we've shared this information?"

"I hope so." The officer squished the last of his cigarette into the ashtray.

"I'm talking about my family."

"I can't make promises."

"No one?"

"You and Shine are brave. His girlfriend sitting outside, too. Brave."

"It's a duty," Josephine said. "I'm going to bet on what Fremont says. It's what I heard, that's all."

"Brave," the officer said. "Listen, these guys are tough."

"What about our safety?"

"I live across the street. That'll be double protection."

"I can't see this young man Fremont making up a story this crazy," Josephine said. "Elmer, do you know his family story? You know how hard it's been for that boy? What he has to go through each day deaf and mute as he is? I know deaf people. I work with them."

While she talked, there came a point when Josephine oddly lapsed into using sign language in front of the officer. To Shine, it had become a natural habit. In a police station, it was terribly odd. She engaged Klump in a way he could not have predicted. He watched Josephine jerk and slap her arms and hands as she expressed concern for Fremont.

She said: "A boy like that needs protection. His small family pays taxes. We pay taxes. And he's done an admirable thing, talking about what he saw. Quite often, I've learned, deaf people get to the truth - and they want the truth."

Josephine continued to flex her arms and hands, signing and describing the way Fremont sacrificed a part of what he knew. "Now he might be living in fear, Elmer. I don't want this boy to live in fear. Can we make that not happen?"

The officer didn't remind her that he wasn't deaf and that she didn't need to sign in front of him, waving her hands like a mad woman.

Then Josephine, who'd been standing, sat back down in her chair and fanned her face with a bookmark. She looked toward the windowless door that lead to the cluster of jail cells.

"I'd better check on Cynthia, mom," Shine interrupted. "We've been in here pretty long."

"Go."

"No, wait," Klump said. "Well, no, go ahead. Hey, come over and swim later if you want to. Take your mind off stuff."

Shine shook off the stale odor of the police room, the scent of old wood and Pine-Sol. The air conditioner churned so loudly Shine thought it could explode. The more he sat and listened to his mother and Klump, the more he thought of Cynthia. She was wise not to involve herself. She stayed detached, except to get news from Shine.

Cynthia had given Shine and his mother their personal space. She dignified their information by not butting in, and that impressed Shine.

What he wanted most to do now: go outside and wait with her on the bench at City Hall.

He did just that.

WILL

SHINE EXPECTED SWIMMING UNDERWATER WOULD be easygoing, as much as he loved it underwater. He didn't expect his morning swim would be soundly defeated.

Just before he planned to execute another one of his perfectionist-dives, toes pointed, with his outstretched arms clamped in a V around his head, hands locked in a similar V, Shine reared back, unclasped his hands, and began belting out the worst, most explosive sneezing fit he'd had all summer. Uncontrollable snorting.

A nasal ambush. A cannon firing from his head.

His nose. Once a wasteland on his face because of his Hay Fever, also known as rhinitis, his nose had filled with mucus.

Shine couldn't make it to the side of the pool in time, so the pool itself received part of the mucus ambush. There was no other alternative. It was as if every pollen-bearing weed in Bedlam schemed to raid Klump's pool and drown

Shine with their contributions, until he surrendered, got out, and dressed for the day.

He lost that battle with whatever substance in the air blindsided him. He used the towel as a handkerchief. He didn't think twice about it. The swim turned into a failed option. He'd lost interest. His eyes were watery. His nose felt like a brick. His ears thrummed.

Shine lingered at Breezy's a while longer.

He considered what he needed to do, but was slow to move: get a few groceries at Hattendorf's for his mother who'd taped a short list to his bedroom door, along with a ten dollar bill; shoot basketball; practice trumpet; and check in with Moondog. Yes: call Cynthia. He shouldn't forget a priority, his girlfriend. Shine's sister wanted an answer from Cynthia. Allison and Ulysses wanted to take them to see a new movie at The Swashbuckler. It was a new Clint Eastwood western called "Hang 'Em High."

It was early morning. Not only had Shine barely set foot in the pool, but he'd barely slept through the night. Numerous times he'd kicked off the bed sheet, waking uncovered, while intermittently thinking that he heard strange voices and dreaming that Cynthia was calling him down from a boxcar. "Jump, Shine. Don't you leave me standing here near a hobo camp," she said in his dream. The train moved. He and Moondog, standing on the lip of the moving box car, saluted her.

Anyway, he slept horribly. He had hoped Breezy's pool would energize him.

He still hoped for a decent day, in spite of the sneezing, and in spite of the sad fact that, tomorrow, he would still have to accompany his aunt to the tired old doctor for his allergy shots. They'd waste hours waiting for the old man to give them injections.

THE OFFICER CAME OUT OF his house, flaunting his usual Bermuda shorts, yellow t-shirt, flip-flops. He pitched a clean towel to Shine. "You ok? You could wake the dead with that sneezing."

"It hits all the sudden," Shine said.

The officer picked at weeds around the pool and his tomato garden, giving Shine his space. Breezy finally took a break, went into the house, and returned with two glasses of iced tea. "Drink up," he said.

Shine squeezed juice from the lemon wedge into his tea. Breezy twirled ice cubes with his finger.

"I've got a busy day," the officer said.

"How so?"

"We're nailing a couple of drag racers. The Armantrout kid is one. Hate doing it. He's the ring leader along with deLong. Quiet kid. No driver's license. His dad lets him drive his Camaro. He and deLong have set times to drag. We'll set up a net."

"They've got great cars to get out there for not having licenses," Shine said.

"If you talk much to the Armantrout kid, don't say anything. I hold you accountable." Breezy smiled.

"I hardly see him."

"Good. Armantrout's sowing his oats. He's got happy feet with the accelerator, and his dad gives him his blessing. He's not in the clear himself."

***

LATER IN THE DAY, A strange and ironic thing happened: Shine dribbled his basketball down to the outside courts; he passed the school and came up on City Hall. He looked up to discover officer Watson leading Alphonso Peace into the police station. He wasn't cuffed, though he looked angry.

Shine wanted desperately to run over to Moondog's to see if anyone was home. But, he decided not to rush it. Just pace it. Involve himself as little as possible. He didn't want to jeopardize any little thing he'd accomplish this summer by putting himself in proximity right now of the Simms brothers or anyone who might remember him later.

He was just going to shoot a few baskets and be done.

Even though he occasionally encountered Alphonso while at Moondog's house, he could slip by Alphonso at any time.

Shine practiced some jump shots, though wound up toying with attempts to sink the basketball from half-court. He fantasized time running out in a game, and so it was up to him to hit the game-winning shot from half-court. He heaved the ball repeatedly. Every shot either smacked the backboard or struck the rim. A lot of fantasized games were lost. He decided to shoot free-throws.

When he left, dribbling mindlessly, a second strange and ironic thing happened: just as Breezy said, officers planned to put a halt to the Armantrout-deLong drag racing feat. Shine looked up and across the street and saw an officer he didn't recognize lead Wayne deLong into the station. Wayne's 1966 Chevelle SS was parked in the back of the police lot, and a second officer was searching its interior.

On his way home, he saw Raymond Armantrout

"What happened, Raymond?" Shine said. "I just saw deLong head into the cop station."

"They got him." Raymond swallowed the last of his hamburger. "I pulled into Golden Point. I'm just checking now to see if they impounded his Chevelle. Wayne ain't smart. He kept driving and swerving. I stopped, pulled in fast to get a burger. They didn't get me."

"You guys dragging?"

"Hey, no. Nope."

"You leaving your Camaro at Golden Point?"

"Until my dad gets home. Then he'll get it. I ain't taking chances without a license, since they got Wayne."

Raymond started to walk away and head toward downtown Bedlam and back to his house. He glanced back at Shine. "They're not gonna stop us for long. Wayne ran a red light. He should've hit the brakes some more. Speed ain't the thing. We're always fast."

***

SHINE AND LARRY LOOMIS WERE sweeping the concrete floor of the rec shelter when they watched Baldy Babcock drive his tractor across center field to meet them. Larry had been collecting bottles and noticed Shine by himself; it was his last designated job before he could receive his last summer paycheck. Larry put down his bag of bottles and held a dustpan.

Baldy Babcock had another idea.

"Hey, Shine," he called from his tractor, "want another go-round around the infield? I need a good laugh."

"No way," Shine said. "Not after the trouble I got in. Maybe next summer."

"I might not let you then."

When Baldy noticed Maury Riggs' car coming down the hill, he shoved the gearshift into place and sped off, leaving Shine and Larry Loomis standing in center field. Baldy's tractor crept around the base path. He knew not to kick up dust. Riggs pulled next to the shelter and waited in his car. He rolled down his window.

"I need to talk to Shine here for a minute."

"You want me to back off?" Larry said. "Could you give me ride?"

"You can't walk?"

"I could. But I got all these pop bottles."

Riggs sized up Larry Loomis and the half-full bag. A hefty breeze whipped against the bag rattling the bottles, and it brushed Larry's big feathery afro to one side of his head. Infield dust from Baldy's tractor caught a current and whirled up Garland hill.

"I'll give you a ride in a minute."

Larry walked back and finished sweeping where Shine left off.

"That's something about that Jones boy. He's a big help," Riggs said. "Might be deaf but he's a help. I think it's going somewhere." He pressed his lips down on his cigar and puffed.

"What is 'it'?" Shine said.

258

"Well, I mean 'it' as in what the police and fire departments might discover."

"About the fire?"

"That one."

"Are they close to knowing?"

"I wouldn't know. But tell your mom thanks. She was a help. You take care." He partially rolled up the window before Shine tapped on it.

"But, Mr. Riggs, that young guy Fremont? He's not even fifteen by a long shot. Maybe twelve? Maybe next summer can you get him a job just sweeping around City Hall, just pay him a little cash? He's a good kid. Even a kid like that can work. Have him vacuum city cars? He's deaf. You've probably seen him on his bike."

"I'll have to think about that. Maybe run it by the Mayor."

"Please."

"You say pay him cash? Who's cash?"

"The city's."

"What makes you think the city can pay cash?"

"You can do anything you want. My dad said."

"I have to think about that." Riggs' booming laugh prodded his cigar to jiggle between his fingers, almost to a point he nearly fumbled it.

"Evidently, we can't rescue a parrot," Riggs said. "Sorry about your parrot. Gorgeous things, those parrots."

"I hate thinking about it," Shine said. "Could you do that, a favor, for Fremont Jones?"

"Let's wait til next summer. Meantime, have yourself a good school year."

Shine wasted one last sentence: "You know Fremont might have helped give ideas as to who maybe was around the Empire at the time of that fire?"

"Is that right?" Riggs seemed clueless. "I'll look into that."

Riggs motioned for Larry Loomis to get in the backseat.

Larry slapped Shine's hand with a goodbye, see-you-soon confidence. The whole time Riggs drove up the hill he watched Baldy Babcock on his tractor, waving to him with his cigar hand, definitely taking stock of Baldy's tractor speed.

Shine felt edgy. He sensed he knew more than his boss, Maury Riggs. He could hold information against Shine who never quite trusted the man, anyway. Riggs was a boss for a reason. He was one official position under the Mayor. He had clout. Judson Ross once told his son, in a postcard, that a boss can hold secrets and deal them out - outright make up things - according to his whims and needs. Shine never forgot this. It unnerved him to think that Riggs might resent how much Shine knew, or knew more than he did about certain people in the city.

Shine also had a feeling that his boss somehow knew he'd carried a Band-Aid box most of summer and lit up in the woods.

He never doubted that Maury Riggs knew certain things he kept to himself.

***

IN A WAY OF THINKING, Shine disobeyed his father.

In another way, he argued that Allison was older than he and that she, as the big sis who was basically a grown young woman, could protect their mother. He didn't see the need to be cooped up in the house on this particular night of August 10.

So, Shine looked at his decision this latter way: He wasn't disobeying.

His mother didn't seem to care, either. She didn't say word one to him.

Judson Ross had wanted Shine to stay home and act as "a support," he said, to his mother and sister, in case someone happened to ease out of the darkness of eleven o'clock and came knocking unexpectedly at the door.

"What do you mean by support?" Shine asked his father.

"Scare off anyone you might hear rumbling around outside. If you don't know who it is."

"Scare off how?"

"Make noise. You're good at that."

"Allison can do that. Or mom."

"Your mom doesn't raise her voice, and Allison is a girl. You're getting to be a man."

"What if I can't?"

"Point the gun. But don't fire. Don't ever use it."

"I don't want to hold it. Nothing's going to happen."

His father upset him. Shine decided right then that he'd go to Moondog's. He hated obligations that he questioned, and he spent a lot of time in west Bedlam, anyway. He just wouldn't be near the rally. On the street, that is. He'd be inside a house. Moondog had not cared one bit that H. Rap Brown was coming.

Still, it would soon be the eight o'clock hour of H. Rap Brown.

It would be the hour for the Black Panther Party's chairman of the Student Nonviolent Coordinating Committee to deliver his speech to west Bedlam residents.

Shine wasn't always that defiant. He loved his father and missed him, although he was never outspoken about it. He'd never outright said to his father, "Stay home and I mean it. I need you to watch me play basketball. I need you to listen to my horn." Shine let it go.

He wanted to see his friend Moondog, who was also a kid and best friend, and he happened to be black. Besides, Moondog had earlier bragged that he would beat Shine in any number of games of checkers.

Shine said, "You're on."

HE LEFT HIS SISTER AND mother alone in the house with his grandfather's shotgun.

His grandpa, Josephine's father, brought it down that afternoon of the rally. He left it on a chair by the front door. He taped a hastily-scribbled note to the barrel: "Be back to get it tomorrow. Careful, it kicks heavy when fired."

Shine never bought the fear that some north Bedlam residents showed over their insistence that a Black Panther Party leader could stir up an audience to march around Bedlam at midnight, disturbing the peace. Shine never did believe he needed to stay home the evening of H. Rap Brown. He put his plan into place: checkers.

Shine sometimes watched the eleven o'clock news with his mother. He saw the peace movement rising in the Midwest, in parts of St. Louis, Chicago, Detroit, Cleveland, and Cincinnati. He saw spray-painted posters: "Stop the War," "Get Out of 'Nam." "Make Love Not War." He saw protesters file up and down streets thrusting their posters toward cars and anyone they'd pass.

The peace movement had grown with the murder of Martin Luther King on April 4th in Memphis. And especially since the murder of Bobby Kennedy less than twelve weeks ago, in June, in Los Angeles.

Protesters came out in droves when more bombings in Vietnam were announced.

The t.v. news always covered the East and West coasts. Now in the Midwest, things were different. Situations changed each day. Shine took more seriously the news his father brought home about a protester getting his head fractured, or a civil rights activist chaining himself to a mailbox in downtown Detroit. The degree to which some counter-protesters clashed with peace protesters made the Midwest more and more attractive for reporters.

As usual, Shine was happy tonight to get out of the house no matter what.

THE HOUR OF EIGHT O'CLOCK. The hour of H. Rap Brown.

All the traffic lights in Bedlam still operated. Crosswalk signs blinked. I-75 traffic still roared next to the city limits.

Trucks still emitted diesel exhaust.

Peopled still walked to Hattendorf's, Bettman's, Kroger, and Golden Point.

It was a humid evening. The pillar of the west Bedlam community, councilman Al Tillman, helped H. Rap Brown's three assistants set up a portable wooden stage outside Drake school. The assistants wore black t-shirts and black dress pants. Councilman Tillman wore a red dress shirt with tan pants and a white fedora.

Inside Moondog's house, Shine had already lost two games when the muffled voice of H. Rap Brown released through loud speakers got even louder. They could hear the leader pep up the crowd, instigating cheers and clapping. He asked listeners to understand the power in the Black Panther Party's points. At one point, it sounded as if H. Rap Brown's voice was cracking.

"What do you think he's saying?" Shine asked.

"He's getting people to wake up. He's getting people to believe in themselves and what they can do. That's what Pop said he does. He's like a President. That's what they do."

Moondog had taken a break so he could play a newly-learned tune on his sax. Before he finished, the boys heard what sounded like gunfire. Instead, it was a round of firecrackers. Someone set them off behind the house.

"You know how I know they're firecrackers?" Moondog said.

"How?"

"Listen. Hear them? One after the other. Like Fourth of July in the backyard."

Shine looked out the front door. He saw a scrawny cat sitting in the middle of the street. It had a forlorn yet affectionate look. Shine couldn't put a finger on it; the cat had an almost comical stare. It looked abandoned. On the scrawny side, it was amusing looking.

Shine walked outside to pick up the cat before any more traffic passed. The cat took immediately to Shine.

"No tags," Shine said. "You know whose it is?"

"Cat's not from around here."

"I'll take it for now. It was just sitting in the middle of the street. It looked at me."

The cat stretched its legs in Shine's lap. "Something clicked. Scarecrow. It's a her. I'll call her Scarecrow."

"Looks like a scarecrow," Moondog said.

It was a black Calico with its partial brown and white markings.

"I might take Scarecrow home to remind me of losing four games of checkers," Shine said. "Play your sax like it's checkers and you'll be fine."

When they peered out the front door again, when there appeared to be a lull in the amplified voice of H. Rap Brown, they saw Fremont Jones on his bike waving to people as they went back into their houses. "He's deciding which house he wants to peek into," Moondog said.

The speech must have ended. No evidence suggested people were assembling for a parade. Moondog's neighbors carried rolled up pamphlets but that was all.

All remained peaceful. The lights came back on in houses.

Officer Watson drove down the street without police lights beaming on top of his cruiser.

H. Rap Brown and his assistants were escorted out of Bedlam by Watson and by councilman Tillman, who was driving a Cadillac.

The factories' engine-houses still thrummed.

Music poured from the jukebox in the Touchdown Bar & Grill in downtown Bedlam.

Three teens, well past ten o'clock, rollerskated on the school's playground.

A stunning Amazon parrot named JoJo flew westward in the direction of Arizona.

And people in north Bedlam and downtown Bedlam turned off lights and eventually went to sleep.

Pop returned about ten-thirty from the rally. Still sweating, he toted a "Black Panther Party" poster under his arm. "Don't know what I'm gonna do with this," he said. "Tillman gave it to me, said it's a souvenir and it'll be worth serious money some day. I'm not into it, but I didn't want to ignore the man."

Pop asked the boys to sit down and listen to a brief recap of the speech.

He told the boys H. Rap Brown said the Panthers were creating a national health education summit and creating a team that was going to bring better health awareness to minority communities in big cities.

"What you gotta know is they're on a social mission," Pop said. "They're getting out food distribution posts. Brown said the Panthers say, 'Put a loaf of bread on top of every grocery bag.'"

"All those balloons out there," Pop said. "Who blew up three hundred balloons? I'd like to know. Never seen so many balloons. Folks passing out balloons to everybody down there. I popped mine by mistake. What would I do with a balloon? Faces of Black Panther Party leaders on the balloons, neatest thing ever. Cleaver, Fred Hampton, Rap Brown. Face of Bobby Hutton who was killed out in Oakland. Smile on his face."

The subject and optimistic tone changed dramatically after Moondog glanced at the stairs leading up to the second floor.

"Where's Alphonso today? You see him?"

Pop played ignorant for a moment. He turned his good eye toward the boys. His playful demeanor changed. He became outright unsteady on his feet. "Let me sit a minute, drink this water before we leave."

"He here?" Moondog said. "Was he at the rally? That's his thing."

"No."

"Where? Something up?"

"Something's up."

"What?"

Seeing Eye scratched his head. "Lookit, a cop came and took him off in cuffs earlier. You weren't here. He just walked away with them."

"He got arrested?" Moondog said.

"Looks like it. Cop said it might be a few days, hang tight. Alphonso didn't look me square in the eye or nothing."

It was impossible to persuade Pop to share anymore information. He tied his shoelaces without looking at the boys again, and seemed anxious to drive Shine home. They knew it was time, and they knew not to prod him for any more insight.

When Pop and Moondog dropped off Shine and his new cat, Scarecrow, it was past midnight. The front door was unlocked. Pop flashed him a thumbs-up sign, and Shine could still hear the muffler rattle. He thought if Rap Brown's booming voice didn't bother anyone in north Bedlam, then Pop's bad muffler might do it.

***

SHINE HAD NO IDEA WHY two basketballs were rolling around on the backseat floor of Ulysses' CAPRICE, knocking against his shins.

Ulysses hit enough bumps to jostle the balls. They were on Shine's side, too, cramping his legs more than Cynthia's. She inched closer to Shine with every mile, it seemed, and she had plenty of room on her own side.

Shine resisted complaining to Ulysses because he'd generously offered to give Cynthia and him a ride to Coney Island for the day. It was a forty minute drive from Bedlam to the Ohio River and the amusement park alongside it. Shine had just enough money from his final, summer rec shelter paycheck to fork out for two tickets.

He had never known Ulysses to play basketball, much less haul a couple of balls in his car. It was completely unlike his sister's boyfriend. Ulysses rarely talked sports, although he was a natural athlete; he was fast and powerful. Shine knew his sister hadn't taken up the game.

He reached down and picked up both balls. He tried spinning one on his finger, Pete Maravich-style. It danced off his finger and bounced off Ulysses' head.

"Hey, man, I'm driving," U.S. said.

"Sorry. It got away."

"Put them up here if they're in your way. Hold him down back there, Cynthia."

"They yours?" Shine said.

"Nope. Larry Loomis'. Both of them."

"Larry's?"

"Yep. I gave him a ride to drop off his bottles for refund cash. He had these two balls, one tucked under each arm. Plus that bag of bottles. Crazy. I told him to hop in."

Shine pictured all that Larry Loomis must have tried to carry.

"You and Loomis o.k. now?" Ulysses asked.

"I guess so. I helped him collect some bottles the other night. I was staying up late, sleeping out back. I walked over to Angilo's and back with garlic bread. I saw Larry out with his bag, after midnight."

"That late, huh? He's desperate."

"He won't say it," Shine said. "He sure wanted to fill that bag."

"He probably did want your help. Stuff is heavy."

"Yeah, I dragged one side and he got the other."

Ulysses turned onto the two-lane road that lead to the blue and green sign with tiny lights forming the words, "Welcome to Coney Island".

Shine mentioned he wouldn't see Moondog until the next day, creating an avenue for him to also quiz U.S. on his cousin Alphonso. But, U.S. hesitated, offering only one nugget he confided to the two in the backseat. He said, "He may not be back for awhile."

"How long is that?" Shine said.

"Police said he would need a lawyer. They told Pop to ask a lawyer. That's all I know."

Shine didn't want to speculate about any involvement Alphonso might have had in the Empire fire, if any. Nor did he want to share his scarce opinions about what Fremont Jones testified to seeing. He could tell any more talk would disgust Alphonso further. He already faced another long drive back to Bedlam.

"Police did say that if nothing panned out fast, they would let him go fast," Alphonso said.

"I wonder about him." And that's all Shine offered.

"Allison will pick you guys up in this car. I've got to work," Alphonso said. "Meet her here."

THE COUPLE WANDERED INSIDE THE park before deciding to ride The Lost River. It was the first legitimate ride inside the entrance gate. They'd passed the line for The Lost River several times, walking up and down a lane that highlighted the grassy promenade, which split the park into two sides of rides.

The Lost River's wooden boats held four people. They were like wooden boxes floating in a walled-in stream of water.

Anyone could see The Lost River from the road outside Coney Island. Anyone could see the climactic steep drop.

Shine got in first, legs forward, back arched against a rugged seat which irritated his skinny rump. He took

Cynthia's hand as she climbed in, leaning back against his thighs. The gentlemanly way: girl in front. Be cool. Don't squeeze her. Relax. Don't kick her when the boat bangs around curves. Feet flat. Focus on the final plunge like you would first wild dip of a rollercoaster. Shout like a girl, impress her, because it would seal your interest in hanging with her. Mimic Cynthia. The drop was deep, and one's legs flopped around.

He could hold her shoulders then. Squeeze her arms. Not too much. Be a man about it, Shine thought.

The box-boat slogged around the snake-shaped stream. It pounded against metal sides.

They didn't get too wet coming down the drop. Shine slipped down in his seat, cowering to the fountain of water, and grabbed Cynthia. She was steadier, not as wet. Shine's hair was soaked. He played it off, walking a little in back of her, vigorously running his fingers through his hair to calm it down.

"Go again later?" she said. "I like to see you all wet."

"Maybe," he said. He took her arm and guided her toward the Wild Mouse. "This next one'll dry my hair fast. It might give us whiplash."

"I thought we could dry off more in the Haunted House," she said.

"Can we work up to there?"

She nudged him and headed for the Wild Mouse. He screamed in her ear in the middle of the ride, and that's when she really tilted back and wedged her body into his.

THEY SLIPPED IN AND OUT of rides for hours.

271

They even worked their way through Kiddie Land. They squeezed into a beetle-shaped car on a herky-jerky rollercoaster whose track was a small circle with one little bump. Cynthia bit her lip. Shine dabbed at a speck of blood with his handkerchief. She let him hold it there.

He wound up knocking his knee on a handlebar inside the Whip. It should have been called the Whiplash. Cynthia rubbed his knee while they sat outside the Haunted House.

The hoopla in Bedlam seemed so far removed. No early store closings. No drag racing in the middle of the night - or day. No cop in sight. No factories. No fire to put out. No creek rats. No bullhorn or loud speakers. No cunning summer boss. No middle-of-the-night train whistles. No hobos. No second-guessing about what necklace to buy a pretty girl.

Shine emptied most of his dimes into the Skeeball machine in the arcade. Skeeball: a contraption like one miniature bowling lane. There was a row of lanes like with bowling. Any one of four numbered slots that Shine rolled a hand-size ball into ate the Skeeball, returned it, and spit out tickets near the coin slot.

He was down to one quarter; he saved it. He and Cynthia rolled close to a hundred Skeeballs. They bagged 175 tickets which allowed Shine to pick out a Coney Island ballpoint pen.

They lost track of time.

The moment under the Giant Genie's legs arrived.

Shine and Cynthia walked underneath the twenty-feet tall, thick legs of the Giant Genie. They leaned against a leg. A fake giant's voice droned from speakers inside the head: "Enjoy your time at Coney Island, one and all." They stood there listening to the Genie speak to them at two minute intervals.

"Come here a minute, closer," Cynthia said, and put a finger in Shine's belt loop and pulled him. She jammed an envelope into his back pocket. "Ok, read this later." The Genie's legs formed the entryway into the picnic area with sheltered tables. The Ohio River was a streak just over a ravine.

They walked to a picnic table and finished their ice cream cones that Cynthia bought. They could see boats dotting the river. Only a few zigzagged across it. Even with no breeze, the evening's humidity seemed to kick up more under the shelter's shade.

He pulled a wrapped box from his other back pocket with part of the paper torn. "Here you go."

She opened it, held the dime store necklace up to the light, and focused on the heart. She tilted it at so many angles that Shine thought she might be regretting holding it. "I think it's gorgeous," she said. "Where'd you get it? Really?"

"Someplace special," he said.

"Well, yeah, special," she said. She held it in her hand. "Who took you shopping? Your dad?"

"Are you kidding?"

He fumbled with the necklace's clasp. She turned around and he stared at the necklace. This was the longest he'd ever stared directly at Cynthia, though from time to time earlier in the day he sneaked incredibly long glances at her while she gazed at other rides.

"I'll be right back," he said. "Restroom. Don't leave me alone just yet." And he touched the necklace heart.

He went into a stall. He sat on the toilet seat with his pants still buckled. He hadn't needed to use a restroom. He needed to read her note.

He peeled back the folded triangle of pink paper. He admired her beautiful handwriting. He read slowly, trying to be mindful of the time: "Dear Shine, You are a sweet friend, and I think my sweetest. Let me see, I'm thinking. At least you're up there as my sweetest. Right there at number one. I want to be with you. I had a good summer. Most of the time we grew to like each other. I'm glad. We can be anything we want. I kind of want that. I've known you since first grade. I still like you. How's that for growing up together? I hope this doesn't embarrass you, and I hope during this school year we don't mess it up. You are talented. You are smart. You're funny in a goofy way - a fun way. Now, stop your smoking. I hope. Anyway, I liked being locked in the trunk of Ulysses' car with you. Love, C."

Shine clicked his Coney Island pen and tore off one ply of toilet paper. It was rough, perfect to write on. The toilet paper was like notebook paper. Only, it was far less than perfect. As he attempted to write to Cynthia, his pen kept smudging and tearing the toilet paper, enough to persuade him to stop and flush it.

He'd have to remember what he wanted to write. Something like, "Thanks for your letter, C. It made my summer to be with you. I'm glad you put up with me. I will do better, I hope. I wish I could word this better and more fulfillingly (is this even a word?). But, I'm not a writer. I'm a basketball player and trumpet player. Hard to believe, I know. Don't laugh. Anyway, I look forward to being locked in a car trunk with you again. I hope our dreams are good ones our sophomore year. Yours in Coney Island, Shine.

Cynthia had waited for him just outside the restroom all along.

The amusement park's fireworks began to stretch the sky. They walked the promenade back toward the entrance - and its exit - to look for his sister who was surely waiting for them by now, as late as they probably were. The fireworks carved initials of light above The Shooting Star roller coaster. They lit up the The Lost River's fake waterfall also bathed in a rainbow of lights.

Red, yellow, and violet streaks formed a kind of heart in the sky, and Shine could only wonder if he would remember those words he wanted to write to Cynthia. He could have been lost in a dream. It would be a dream in which he'd be happiest.

Action Steps

Reviews from readers like you play a huge part in helping me spread the word about my fiction. If you liked this novel, please consider taking a few minutes to leave a review on Amazon, Goodreads, or Facebook. But, especially Amazon. I greatly appreciate your time and your kind words.

Keep up with the publication of the next Shine in Bedlam novels. Sign up for my email mailing list at www.jeffreyhillard.com. On the site, I have a free copy of a short ebook on writing creatively that I wrote, and I want you to have it for signing up.

Expect future novels in the Shine in Bedlam YA series shortly.

Jeffrey Hillard
Cincinnati, Ohio

A Note from the Author

The following print and visual works were invaluable resources in my writing this novel. They proved indispensable in providing a far deeper understanding of the 1960s, and they enriched my vision for the novel: The 60s: The Story of a Decade by The New Yorker Magazine (Henry Finder, editor); The Age of Great Dreams: America in the 1960s (American Century Series) by David Farber; Black against Empire: The History and Politics of the Black Panther Party (The George Gund Foundation imprint in African American Studies) by Joshua Bloom and Waldo E. Martin Jr.; Black Panthers: Vanguard of the Revolution (Stanley Nelson, Director).

Acknowledgements

I owe a special debt of gratitude - a champion's shout-out of accolades - to the following for their extraordinary help in making the publication of this novel possible. Their talents, boundless. Their presence in my writing life, priceless. Thank you: Trace Conger, Brenda Elam-Huff, Christine Grote, Chelsea Hillard, William Lambers, Jacqui Slabach, and Jennifer Vogel. And to Mount St. Joseph University and the Mount community and to The Public Library of Cincinnati and Hamilton County.

I am so grateful to the following friends, colleagues, and family members for their support of my work over the years. Many thanks to Thom Atkinson, John Ballard, Elizabeth Barkley, Andy Bockhold, Robert Bodle, Chris Boland, S. Mary Bookser, Greg Brugger, Karen Carroll, Joe Dougherty, Mary Ann Edwards, Larry Garner, Karen George, Susan Glassmeyer, Roger Grein, Tom Groh, Richard Hague, Randy Haight, Pauletta Hansel, Fran Harmon, Betty Hillard, the late William C. Hillard, Caron Hofer, Wayne Hofer, Sue Howard, Jon Hughes, Susan Hughes, Lynne Hugo, Bucky Ignatius, Paul Jenkins, Jerry Judge, Donna Kermos, Mike Klabunde, S. Marge Kloos, Gene Kritsky, Carol Feiser Laque, Craig Lloyd, Tim Lynch, Dan Mader, Elizabeth Mason, S. Peg McPeak, Jennifer Morris, Robert Murphy, Ryck Neube, Kathleen Owens, James Riggs, William Schutzius, Bob Shacochis, Drew Shannon, Keith Sherrill, Charles Skillman, Michael Sontag, Loyola Walter, the late Dallas Wiebe, and Karl Zuelke. Many thanks to my friends and colleagues at

Mount St. Joseph University and to members of Cincinnati Writers' Project and the Greater Cincinnati Writers League.

About the Author

Jeffrey Hillard is an award-winning writer and teacher. He is the author of four books of poems, a chapbook of short stories, and a book of nonfiction. His novel, Shine out of Bedlam, is part of the "Shine in Bedlam" Young Adult/Adult series. In addition to working as a former publisher, editor, anthology co-editor, and literary advocate for over 30 years, Mr. Hillard also taught writing and mentored individuals in incarceration facilities in the 2000s. Among his numerous awards, in 2015-2016, he worked as Writer-in-Residence for The Public Library of Cincinnati and Hamilton County. He teaches writing and literature at Mount St. Joseph University in Cincinnati, Ohio.

Visit online at:

www.jeffreyhillard.com (& receive a free book at the site)
www.facebook.com/jeffreyhillard
www.twitter.com/JSHillard (@JSHillard)

www.ingramcontent.com/pod-product-compliance
Lightning Source LLC
Chambersburg PA
CBHW030237200626
46816CB00002BA/404